WHEN THINGS OF THE SPIRIT COME FIRST

WHEN THINGS OF THE SPIRIT COME FIRST

SIMONE DE BEAUVOIR

FIVE EARLY TALES

TRANSLATED BY PATRICK O'BRIAN

PANTHEON BOOKS, NEW YORK

All rights reserved under International and Pan-American
Copyright Conventions. Published in the United States by Pantheon
Books, a division of Random House, Inc., New York, and
simultaneously in Canada by Random House of Canada Limited,
Toronto. Originally published in France as *Quand Prime le Spirituel* by
Editions Gallimard. Copyright © 1979 by Editions Gallimard. First
American edition published in 1982 by Pantheon Books, a division
of Random House, Inc., New York.

Library of Congress Cataloging in Publication Data

Beauvoir, Simone de, 1908–
When things of the spirit come first.

Translation of: Quand prime le spirituel.
Contents: Marcelle—Chantal—Lisa—[etc.]
1. Beauvoir, Simone de, 1908– —Translations,
English. I. Title.
PQ2603.E362Q313 1982   843'.914   82-47872
ISBN 0-394-52216-8   AACR2
0-394-72235-3 (pbk.)

Manufactured in the United States of America

9 8 7 6 5 4 3

❦ ❦ ❦ ❦ ❦ CONTENTS ❦ ❦ ❦ ❦ ❦

When I started this book, a little before I was thirty, I already had
the beginnings and the rough drafts of several novels behind me.
In these I had given outward expression to various phantasms;
they had almost no relationship to my personal life. Not one of
them was finished. After thinking about the matter for a year I
made up my mind to write something completely different: this
time I should speak about the world I knew, and I should expose
some of its defects. A few years before this I had discovered the
harm done by the religiosity that was in the air I breathed during
my childhood and early youth. Several of my friends had never
broken away from it: willingly or unwillingly they had undergone
the dangerous influence of that kind of spiritual life. I decided to
tell their stories and also to deal with my own conversion to the
real world. I linked the characters of these five tales, but the
connection was loose and each tale was a self-sufficing entity.

In *Lisa* I described the withering away of a girl whose shy
attempts at living were crushed by the mysticism and the
intrigues of the pious institution in which we were students
together. At a time when her body was insidiously working upon
her, she tried to be nothing more than a soul among other souls;
and she tried in vain.

I took the idea of *Marcelle* from a young poetess with a large pale
forehead whom I had known in Marseilles during the year I was
teaching at a lycée there. I had come to realize that when I was a
child there was a very close connection between my piety and the
masochism of some of my games. I had also learnt that the most
devout of my aunts used to make her husband whip her heartily
by night. I had fun drawing a picture of piety gradually shading
off into shameless appetite. In these two stories I used a tone of
false objectivity, a veiled irony after the manner of John Dos
Passos.

In *Chantal* I tackled one of my fellow-teachers at Rouen: she taught literature and I saw a good deal of her. She tried to give those who came into contact with her a brilliant image of her life and of herself, and she did so by means of a continual clumsy faking. I invented a private diary in which she pursues 'the wonderful', turning every one of her experiences into something far more glamorous and providing herself with a fictitious character, that of a broad-minded, unprejudiced, intensely sensitive woman. I worked out a plot that made her take off her mask. This tale was an advance on the others: Chantal's inner monologue and her diary showed her both as she longed to be and as she really was. I had succeeded in conveying that distance between a person and himself which is the essence of bad faith.

In my drafts of novels I had already made vain attempts at bringing Zaza back to life – Zaza, the friend who had meant so much to me. In this book I kept closer to reality. *Anne*, at the age of twenty, was tormented by the same anguish and the same doubts as Zaza. I drew a more faithful and a more engaging portrait of her than I had done in the earlier versions: yet one does not quite believe in her unhappiness and her death. Perhaps the only way of convincing the reader was to give an exact account of both, as I did in *Memoirs of a Dutiful Daughter*.

The book ends with a satire on my youth. I give *Marguerite* my own childhood at the Cours Désir and my own adolescent religious crisis. After this she falls into the pitfall of 'the wonderful', as I did when I was influenced by my cousin Jacques (though Jacques had scarcely any resemblance to the character Denis). In the end her eyes are opened; she tosses mysteries, mirages and myths overboard and looks the world in the face. I think this is the best part of the book. I wrote it in a lively style and with a fellow-feeling for the heroine.

The book is a beginner's piece of work. But looking back at it from a distance of forty years, I felt that in spite of its obvious faults it had merit enough for me to wish to see it published. There are readers who have liked it. I hope that in England and the United States there may be some others who also find it moving.

Simone de Beauvoir

Author's Preface

Editor's Note: The book's original title was *Primauté du spirituel*, but since that title was used by M. Jacques Maritain for one of his works, Madame de Beauvoir changed it to *Quand prime le spirituel*.

❦ MARCELLE ❦

MARCELLE DROUFFE was a dreamy, precocious little girl: as early as the age of ten months she gave signs of being extraordinarily sensitive. 'When you hurt yourself, it wasn't the pain that made you cry,' her mother told her later. 'It was because you felt the world had betrayed you.'

Her parents cherished her, and she was so good that they never scolded her at all; but early in life she knew the taste of tears. As dusk fell she would slip under her father's desk or behind the heavy drawing-room curtains and let sadness and the night flow into her. She would think of the poor children and the orphans she had read about in story-books with gilt covers; she reflected that one day she would be a grown-up and that her mother would no longer take her on to her lap; or she imagined that her parents were dead and that she was alone in the world. Then the tears would roll down her cheeks and she would feel her body swoon away into a delicious void.

She liked crying in churches best: on holidays Mme Drouffe took her to admire the wax Infant Jesuses in their cradles or to breathe in the scent of the shrines. Through the shining haze round the candle-flames Marcelle would see wonderful visions. Her heart melted within her and, sobbing, she offered a young fair-haired God the sacrifice of her life. She had seen him once, at the cinema: in bed, at night, she told him her secrets and went to sleep snuggled in Jesus' bosom: she dreamed of wiping soft bare feet with her long hair.

One of Marcelle's great-aunts had a reading-room in the rue Saint-Sulpice: she was an old lady with a croaking voice, and she always wore a ribbon round her throat. Marcelle's greatest pleasure was spending a day at Mlle Olivier's. She would choose among the works intended for the young (they had a Y after their titles in the catalogue) and then she would go and sit at a little table in a dark passage lined with books in black uniforms: there, by the light of a candle, she devoured Schmidt's tales, Reynes Montlaur's novels, or historical memoirs as bowdlerized by Mme Carette. Customers were not allowed into the corridors and the

11

only person who occasionally stole through the gloom was an assistant in a high-necked blouse; she would climb a ladder, encumbered by her long skirt, and shine a torch along the shelves. When this happened Marcelle knew that another customer had just come in and had sat in silence on one of the leather chairs; looking curiously into the main room she usually saw old ladies and priests. Mlle Olivier, perched on a kind of rostrum, supervised the room with an austere expression; a large register, green and black, lay open before her, and before giving the customers their books – a red label on the back for novels, yellow for serious works – she wrote the title and the author's name in a round hand.

Some of the library's regular visitors aroused a passionate interest in Marcelle: middle-aged men with a pensive gaze, their faces matured and refined by thought. In their handsome greying hair, their overcoats, and their white hands she discerned an exalted elegance that seemed to come from the soul. Perhaps they were writers, poets: they certainly belonged to that intellectual élite that M. Drouffe often spoke about with a mysterious air. Marcelle gazed devoutly upon them. She ardently longed for one of them to notice her some day and to say in velvety tones 'What serious books that pretty little girl does read, to be sure!' He would ask her questions and he would be astonished by her replies: then he would take her to a beautiful house full of books and pictures and he would talk to her as though she were a grown-up.

Marcelle could not wait to be older; she wanted to be a well-known writer and to have high-minded conversations with great men. Nothing pained her more than being treated as a child; she always remained in the drawing-room when her parents had visitors, and she liked being with these middle-aged men and women with their soft smiles, grave voices and restrained gestures. When M. Drouffe read them the tales and poems Marcelle wrote for her little brother Pascal, she felt rather shy but very happy. She was never unsociable except in the company of children of her own age: their loud laughter, their shouts and their wild, disorderly games filled her with horror. Mme Drouffe would have liked to send her to a private school, but Marcelle was so sensitive it scarcely seemed right to cross her and she was allowed to have lessons with an elderly spinster; her

12

father, who taught grammar, undertook her literary education, correcting her stylistic exercises and reading her the great classics in the evening.

Yet when Mme Drouffe took Marcelle to the Tuileries or the Luxembourg Gardens she did not let her stay sitting there at her side. 'Go and play with your little friends,' she would say firmly: it was the only point on which she displayed authority. Marcelle obeyed, but she thought there was nothing so stupid as running about and pulling and pushing one another. She was not an agile child and she dragged along, hating the whole thing.

Later she often thought tenderly of those times, calling up the picture of that thoughtful little girl who hid in the window-recesses when Christmas trees were lit up and when they danced in a ring under the drawing-room lights: the other children were too busy stuffing themselves with chocolate éclairs or putting on paper hats to bother about her, and far from their red faces and noisy laughter she escaped into an imaginary world.

Mlle Olivier, who had taken such pains with her catalogue of books for the young, would have been astonished to learn the kind of sustenance that her niece's dreaming drew from certain harmless stories and from Canon Schmidt's improving tales. Bluebeard's cruelty, the trials imposed upon the gentle Griselda by her suspicious husband, the Duke of Brabant's meeting with the unfortunate Geneviève, stark naked under her long hair – all these perturbed and excited Marcelle to a remarkable degree. The story of a woman, cruelly and harshly treated by an arrogant master, who eventually wins his heart by her submissiveness and her love was one that never failed to delight her. She identified herself with this heroine, sometimes imagining her innocent and misunderstood, but more often guilty of some grave offence, for she was fond of quivering with repentance at the feet of a sinless, beautiful and terrible man. He had the right of life and death over her, and she called him 'Lord': he made her strip herself naked before him, and he used her body as a step when he mounted his splendidly decked charger. With a sensuous delight she drew out this moment of feeling the harsh spur flay her servile back as she knelt there, her head bowed, her heart full of adoration and passionate humility. And when the stern-eyed avenger, vanquished by pity and by love, laid his hand on her head as a sign of forgiveness she clasped his knees in an exquisite swoon.

She was thirteen when she happened to see a *Petit Parisien* serial in a public lavatory – a man covering an alabaster breast with eager kisses. Marcelle could not put the picture out of her mind all day long, and that night, when she was in bed, she gave way to it without resistance, her cheeks on fire. From then on every night, when she was half asleep in her warm bed, she offered her bosom to searching, greedy lips: insistent gentle hands ran over her flesh, a warm body pressed against her own. In the morning she was ashamed of these thoughts, but with the fading of the light she became impatient for her heated phantasms to come back. She did not go to sleep for a long while: her dry throat and lips were painful and sometimes she had shivering fits and cold sweats. After about a year her nights grew calm again: she stopped indulging in fanciful imaginings and began looking forward, looking anxiously forward, to a future that should prove worthy of her.

Her heart was too exacting to be satisfied with the commonplace affections of her everyday life at home. Mme Drouffe was passionately devoted to Marcelle, but she was neither very clever nor very highly cultivated; Marcelle adored her, of course, but she felt very much alone when she was with her mother and often she could not prevent herself from giving a cross answer. She had hoped that as she grew older she would become her father's friend, a friend he would confide in; but M. Drouffe was just as interested in Pascal, who was beginning to learn Latin, and in the little Marguerite as he was in Marcelle. Indeed, he would frequently tease his elder daughter about her shyness and the fact that her hands were big and that she did not know what to do with them. Marcelle was cruelly disappointed. Often and sadly she whispered 'Who will ever be capable of loving me?' One evening, when she came back from a party where no one had asked her to dance and her father reproved her for looking glum, she burst into tears, ran to her bedroom and locked herself in. Several times Mme Drouffe came and tapped softly on the door, but Marcelle would not open it; she lay there on the bed in the darkness, staring at the ceiling, lit from time to time by the glow of a passing tram: she was immeasurably sorry for herself. She never would be like those frivolous thick-witted girls that people in general thought more attractive: she never would consent to smother her soul.

'I am different from the others,' she said to herself passionate-ly. She got up, opened the shutters and stepped out onto the balcony: Paris was covered with a sky as mauve as a field of autumn crocus and the night was so soft and mild that Marcelle's heart began to beat faster. She thought of Mme de Staël, of George Eliot, of the Comtesse de Noailles; and it was then, all of a sudden, that she had the wonderful revelation of her destiny. 'I shall live with a man of genius: I shall be his companion,' she said, in an ecstatic whisper.

The winter after war was declared she thought she had met him: he was a lieutenant, and he read Epictetus in the trenches. Marcelle wanted to be worthy of him. She was too young to be a nurse, but she made mounds of lint out of her old skirts and she tirelessly knitted Balaclava helmets; she also collected funds for the Red Cross in the Champs-Elysées. Mme Drouffe took to making her drink an infusion of orange-flowers every evening so that she should not dream of the poor wounded soldiers and the little refugees from the north all night: and it was at this time that Marcelle began to use powder because she wept over the horrors of the war so very often and so very much that she was always afraid of having red eyes and a swollen nose. She stopped believing in God: with the immensity of human suffering before her, she felt quite sure that Providence did not exist.

Those were terrible years for Marcelle, and in later times it often surprised her that she came through the crisis unbroken. She missed the presence of God; and men betrayed her. The heroic young lieutenant married one of her cousins. Every day the world grew more hostile, human contacts more disappoint-ing. Marcelle longed to escape, to go a great way off. If she had not been afraid of hurting her mother she would have gone to nurse lepers in Madagascar. She went for long, long walks, and in the Bois de Boulogne she kissed the trunks of trees, rubbing a loving cheek against the rough bark of these living beings that would let themselves be loved without wounding her.

She was twenty when her father died, not long after the war. Pascal was working for his baccalauréat, his university entrance examination. Marguerite had just been moved up to the fifth form at school, among the twelve- and thirteen-year-olds. Paying her a modest sum, Mme Drouffe took over Mlle Olivier's reading-room, which brought in quite a considerable profit.

Marcelle did not wish to be a burden on her mother and she wanted to give her life a meaning: she made up her mind to take a job. It had to be work that would appeal to her heart, and after two years of preparation she found a place as a social assistant at a welfare centre in the rue de Ménilmontant.

The Centre was run by a gentle, sensitive woman of forty whom life had treated cruelly: from their first meeting she was charmed by Marcelle's youth, the vivid life and eagerness in her voice and look; and Marcelle experienced the delights of friendship. Germaine Masson knitted filmy scarves for her and almost every Sunday she invited her to tea. Marcelle told Germaine about her childhood, and, speaking confidentially, about her hopes, her disappointments, and the peculiarities of her character. Germaine conceived a positively servile affection for her. But Marcelle did not find her work as rewarding as she had hoped: the Centre was concerned with distributing material help to the local poor, finding work for the unemployed young, and looking after sick or ill-treated children; it also provided medical consultations and free treatment, either at the Centre or at home. The nurses were competent, conscientious women, but they looked upon their calling merely as a means of earning a living; and during her inquiries Marcelle never heard a word of anything but worries about health and money. Never did she come into contact with a single soul.

In the evening, as she went home in the crowded métro, Marcelle wondered sadly whether the emptiness in her heart would ever be filled: she gazed despairingly at the horny-handed men and the sickly-looking women – eyes that never showed the least gleam of an ideal. They had been toiling all day long and now they were going to eat: no beautiful memories there, no hopes, not even a sweetly running line of poetry to soothe their unhappiness. Lives as dark and subterranean as the tunnels into which the train kept plunging. In the foul-smelling carriages the atmosphere was stifling. Marcelle felt a wave of intense pity, and it seemed to her that she bore all the sufferings of the world on her shoulders; she would have liked to talk to these unfortunate people about beauty, about love, and about the meaning of pain and sorrow, speaking so convincingly that their lives would be transformed. She could do nothing for them: as well as the uselessness of her charity there was the physical distress caused by the smell of human sweat; and contact with coarse, rough bodies made her feel so sick that she was often compelled to get out and finish the journey on foot. At home once more she gazed a long while at her face in the mirror: the skin beneath her soulful eyes was somewhat worn, transparent and flecked with reddish-brown, like the throat of a foxglove. This pathetic face deserved the love of a hero.

'Oh beloved,' she whispered.

Marcelle had been working at the rue de Ménilmontant for a year before she had a chance to spend her unused treasures of strength and charity at last.

It was a morning in April: she was in her office, busy with accounts. 'To be strong, and to wear oneself out in base, unworthy occupations,' she muttered as she checked the totals. The concierge knocked on the door and gave her two visiting-cards: Maurice Perdrières, Director of 'Social Contact', and Paul Desroches, Government Civil Engineer, names unknown to her. A moment later she was in the company of two men of about twenty-five with intelligent faces and cheerful expressions: they seemed almost to be related to each other. Without wasting time on preliminaries they told Marcelle that they had come to ask her to collaborate with them, and they did so in a blunt, straightforward, trusting fashion that pleased her.

The idea of 'Social Contact' had arisen from the war: Perdrières and his friend Desroches had spent a year at the front, and, where others had seen only mud and slaughter, they had discovered that wonderful thing called brotherhood. When they went back to their books and their studies in 1919 they were at a loss: the purely intellectual life that had once satisfied them now seemed dry and sterile and they retained a longing for the fraternity of the war. Perdrières and Desroches decided to revive the deep, simple comradeship of the trenches – to revive it between the classes. Enthusiasm and good will vanquished all obstacles, and soon they had won over a large number of eager young people. Groups were set up: they were called teams, and in the evenings they travelled to the outlying districts to give lectures attended by apprentices and young workmen and to gain their friendship. The movement did not have the least political attachment, and, although Christian in its origins, it did not undertake any religious proselytism: disinterested exchange was the goal, and nothing else. The students brought the young workers the spiritual nourishment which alone gives man an inner dignity; in return they were quickened and invigorated by the blaze of generosity, good humour and courage which burns in the heart of the common people.

'We have been more successful than we hoped,' said Perdrières, 'and material difficulties are all that hold us up, particularly the question of premises: the meetings often have to take place in bistros.' He smiled. 'A bistro is fine, but it costs money, and after all one is not in one's own place. If you could give us some kind of a shelter, that would help us enormously.'

Leaning her chin on her hand, Marcelle gazed at Perdrières with the greatest interest: these men were quite outside the common run. 'Social questions concern me very deeply indeed,' she said. 'I am entirely at your service. Here we only look after people's bodies and it has often grieved me: man does not live by bread alone.'

'You could do a great deal for us,' said Desroches. 'You know this district's needs and its resources. Your help would be invaluable for setting up a team here.'

Marcelle gave her wholehearted agreement and asked them to dinner in two days time so that they could look into the question more thoroughly. When she was alone again, an immense happiness flooded into her: at last she was going to be able to show what she was made of! She opened the window and leant out over the garden: thousands of sticky little leaves twinkled in the sun and all springtime murmured in her bosom – the inner wealth accumulated in solitude was yearning to blossom into action. Ecstatically, Marcelle greeted the renewal of her heart as the dawn of the renewal of the world itself.

The dinner took place in the Centre's dining-room; Germaine was not there. Marcelle had ordered a pleasant little meal, and she had covered the table with an embroidered cloth belonging to her mother. Perdrières and Desroches did not seem to pay any attention to their food; they talked all the time, with great eagerness, about social questions, pure poetry, and the fate of mankind. Marcelle had never heard such interesting conversation. They explained that what had to be done was to bring the people up to culture, not to bring culture down to the people, and

Perdrières quoted the instance of a young printer who understood Valéry better than the professors at the Sorbonne. With dessert Marcelle gave them Benedictine, and she drank a finger herself. It was agreed that Perdrières should take charge of a study-group every Thursday: between them Desroches and another member of the team would give lessons in English, book-keeping and French. These lessons were intended for the young only. 'It is the young who must change the world,' said Perdrières. But to enter into contact with their families there would be lectures on subjects of general interest once a month in the hall to which members could bring their friends and relations. Perdrières also intended there to be group excursions, for he believed that picnics, marching in step, and songs with everyone joining in the chorus were of use in restoring the people's sense of spiritual values. As the Centre was empty after six o'clock, Marcelle proposed setting up a kind of club-room at that time; she would undertake the supervision until eight, and would see to it that there were books, magazines and a billiard-table.

The suggestion was eagerly adopted and Desroches spoke with great enthusiasm of the splendid way the rue de Ménilmontant team was going to spread and grow, thanks to Marcelle's brilliant ideas. While he was talking, Marcelle noticed that he had a little scratch at the corner of his mouth; she also noticed that Perdrières did not wear sock-suspenders and that when he crossed his legs his calves could be seen: this touched her heart. These exceptional beings were also men, big awkward children like all other men. She would have liked to tidy their rooms, arrange the knot of their tie and sew on their buttons, as she did for Pascal. A motherly affection blended with her admiration for them.

For some time now Germaine's soft, demanding friendship had been wearisome to her; Germaine was always wanting to find parallels between Marcelle's experiences and her own, and between their two characters; she badgered Marcelle with questions and she monopolized all her spare time: she was almost an old woman and she fed on her friend's youth and zest for life like a vampire. Contact with her was depressing. Friendly contact with men, on the other hand, greatly increased one's strength of will and one's spirit: it was direct, open and straightforward.

'In a way I am very feminine,' said Marcelle to Desroches one day, 'and yet I can only get on with men.'

She stopped seeing Germaine so often. When Marcelle had telephoned to cry off on Sunday, on Monday Germaine's eyes would be full of silent reproach: and at this Marcelle felt with pride that her untamable spirit could never submit to the bondage of Germaine's affection.

Marcelle gave the team all her free time. Many youths joined 'Social Contact'; but there were few who came out of a genuine wish to improve their minds and Marcelle nourished no illusions about their membership. They came to be among friends, and because nothing was asked of them, and because they could not afford to go to the café every evening. Some of them, reflecting that one day they might need a job or medical advice, wanted to be in favour with the Centre, which was looked upon as a power in the neighbourhood; their parents encouraged them to go to the hall – it might one day prove useful. Germaine, with her embittered, sceptical cast of mind, did not fail to point out these interested motives; but Marcelle looked upon all ways of getting members as justified. She carried out active propaganda with the families and the young people she knew through the medical side of the Centre or its employment agency; and gradually they brought in others.

The hall was very large: Marcelle settled discreetly at the far end and pretended to be absorbed in some sort of work; the young men played at cards or billiards, read the papers and talked among themselves. Marcelle had arranged with the head of a people's library that books should be available and she took advantage of their borrowing or returning them to enter into conversation. They spoke about the last study-group or the next lecture; and sometimes the talk took a personal turn. Marcelle felt that in order to acquire an influence over these children she should in the first place be a friend, a comrade; presently she grew more familiar, leaning over their shoulders to see what they were reading and sometimes unceremoniously sitting on the table as she spoke to them. She liked this warm, youthful atmosphere: when she was joking with a young mechanic or a shop-assistant it was perfectly obvious to her that the barriers between classes were brought into being by hatred and prejudice alone; and she did not look upon their reserve towards her as the evidence of a social difference but rather as a discreet and flattering tribute. Most of the team-members were well behaved young people with serious tastes, belonging to respectable families; but as the movement spread, more dubious elements found their way into the group – even Communists and downright undesirables appeared. The best part of Marcelle's affection was kept for these lost souls: she undertook the task of awakening their moral sense and of pulling them out of their corrupted environment. On warm evenings, when they sat on the sills of the open window in their shirt-sleeves, looking like graceful animals, Marcelle felt an overwhelming longing to grasp them in a motherly fashion and press their heads against her bosom.

There was one in particular, one whom Marcelle would have liked to hold in her arms to keep him from evil ways for ever. Fradin was his name: his features were irregular, his eyes velvety, his mouth childish and sensual; his open shirt shamelessly displayed a sunburnt chest and his sweat smelt of mint; it was said that he lived off women. Marcelle often asked him to stay after the others to help her tidy the room a little: he agreed in a good-natured way, but she never managed to make him talk. As soon as he had done he took his cap and in a guttersnipe voice bade Marcelle good night.

She watched him go off to his own amusements with intense anxiety. Presently, in some low dance-hall, girls covered with make-up would cling tight to him and smell his scent, resting their heads against the opening of his shirt: sitting on his knee, one of them would stroke his hair and then his neck, her hand slipping gently under his collar. Marcelle almost felt the touch of the warm, satiny skin under her palm. She quivered. How should one set about teaching these young creatures purity? The idea of the risks that Fradin was running – the risks to his soul and body – quite overcame her. Although her calling had brought her into contact with the harsh facts of life the words vice, syphilis, and venereal disease still filled Marcelle with disgust and fear.

For a moment she stood there in the empty room, sad at heart: they had all gone off, respectful and uncaring, leaving her to her purity and her loneliness. She put out the lights and walked down to the Ménilmontant station. She thought about Vigny's *Moïse*, and *Christ on the Mount of Olives*. 'I give, I give, and who will give to me?' she whispered when she was back in her bedroom with its pale green wallpaper: sadly she brushed her lips over the cool petals of the flowers – there was always a bouquet on her table. She liked talking to things that had no life, and caressing them: they required nothing of her and they never refused themselves. Often, in the gentle glow of her lamp, she wept in spite of the scent of the roses.

Neither Perdrières nor Desroches had any inkling of these tears. They were men and they believed that ideas were enough to transform the world: their social theories interested Marcelle at first, and then they wearied her. In the company of these intellectuals she felt rich with a mysterious femininity, and lonely once again. They valued her because she was energetic, intelligent, calm. But who would ever be capable of understanding her and loving her weakness? 'The touching weakness of the strong,' she jotted down in a note-book; and she promised herself to write a poem ending with those words.

Marcelle got on better with Desroches than with Perdrières; there was greater subtlety in his character and he was more understanding; although his culture and his mind were somewhat unsophisticated and his sensitivity still childish, he was capable of melancholy and tenderness, and he had an inner life. As she was afraid of evil tongues if she were to see him often at her office, Marcelle sometimes met him away from the Centre. They went to lectures and concerts and they had tea together. She was not at all flirtatious with him: she looked upon flirting as a lack of candour, as something contemptible; but she did want him to know what she was really like, and as he was not very quick-witted she was obliged to emphasize certain aspects of her character. One day she welcomed him very soberly and spoke about the tragic state of the humble in such a feeling way that he had tears in his eyes when he left her: the next day he found an idle, frivolous woman who made fun of serious remarks. As they left a moving talk given by Claudel, instead of seeming touched, she mocked the poet's fatness and his thick spectacles: Desroches looked so taken aback that Marcelle burst out laughing. 'There's more than one woman in me,' she said.

In the early days Desroches always talked about 'Social Contact', the duties of the élite and the Christian's attitude towards economic and political questions – he was a practising Catholic.

Marcelle was more interested in people than ideas, and for her friendship was not an exchange of viewpoints but a deep communication between souls: she questioned Desroches about his childhood and she told him some secrets of her own. They became more and more intimate. Desroches grew bold enough to give her violets from time to time, and he tried to define the precise shade of her beautiful hair.

'You are not only a superior woman,' he said to her one day in an earnest voice, 'you are also quite simply just a woman.'

'Yes,' said Marcelle tenderly, 'a woman.'

She did not find that Desroches had an outstanding personality, but she did like being understood and revered. When he asked her to marry him she accepted. Desroches did not want to be married until he had a position that would allow Marcelle to stop working, but to avoid any gossip they announced their engagement right away. There was a cheerful party at the Centre, and Perdrières, proposing the toasts, made a very successful speech.

A little while after this Marcelle spent a month in the country with her mother and she had time to appreciate and relish the full extent of her happiness: she sent Desroches and Germaine letters like welling springs. 'I spend my days lying on the grass in the meadows, drunk with sun like a young animal,' she wrote. 'I do not regret the weary years that I spent alone, without love: my joy would not be so splendid if I had not waited for it in tears. How wonderful it is, Germaine, to give myself up to the wafting air of a great love at last, after having borne the weight of my useless heart like a burden for so long.'

Marcelle was not one of those who are made selfish by happiness: once she was back in Paris she organized a women's team and took charge of the study-circle. Every Saturday she gave talks on Claudel, Péguy, women's social mission and the meaning of pain to an admiring audience. In order to spread the movement she also persuaded Germaine to give a monthly dance, at which the young people belonging to the Centre could indulge in the pleasures suitable to their age. The first evening passed off very well indeed. Marcelle danced with Desroches: she also danced with Fradin and Linières. Every time their arms diffidently went round her waist she felt the beauty of this fraternization so intensely that her heart beat high and fast.

When she left the dance she was too uplifted to want to sleep; she asked Desroches to see her home on foot, and they walked cheerfully along the deserted streets.

'An evening like this really makes one feel that bringing the classes together is merely a question of good will!' cried Desroches eagerly. Marcelle thoroughly agreed. But then all at once it occurred to her that men of good will were very rare; sadness overcame her and shivering she pressed herself against her fiancé. He put his arm round her and for a moment they stood there, linked in a silent communion: Marcelle closed her eyes: Desroches' arm round her shoulders burnt exquisitely: she turned her face to his.

Desroches hesitated a moment: then Marcelle felt two hot lips against her own: she returned his kiss passionately, in an ecstasy of tenderness and surrender. Almost at once he gently freed himself and walked on by her side without touching her. He seemed embarrassed, and Marcelle could no longer think of anything to say to him. All her happiness had vanished: now, after these hours in which she had spent herself so generously she had a sudden revelation of the vanity of all action, the vanity of all love. It appeared to her that even happiness itself was too small a matter for great souls.

Marcelle remained in low spirits and on edge during the days that followed. She wished she still believed in God so that she could go and cry in a church as she had done when she was a child: human things always left her deeply unsatisfied. She had imagined love as a wonderful fulfilment; but no doubt there would never be peace on earth for her troubled, restless heart. When she was away from Desroches she longed for his coming so intensely that her dry throat and her burning lips were really painful: when he was there she found his presence stifling. Desroches always had stories to tell her and ideas to impart and he never stopped smiling. While he talked Marcelle gazed despairingly at that stranger's body within which a soul was hidden, precious and inaccessible: she was so weary of herself that she would have liked to be lost in him for ever. But two beings who love one another and who sit side by side are still two separate, solitary entities: Desroches did not seem to have any notion of this tragedy. Yet one Sunday afternoon Marcelle was so gloomy that eventually he became concerned: half-sitting, half-lying on the divan in her pale-green room, she answered only in monosyllables; she saw the delicate harmonies of the carpet and the walls through a grey mist; the outlines of the things in the room seemed blurred and the daylight dull; her own body was as heavy as lead.

'What's the matter, darling?' asked Desroches, leaning over her.

She gave a faint smile: she was by no means sure what the sorrow was that needed soothing. 'Sit there, close to me,' she said. He sat down, taking her hand rather awkwardly: she laid her head on his shoulder. 'Oh, the world is too horrible,' she said, with tears in her eyes. He pressed her close. 'Let's stay like this,' she said. 'It's so comfortable.' With her cheek against the roughness of his jacket, the warmth of his body flooding into her and his strong arms about her, she forgot the inadequacy of happiness. The moment was heavy with a melancholy sweetness that words could not express: it was by a kiss alone that Desroches could have gathered the heart she was offering. He did not kiss her: he stroked her hair and then stood up. When he had gone, Marcelle lay there for a long while, exhausted, with no strength, no desire: she would have liked to vanish, to dissolve into nothingness. When she came out of this painful torpor she could not bear her own company and she went out: for two hours she walked wherever her feet happened to lead her along the streets, shaken by sobs, she could not tell why; sometimes she felt that she was going to faint and she had to lean against a wall.

Some days later she had a long talk with Desroches: he told her how much the restraints he imposed upon himself made him suffer and how often he had a violent longing to take her in his arms. But he was of the opinion that a Christian should not experience carnal joys before their sanctification by the sacrament of marriage; and even then, he thought, the degree to which these pleasures were allowable presented a serious moral problem.

'The sacrament of marriage is not a glorification of the body,' he said. 'It is the acceptance of our animal nature. But at the same time it insists that this aspect must remain under the control of our will and reason: we must not allow it an independent existence. Yielding to merely physical drives is the denial of our human dignity.'

Marcelle thoroughly agreed. She felt that the act of love should not be the brutish satisfaction of an appetite: it had to be freely granted on both sides and as it were rendered spiritual by an intention of kindness and affection. 'But it is no unworthy pleasure that we expect from kisses and embraces,' she said. 'Often there is no other language that allows hearts to speak to one another.'

Desroches eagerly replied that he saw the matter in just the same light. Only their engagement had to be long: and so that their wedding night might retain all its touching solemnity they should take care that their bodies did not grow used to each other, even through the most chaste of caresses.

Marcelle thought it admirable that an engaged couple should be able to talk about such things with no false shame, and she told Desroches how much she appreciated his delicacy. Yet afterwards it grieved her to see how easily he obeyed the rules he had set himself. His was neither a passionate nor a troubled nature.

'I do not blame him in any way,' she said sadly to Germaine. 'But there you are: I was looking for giants, and there are only men.'

Marcelle met with cruel disappointments at 'Social Contact' as well. Although, in his articles and lectures, Perdrières asserted that uncultivated spirits were the best suited for enjoying the everlasting masterpieces of the human mind, the working girls and shop-assistants of the team were not very interested in Racine, nor in Baudelaire. They could not understand why a married woman should give up her job to look after the house. And Marcelle's fine lectures on resignation and self-sacrifice did not move them at all. When she left the Centre she was completely worn out from giving the best of herself, and all in vain. In the spring she had serious difficulties with the women's section: the young men and the girls who had been meeting regularly at the dances took to seeing one another in secret: on Sundays they would often tell their parents that they were going out in a group, some with Marcelle, others with Perdrières, when in fact they went off together without the least supervision. When this was discovered it caused a minor scandal in the neighbourhood. The dances had to be stopped, and from then on great care was taken to avoid all contact between the sexes.

Marcelle took to hating the team, the Centre, and the rue de Ménilmontant: when there was a lecture and all the members, their relatives and their friends gathered in the long building smelling of rotten wood, the atmosphere was so oppressive that Marcelle felt despair overcome her. The girls never stopped their silly tittering; their mothers' eyes rested on Marcelle with distrust, sometimes with dislike; the students and the learned men who came to talk about Péguy, the United States, or prehistoric man, according to their speciality, were all most disappointingly commonplace. Looking over the grey mass of the audience, Marcelle gazed at the sheets of oiled paper that served as window-panes and she reflected that her youth was being frittered away uselessly. The evening Perdrières introduced Denis Charval to her she was agreeably surprised; he was different from the other lecturers – an elegant, offhand young man with a lock of black hair falling over his forehead.

'Is he a friend of yours?' she asked Perdrières as Charval sat down at the green-covered table.

'He's the friend of a friend's brother,' said Perdrières. 'It seems that he has published some very remarkable verse. Do you think a talk on Rimbaud can amount to much?'

'Why not?' said Marcelle. She directed an interested stare at the young poet: his green eyes gave one the impression of an artless, capricious spirit, given to extremes. Marcelle felt that in speaking of Rimbaud he would present a picture of himself.

Charval spoke with feeling, and he spoke skilfully. He described Rimbaud as a man who had refused to stifle his thirst for the infinite, and as one who had turned down all the commonplace advantages and benefits that delude others – affection, family, love, fame, and even his own genius. When he spoke of the beauty of this refusal, Charval's voice assumed a tone so grave and tender that Marcelle felt she could see his heart laid bare and interpret it. 'We admire Rimbaud for the matchless harmony of his poetry and his prose,' he ended. 'But the reason why we love him like a brother, like a pure and terrible angel, is because he refused even that beauty which delights us: it is because of all the sublime pages he never wrote.'

There was a certain amount of applause: Perdrières leant towards Marcelle. 'I think we made a mistake,' he said in an anxious voice. Marcelle shrugged. 'Obviously Rimbaud can't serve as an example for this herd.' She pushed back her chair and went up to Charval to thank him in the team's name and to tell him how much she had admired his lecture. Charval modestly disclaimed all merit and then invited Marcelle, Perdrières and Desroches to have a drink with him. Marcelle had never set foot in a café: when she passed through the door of one of the big Montmarte establishments she felt that she had suddenly been transported into the middle of a fantastic dream: she had observed that the taximeter showed twenty francs, she reckoned that the white cashmere scarf that went so well with Charval's greatcoat must have cost over a hundred francs, and all this splendour dazzled her, though at the same time she found it slightly shocking. She would have liked to know Charval better: his mouth was rather like young Fradin's, and it had a disillusioned line at the corner; comparing these features with those of Desroches, which were devoid of mystery, she felt that Charval had already seen a great deal of life.

The conversation was less interesting than it might have been because Perdrières kept talking about the people and about culture. With real vexation Marcelle thought that Charval was going to vanish from her life before he had been able to appreciate her. 'Life is already quite good enough at condemning people to loneliness,' she reflected. 'We ought not to turn ourselves into its accomplices.' She told Charval that she would very much like to read his poems and she asked him to tea the next Sunday.

It was a wonderful encounter. From the very beginning Marcelle gave their conversation an intimate, personal turn: she confessed that she no longer believed in action and Charval told her confidentially that for his part he had never believed in it. Nor did either of them believe in friendship any more. Marcelle said that her dreams and the poetic essays she sometimes confided to her note-books were her only refuge and she was overwhelmed when she learnt that for Charval even poetry often seemed a useless amusement or a falsehood: he lived for a few pure, precious impressions that he could not translate into words without betraying them. Marcelle protested: in a voice trembling with emotion she told Charval about the poet's mission and she begged him to believe in himself. She would have liked to take his handsome, bitter face between her hands and transfuse some of her own faith and ardour into him.

Charval was too young and too shy to court her friendship, but Marcelle generously set the pace: she perceived that she had a part to play in this sad child's life. Together they went to the new show at the Vieux Colombier, to a Picasso exhibition, to the Studio des Ursulines – they saw one another almost every day. Charval questioned Marcelle about her job, her pursuits, her family: he told her about the entrancing sadness that drifted through the bars, saloons and night-spots after dark, about modern aesthetics and the absurdity of life. Marcelle wanted to know his friends: sometimes she went with him to cafés where he talked about cubism, dadaism, Cocteau's latest poems, and the fourth dimension with writers and poets dressed in light-coloured suits and soft shirts; it was not easy to follow the conversation, because it skipped from one subject to another, interrupted by jokes and allusions comprehensible only to the initiated, but Marcelle was delighted at being transported at last into the only atmosphere in which she had ever wanted to live – in this very strange and subtle world, surrounded by young geniuses, she could at last come into bloom. Of all these chosen beings, Denis was the handsomest, the youngest and the most elegant; his voice was the most caressing, his eyes the dreamiest. On no other face did Marcelle see such heart-stirring promise. His opinions were often paradoxical and she listened to them indulgently: if she ever gained any influence over Charval she would bring him back to a sounder way of thinking. But she loved his careless, off-hand phrases and their delightful, unpredictable turns.

It was scarcely three weeks after their first meeting that Denis asked Marcelle to dine with him at a restaurant on the banks of the Marne. It was a beautiful summer evening and Marcelle was wearing a wide-brimmed straw hat and a green print dress with puffed sleeves: she looked at the pale sky, she looked at Charval's smooth cheeks; and she hesitated because Desroches was invited to dinner that evening at the Drouffes'. A week before, Marcelle had had a violent scene with her fiancé: she had accused him of being timid, obtuse, insensitive; she had told him that she was sick of his tender care and his unfailing good humour, and since then their relationship had been strained; but Marcelle did not wish to do anything grossly uncivil.

'Telephone your home. Make something up: it doesn't matter what,' said Charval in a sulky, peremptory tone. Marcelle smiled: it was a curiously pleasant experience, giving way to the whims of this child. 'One can't refuse you anything,' she said.

They ate fried potatoes and a matelote of eels in the open air: Marcelle was not very fond of wine, but she drank nearly half a bottle. After the meal they lay on the grass, side by side, on the river-bank. Paris was a great way off; the rue de Ménilmontant, 'Social Contact' and Desroches had ceased to exist; it seemed to Marcelle that she was being carried along like an obedient toy by a fate that was quite out of her control. She was no longer aware of anything but the beating of her heart and of the warm breath close, very close to her face. Something was going to happen, and she would not do anything to prevent it: motionless and passive she acquiesced. For years she had filled the role of a strong, affectionate, anxious woman and now she yearned to give it all up, if only for a moment, and think of nothing, wish for nothing.

At first it was a shower of urgent kisses on her eyes, the corner of her mouth, then the warmth of a body against her own and a long deep kiss full on her mouth: she let herself go – there was nothing in her but well-being and weakness, and lying there in Denis' arms she discovered the sweet experience of communicating with the void.

All at once fear shot through her like a lightning-flash; her muscles stiffened and with both hands she thrust at the man whose weight was upon her. This was how seducers enticed girls far out into the deserted countryside to betray them. 'Let me go,' she said in a choking voice. 'You are out of your mind.'

Charval drew back. 'Forgive me,' he said, 'I let myself be carried away . . .' She had stood up and he put his hand on her shoulder. 'I preferred relying on kisses rather than words; you mustn't hold it against me, Marcelle – I'm shy with you.' He looked uncomfortable, awkward, and charming. 'I love you – extraordinary creature.' He took her in his arms again and pressed her close: now that she was out of danger she let him fondle her breasts and the back of her neck without resisting.

They walked by the river most of the night. Marcelle thought of the future that lay in wait for Charval if a loving woman did not devote herself to him, and she pictured it with horror; he was sceptical, disillusioned and wounded, and he would waste his precious gifts – he would sink into a facile life, perhaps into vice. She alone could save him: she had never dreamt of a finer destiny than being the inspiration of a brilliant man, brilliant but weak. Desroches did not need her to be able to live: on the contrary, it was she who had sought refuge with him, a contemptible piece of cowardice in her – she was not made to receive but to give. When she got home she wrote to Desroches, breaking off the engagement.

Neither Mme Drouffe nor Pascal made any comment: they always approved Marcelle's decisions. Germaine hid her surprise as well as she could; and with a kind of pride Marcelle put up with the nurses' ill-natured astonishment when she told them of her forthcoming marriage to Charval. There was not the least reason for a long engagement: Charval had neither private means nor a job, but he could live with Marcelle until he found something. He explained that up until now he had managed on the money his family sent him: the family no doubt looked upon the marriage with an unfavourable eye, for it gave no sign of life.

Mme Drouffe was very anxious that her daughter should be married in white, and although Marcelle had often expressed her horror of official ceremonies she did not want to deprive her mother of this pleasure. She ordered a very simple dress that could easily be made suitable for small dinner-parties: everyone agreed that with her tulle veil she looked like a Madonna. The wedding was very quiet; Marguerite wore a shot-taffeta dress that did not become her, but Pascal looked very fine in his dark suit; and as he led his sister to the altar he seemed deeply moved. In the vestry Germaine burst into sobs, and Marcelle herself could not keep back a few tears. Nevertheless the modest reception that Mme Drouffe gave after the Mass was very cheerful: Denis displayed great resources of amiability and he was thought infinitely charming.

The young couple had decided not to leave for Brittany until the next day. Having publicly told the chauffeur to drive them to the Gare Montparnasse, on the way Denis gave him the address of an hotel where they booked a room for the night. They went to drink a glass of port in one of the big cafés on the boulevards and then Denis took Marcelle to have a particularly good dinner at Weber's. She was rather surprised to see how much he enjoyed the excellent food: for her part she was so overwrought that the mouthfuls stuck in her throat and she scarcely touched the meal. She was so impatient for the night that shivers ran through her; yet at the same time she was afraid. She had certainly heard that for women of her age losing one's virginity was not painful; but that did not entirely reassure her.

As they went up the hotel staircase her knees gave way beneath her: she wanted to sit by Denis and take his hands, and for both of them to talk soberly about the solemn act that they were going to carry out. By means of their bodies' imperfect union their souls would try to reach one another, perhaps in vain: Marcelle would have liked to weep over the touching splendour of this attempt, cuddled there in Denis' arms, and then to pass gently from tears to caresses.

But Denis did not seem aware of the gravity of the moment: in a perfectly natural tone he said he was dropping with sleep, and he went to undress in the bathroom. Marcelle was already in bed when he knocked; she was wearing a pale-green lacy nightgown, and her heart was beating fast.

Lying there beside her, Denis talked about unimportant things for a little while and then, in no particular hurry, began to kiss her. As he did so Marcelle felt the blood flow to her temples and swell her lips and breasts. 'Now he is going to put out the light,' she thought. 'Is he going to hurt me much?'

Denis slipped the pale green nightgown over Marcelle's head and did not put out the light: then, as he kissed her bosom and her belly, she closed her eyes and began to tremble; the idea that a man's eyes were delighting in her nakedness made her whole being quiver with a shame whose stab was sweeter than the sweetest caress.

Denis drew her close and she felt the warmth, the tender suppleness of a naked body against her own: and a mysterious, quivering, hard flesh throbbed against her belly. But even more than by this animal contact, Marcelle was stirred by the skilful hands that fondled her; it was not only a delightful stroking of her skin, for these hands had an awareness and a will of their own; they were shameless and masterful, they compelled the coming of her pleasure; and it was their tyranny that made Marcelle faint with sensual delight.

She opened her eyes: Denis' face appeared before her, changed with desire, intensely eager, almost unrecognizable: he looked capable of beating her, torturing her, and the sight filled Marcelle with so piercing a pleasure that she began to groan. 'I'm at his mercy,' she said to herself and she was engulfed by an ecstasy in which shame and fear and joy were all intermingled. She groaned so loudly that Denis had to put his hand over her mouth: she kissed the hand – she would have liked to call out to Denis that she was his thing, his slave: and tears ran down her cheeks. All at once he penetrated her: she did not exactly feel pleasure, but this violation of her most secret flesh made her gasp with gratitude and humility. She took every one of Denis's piercing thrusts with passionate submission, and to make his possession of her the more complete she let her consciousness glide away into the night.

When she woke up Denis' face had its usual look once more, and he was smiling; this embarrassed her and she pulled the sheet up to her chin. She would have liked to speak, but she found nothing to say. 'Happy?' he murmured. 'Of course,' she said with a little laugh. In that instant she utterly hated him: angrily she remembered that she had groaned in his arms and that he had known how very deeply she was moved. She blushed for shame and this time there was no pleasure mingled with her confusion.

There was an awkward silence; then with an air of spontaneity she said, 'How funny it is, being in Paris and staying in an hotel. Don't you think it would be lovely not to know Paris, and to come for one's honeymoon?'

Denis agreed. He was very, very fond of Paris: indeed, for him Paris was the only place on earth where it was worth living. The charms of nature, on the other hand, hardly meant anything to him. Enthusiastically Marcelle began to list these charms: she told him how happy she was at the idea that presently she would see the shores of Mont-Saint-Michel and the moors of Britanny, which were, she thought, an exact equivalent of her own internal landscape. Having listened politely for a while Denis cut her short, taking her in his arms and seeking her mouth.

Marcelle stiffened in his grasp: once more the blood came flooding to her lips, but this time she knew: she knew that these eager hands wanted to make her sink down into a bottomless pit of abjection. This man was an enemy, one who would laugh at her fall; she felt the horror of such a humiliation so strongly that she began to tremble with desire and in a jet of passion she bit Denis' shoulder. He started; his hands gripped her body harder and he nibbled the quivering flesh; Marcelle clung to him ecstatically, drunk with shame. 'I'm his thing, his slave,' she murmured to herself; and aloud, 'I adore you.' Abruptly he turned her on her belly and made her kneel. 'Stay like that,' he whispered. 'It's more fun.' She trembled: a man, a being endowed with a conscience, wanted her to join him in an unclean act. He was bending her into this ridiculous position and relishing its ignominy. 'On all fours, like animals,' she thought: the idea made her head spin and he had to tense all his muscles to keep her in this degrading posture – she was like one of those victims the executioners force to dance under the whip. 'He's enjoying me, he's enjoying me,' she said to herself in a paroxysm of sensual delight. When Denis drew away she fell gasping on the bed, almost fainting.

She heard him moving about the room: when he came back and lay beside her she kept her eyes shut: at all costs she had to stay deep down in this drowsiness where shame turns into physical pleasure – she must never wake up again – it was impossible to face that half-affectionate, half-mocking look, impossible to allow a clear recollection of the caresses she had undergone. Yet Marcelle felt, and felt with a dreadful anguish, that in spite of all she could do the gentle mist was slowly, ineluctably fading: the nervous tension became so great that her teeth started to chatter.

The chattering was only slight at first and she could have stopped it by opening her eyes; but they remained tightly closed. Gradually the sound grew louder and louder. With a kind of relief Marcelle listened to the sound of clashing bone resonating in her head: it took up all her attention, her awareness, and defended her against recollection. Sobs ran the length of her body, making her shoulders shake convulsively: from time to time she clenched her teeth, but a violent trembling instantly followed this exhausting effort – she had lost all control. Yet she felt that the spell could be broken; all she had to do was to stop believing in it for a moment. But she took pleasure in thinking that she was possessed by unknown forces, and that stiffening her muscles was no use, since they did not obey her. Tears ran down her cheeks: Denis began stroking her hair and talking in an anxious, very irritated voice. 'It's nerves,' she stammered. 'Leave me alone. Let me go to sleep.' She could not bear being face to face with him again. She pulled the blankets over her and turned towards the wall.

The next day they set off for their honeymoon: Marcelle was disappointed by Mont-Saint-Michel, and once more she perceived that life always fell short of dreams. She did find Chateaubriand's grave as imposing as she had hoped it would be, but she liked Chateaubriand less than she had when she was young; and, indeed, she laughed heartily when Denis made disrespectful fun of romanticism. As he often did when he was talking to her, he spoke about the new aesthetic that France had to be provided with. For her part she would have liked to tell him memories of her childhood, but it was not a subject that he found very interesting. Sometimes their conversation tended to die away: Denis would then kiss her neck, stroking her breasts. She loathed those brief caresses. At the slightest contact her body prepared itself for a great yielding, a complete surrender, and since she had to regain possession of herself right away she remained all on edge until the evening. She could not prevent herself from being impatient for night to come, and this made her resent Denis – almost hate him.

At the end of a week Denis suggested going back to Paris: Marcelle had counted on spending her fortnight's holiday in Brittany, but she readily agreed to make this sacrifice for him. Denis was very grateful to her, and he was particularly kind and attentive on the train. They talked about the life that was waiting for them in Paris, and Denis confessed how much it grieved him to be obliged to be dependent on her. At this time the Drouffes were very comfortably off: Pascal had left the Ecole des Chartes and he had been given a grant for research. He was supervising an edition of mediaeval texts and, having made some quite good contacts in literary circles, he might prove a very valuable ally for Denis. For the moment Marcelle and Pascal had decided to leave the young writer all the free time he needed to finish his apprenticeship.

'You'll soon manage to get a name for yourself, you see if you don't,' said Marcelle. With much feeling Denis kissed her hands and promised to show himself worthy of such unselfishness: but he had so terribly little confidence in himself. 'I'm so bad at living, so awkward, so ill-adapted, my poor darling,' he said, and his look darkened. 'I can only bring care and anxiety to those who love me.' Marcelle's eyes filled with tears and rapturously she said that she believed in him. 'I shouldn't have married you if I hadn't been perfectly certain you were an exceptional being,' she said; and then smiling, 'I still remember the evening my fate was revealed to me, a completely mauve evening. I had been crying for a long while because the world was so ordinary and commonplace and I wanted to die. And then all at once I knew that one day you would come.' He listened to her with deep emotion, taking her hand: the blaze of genius shone in his gold-flecked eyes. 'I never stopped waiting for you,' she said.

The young couple settled in Mme Drouffe's apartment, taking over a room separated from the rest by a long corridor. Marcelle went through a period of frivolity: even after she had returned to her work at the Centre she went out with Denis almost every evening, going to the theatre, the cinema, the Lapin Agile, the Noctambules, and sometimes having supper in Montparnasse or Montmartre. On Sundays they stayed in bed until noon. Marcelle gave up her voluntary work at 'Social Contact' for good.

'The only thing I believe in now,' she told Germaine, 'is individual action. Influencing the masses may seem more spectacular, but if you want to accomplish anything of real value it is better to give yourself up entirely to one single worthwhile person.'

Germaine was in complete agreement: she had quite seen that Marcelle's generous giving of her best to the team had not been rewarded. Marcelle confessed that her sense that those beings she cared for so wholeheartedly were so remote from her had been a positive torment, and that in her bedroom at night she had often wept with despair. After this talk it occurred to Marcelle that perhaps she had been slightly unfair to Germaine, and she inwardly promised to overlook her little failings: Marcelle often asked her advice, and the renewal of their friendship made Germaine very happy.

As a wedding-present Germaine had given her friend a sum of money that Marcelle, accustomed to a modest way of life, thought quite considerable; and shortly after her return to Paris she was disagreeably surprised to find that she had frittered away more than half of it. 'I'm letting myself be carried away by a whirlwind,' she said to herself.

She would have to speak to Denis. Long before this Marcelle had observed that he did not understand the value of money: he wore silk shirts and at the theatre he took seats in the stalls. He seemed to float above all vulgar realities, and for several days Marcelle could not bring herself to talk to him about a question that seemed to her shabby and mean. It was one evening at a night-club that her duty became perfectly clear. Ever since she had calculated what it cost, this going out had lost its charm for Marcelle, but she had no excuse for refusing: on this particular evening, after a certain amount of pressing, Marcelle had put on her wedding-dress (a little dressmaker had altered it very prettily so that it would do to wear in the evening), put on lipstick and wrapped herself in a Spanish shawl that belonged to her mother. Denis gave her a queer kind of a look, and when they were sitting down with two sherry cobblers in front of them he asked her why she did not have her hair cut short. Marcelle answered curtly that her hair was an integral part of her personality: it was black and lustrous, and everyone had always acknowledged that it was very beautiful.

Denis did not dwell on the subject: he seemed to enjoy listening to the bawling music of the jazz band and watching the women with dyed hair – they all laughed with the same ingratiating laugh, rubbing themselves against the men. Marcelle shivered and drew the shawl over her shoulders. Sorrowfully she called to mind the dreamy, thoughtful child who had fled from the tawdry glitter of balls: she remembered her exacting youth, her proud sufferings and the wealth of her inner life. She must react against this current of frivolity that was sweeping her along: it was her duty to show Denis how to lead a life filled with serious, sober joys, with work and with lofty thoughts. She turned to him. 'I wonder what we are doing here,' she said.

He looked at her with a rather obstinate expression on his face and said 'It's a pleasant spot for dancing.'

She sighed. Sometimes he quite took her aback: the Denis who was so understanding and sensitive, the Denis who had the outlook of a poet, would now and then utter gross or cynical opinions for the fun of it. She would make him confess that he found these expensive, futile amusements depressing. 'We have given in to the insidious temptation of happiness – given in only too much,' she said to herself thoughtfully. She decided to speak to Denis right away. 'What shall we have gained intellectually or spiritually when this evening is over, Denis?' she asked. 'Listen, since we came back we have been satisfied with easy shows and easy music, and we no longer draw anything from ourselves. We are letting our happiness lull us to sleep – it's understandable in a way; but we are confusing pleasure and happiness.'

He looked at her attentively, with an ironical expression on his face. 'As far as I'm concerned, it's a delightful life,' he said. He did not seem to be taking Marcelle at all seriously.

'In any case it's not a life than we can go on leading any more,' she said curtly. 'We can no longer afford it.'

Denis' face hardened. 'Ah? We're broke? You should have said so right away.'

Marcelle gave an impatient shrug. 'But that's only a secondary issue, Denis,' she said. 'Just think how you are wasting your wonderful gifts in idleness. You must set yourself to work. Besides, we can perfectly well go out once or twice a week, you know.'

'Once a week, on Saturdays!' He smiled unpleasantly, and then in an offhand tone he said, 'Oh well, I suppose you're right. Tomorrow I'll start that article on Lautréamont I was talking to Pascal about. It will surely bring me in a little pocket-money.'

'Denis,' said Marcelle in a reproachful voice, blushing violently. Denis' attitude wounded her: he forgot that it was she who earned the money he threw away so readily, but she could not remind him of the fact without looking mean. It was vexing.

Denis was ill-humoured during the days that followed and the atmosphere at home grew stormy. Pascal was perfectly tactful and discreet, but Mme Drouffe was not very fond of Denis; he was often rude to her and sometimes they quarrelled violently. Marguerite admired Denis, and she took his side with a zeal that did nothing to lessen the animosity. As far as Marcelle herself was concerned, Denis changed: he remained polite, but he was irritable and on edge and he made a point of avoiding serious conversations. It was only at night, when he took her in his arms, that Marcelle's faith in him and in his love came back: to see this child she watched over like a mother during the day change into an imperious young male overwhelmed her and she yielded to his whims with intense pleasure. He always went to sleep first: with her body voluptuously relaxed she gazed at his calm features and uttered the loving promise, 'You will never wear out my patience.' She would no doubt have a great deal to suffer, but she would accept these sufferings with joy; and one day, when he was fully mature and at the height of his fame, he would look back over the past and understand.

Yet Denis could hardly be said to be taking the road to fame, and presently Marcelle grew anxious. When she came unexpectedly into the room, she found him lolling on the bed, smoking or reading detective stories: she thought it her duty to make disapproving remarks, and these he did not like at all. 'You can't write a poem as though it were a thesis,' he said irritably. As for the articles that Pascal had suggested placing for him, it was no good – he had never been able to turn his ideas into money. He spoke with such contempt that Marcelle shed tears. The lack of understanding that great men usually met with from those around them had often made her feel indignant, and she had thought she would be an ideal companion for a superior mind: but genius is always disconcerting – Marcelle was horribly afraid that she had inflicted a vulgar scene on Denis and that she had not fully appreciated the rights of poetry. For the whole of one night she had anxiously wondered how she ought to behave. There were child prodigies who never fulfilled themselves, and dreamers who could be made to produce masterpieces only by compulsion. A perfect understanding and acceptance of the weaknesses and even perversities that were the price of genius did not mean that one must not struggle against them. Marcelle bravely assumed the thankless role that fell to her: she insisted that every evening Denis should show her what he had written during the day: she resolutely checked him for his idleness, she patiently put up with his bad moods. And one day he would kiss her eyelids, his heart torn with remorse, and she would smile and say 'Everything you brought me made me happy.'

This idea kept her going for a while: at night she stroked Denis' hair, filled with gentle, sweet thoughts of all the sacrifices she had made for him and of those she was still prepared to make; and her eyes filled with tears. But even these moments became more and more rare. Although she carefully rationed his pocket-money, Denis took to spending his days in cafés and to going out in the evening without his wife: when he came and lay down at Marcelle's side he scarcely seemed to notice that she was there –in an absent-minded way he accepted her kisses and then went straight to sleep. Marcelle was obliged to speak to him firmly: she described his life in unflattering terms and stated that she would not pay his debts. In return Denis made unsparing fun of her bourgeois carefulness and mocked the yearning for the ideal that tormented her. His cruel and unfair words wounded Marcelle's heart: she repeated them to herself during the sleepless nights that she spent by Denis' peaceful, relaxed body; she remembered their earlier embraces and she trembled with disgust and longing. She grew very highly-strung, and particularly at those times of the month when she was unwell she was incapable of keeping back the insulting words that rose to her lips. By way of response Denis assumed an insolent, arrogant manner; and he was insufferably off-hand with Mme Drouffe and Pascal. The only person he was kind to was Marguerite, who was in open-mouthed admiration of all he did. Mme Drouffe thought he had a thoroughly bad influence on her younger daughter, and she held it against him: there were frequent scenes between Marguerite and her mother.

At dinner one day Marguerite asked Denis what was meant exactly by an 'American bar': he readily told her, ending, 'If you would like to see one, it's perfectly easy. I'll take you this very evening.'

'It's no place for a girl,' said Mme Drouffe sharply.

Marguerite shrugged. 'No place for a girl! That makes no sense. What do you imagine could happen to me?'

'I don't want you to go out this evening,' said Mme Drouffe.

'Why not this evening? What difference does it make?'

'Don't start arguing again,' said Marcelle. 'Mama doesn't want you to go out, and that's all. You really might give way sometimes, Marguerite.'

Marguerite's lips trembled with anger. 'I'm absolutely determined to go out with Denis,' she said in an unsteady voice.

Denis began to laugh and made her a sign not to go on. Nothing further arose until they reached coffee. When he had drunk his cup Denis stood up and said calmly, 'Well, Marguerite, are you coming?'

'You know perfectly well Mama is against it,' said Marcelle in a furious voice. 'Your behaviour is indecent.'

Marguerite hesitated for a moment, then she walked towards the door.

'I absolutely forbid you to go,' said Mme Drouffe, growing very red.

'Good night, everybody,' said Denis. He pushed Marguerite by the shoulder and they ran down the stairs laughing.

It was the first time Marguerite had ever so deliberately disobeyed her mother: Mme Drouffe burst into tears. Pascal and Marcelle soothed her and persuaded her to go to bed. Marcelle undertook to wait up for Marguerite and Denis.

She talked to Pascal for a few moments and then she too went to her bedroom: it was not so much the sadness of her lot that overwhelmed Marcelle as the injustice. She had always foreseen that life would make her suffer, because one does not prefer heroism and beauty to pleasure without having to pay for it; but she had never doubted that by her refusal of easy pleasures she was making herself worthy of those joys which are the reward of great souls. Now her faith wavered. Maybe there was something rotten in the world: maybe she had saved herself for a promised land that did not exist.

To while away the time Marcelle looked for a book; but she was incapable of reading. The street noises had stopped: the silence was almost oppressive. Marcelle was extremely afraid of the dark, and the slightest creaking made her start. She walked up and down the room for a while; then she sat down at Denis' desk and leafed through the untidy papers. He had scarcely written two or three pages, and even those were all crossed out: she had staked everything on him and she had lost.

Without thinking what she was doing, Marcelle opened one of the drawers: a little heap of letters lay at the bottom, perhaps a dozen of them. With a certain dread she took the letters and spread them out before her. There were a few trifling notes – appointments with friends, requests for money. Marcelle glanced through one of the letters: 'You tell me that your freedom is the most precious of those golden bowls that we sometimes have to throw into the sea, like the King of Thule, so as to weep for them afterwards,' wrote a man called André on the occasion of his friend's marriage. 'But what will become of me while you sit sadly watching the rings on the water? Without you, shall we still play the dangerous game you taught us – play it wholeheartedly? I am afraid of forgetting how to live.' Marcelle also found a poem by this André and she was about to read it when a blue letter caught her eye: it was a letter from a woman, dated two days earlier. The address, engraved in dark blue at the top of the sheet, was 12 rue du Ranelagh: the woman signed herself Marie-Ange and it was obvious that she was Denis' mistress. At this Marcelle started searching the bedroom without the least scruple. In a coat pocket she found another blue letter dated three months before and signed M. A. Lamblin. The lady asked Denis to come to tea: she wanted him to meet some interesting people. At this time she was still calling him *vous* rather than the intimate *tu*. Denis must have locked away the rest of their correspondence, because Marcelle's search uncovered nothing more.

'He's betrayed me,' she reflected. Denis had married her because he had nothing to live on and because he disliked the idea of working: but now that he was the lover of a no doubt very wealthy woman, he no longer bothered to treat her decently. For two hours and more Marcelle was prostrated: she wept over all those days lost in devotion and tears; and these present tears were no longer the restoring promise of a brilliant future but a sterile bitterness of mind. She was no longer young; she was physically weary; she had committed her life for good and all: presently she would be a useless old woman, one who had never known happiness. She thought of Denis with a cold hatred.

Three was striking when she got up and put the letters back in their place. She compelled herself to spend a long time getting ready for bed: she wanted to regain full control of herself and she wanted to take her revenge on Denis. With a calm, dignified sadness she would make him thoroughly aware of his wrong-doing; she would crush him with her scorn; she would not speak of the letters.

Marguerite and Denis came back an hour later: Marcelle stared at her half-drunk sister in silence and then turned to her husband. 'It seems to me we had better have it out,' she said.

'Do you really think so?' said Denis, following her into their room: he sat down on the bed to take off his shoes. Marcelle folded her arms and looked at him steadily.

'I do not blame you for no longer having any love for me, nor even any respect,' she said. 'But what I should like to know is why, under such circumstances, you married me?'

Denis hesitated. 'Perhaps I was wrong,' he said. 'I thought that with you I should find the peaceful atmosphere I needed – a happy, well-balanced life. I ought to have preferred my freedom to peace.'

'You admit that you never loved me?'

Denis smiled and began to untie his tie. 'What is love?' he said.

'I've sacrificed everything for you,' said Marcelle in a trembling voice.

'I know,' he said quickly. 'I eat the bread you earn by the sweat of your brow: but I do assure you it's very bitter bread.'

This took Marcelle's breath away. 'Oh,' she cried. 'This is too much. You think it perfectly normal to exploit us and then you dare to come and complain!'

He looked at her gravely and there was a deep contempt in his eyes. 'It's true that for you people these questions of money count enormously. You must forgive me, but I've never been able to get used to that turn of mind.'

Marcelle reddened: no insult could have wounded her more. She bitterly regretted her clumsy words. 'I devoted myself to you body and soul,' she said.

'For my part I thought you rather liked it,' said Denis insolently. 'But now, if it no longer satisfies you, there's a very easy answer – we only have to part.'

'Part!' cried Marcelle: the blood left her cheeks and she sank into a chair. She had seen the appalling fate of living with Denis without love and without hope, but never for a moment had she thought of leaving him.

'I can't change myself,' said Denis, 'and you can't accept me as I am. The best thing is a clean break.'

He was young and he was loved; he would be happy away from her and she would be alone. Little did she care now whether she had her revenge or not: she could not bear the idea of sleeping alone for ever, of never feeling a warm, strong body's weight again.

'Would you spoil my life without any remorse at all?'

'Since you're not happy with me . . .'

Marcelle stood up, took Denis' shoulders and looked deep into his eyes. 'You're only a child,' she said slowly, 'a cruel child. But I love you, Denis: I shall always love you, in spite of everything.'

He freed himself, slightly embarrassed. 'I'm not a brute, Marcelle,' he said in a rather unsure voice. 'Believe me, I've a great deal of affection for you.' He smiled. 'Only I'm just not made for family life.'

Denis said nothing more about parting: Marcelle had been so

afraid of losing her husband that she decided to put up with anything at all to keep him. If only he stayed it did not matter if he never became a genius or if he loved other women. 'True love forgives all,' she reflected.

Marcelle spent some unhappy, painful days: instead of being grateful for such a degree of abnegation, Denis took advantage of it to throw off all restraint. During the hours she spent waiting for him to come back at night, Marcelle sadly remembered the free and peaceful time of her girlhood, when her life ran to the rhythm of melodious verse, when she was surrounded by poets and heroes, brotherly figures always ready to respond to her call, and when she thought about the books she would write in the vague future, about the delicate impressions she had gathered during the day, about happiness, death and fate. Now this calm meditation was denied her: now her daily lot was anxiously listening to the footsteps in the street, evoking the picture of Denis with a woman in his arms, hating him, longing for his caresses. Sometimes she had the despairing thought that her passion for Denis was laying waste a spirit which had been meant for a great destiny, and she found herself wishing for no matter what kind of release.

One Saturday, when she came back from the Centre, she found a letter on her bed. She knew at once what had happened.

'Do not think of me too unkindly,' wrote Denis. 'No doubt I shall never find another love like yours; but my poor dear Marcelle there are some beings who refuse even love. Do you know that in Thule there was a king who threw his golden bowl into the sea so that he might watch the rings on the water and sigh. No doubt one day I shall bitterly miss this happiness I am giving up: may you, for your part, find consolation very soon. I do not dare to hope for your forgiveness.'

The wardrobe and drawers were empty. 'He has got hold of some money,' thought Marcelle. 'It's that woman.' Her eyes remained dry. 'My life is finished,' she said under her breath.

She took off her hat and coat and automatically smoothed her black hair as she stood in front of the wardrobe mirror. A strange peace flooded into her. 'My life is finished,' she said again, with a kind of indifference. She was no longer thinking about Denis: she gazed at the reflection of a woman with a broad forehead and soulful eyes, a woman who was still young and who no longer looked forward to anything at all. She lay down on the divan: from the far end of the corridor small noises reached her bedroom – the closing of a door, footsteps, the metallic sound of forks. Unconscious of the tragedy, Mme Drouffe was laying the table: Pascal was running through his index cards.

'All I have left is myself,' said Marcelle. She closed her eyes: it seemed to her that she was coming back to her real self, as if from a long banishment. Once more she thought of the sad, precocious child, crouching behind heavy curtains that separated her from the world or hiding in the shadows of a book-lined corridor. She saw herself as an adolescent, enthusiastic and misunderstood, confiding her sorrow to a mauve night-sky; she saw her lonely youth, full of pride and high, uncompromising demands. This road, so painfully traversed, had brought her back to solitude; and never again would she be tempted to escape from herself. A great exaltation filled her; she stood up and walked over to the window, drawing the curtains back with a sudden jerk. She was not to look beyond herself for the meaning of her life; she was set free from love, from hope, and from that stifling presence that had taken up all her strength and her time for more than a year. Everything was fine.

Marcelle leaned her forehead against the cool window-pane: in rejecting commonplace pleasures, playthings, finery, social success and easy flirtation she had always saved herself for some splendid happiness. Yet it was not happiness that had been granted to her: it was suffering. But perhaps it was only suffering that could satisfy her heart at last. 'Higher than happiness,' she whispered. This great bitter thing was her lot on earth and she would know how to receive it; she would know how to transform it into beauty; and one day strangers, brothers, would understand her disincarnate soul, and they would cherish it. Higher than happiness. Tears came into her eyes: she could already feel the dawn of sublime poems quivering within her.

For the second time she had the wonderful revelation of her fate. 'I am a woman of genius,' she decided.

❧ ❧ CHANTAL ❧ ❧

I Chantal's diary

2 October

As I left the lycée just now I bought this plum-coloured notebook, whose soft leather cover reminds me of the exact shade of violet I admired so much in Fra Angelico's 'Annunciation'. It is almost sacrilegious to spoil the virgin whiteness of these sheets and I am forming my letters as carefully as a child writing its first page in a new exercise book.

My window is open: the massive silhouette of the Tour Saint-Romain and the cathedral spire stand out sharply against a pearl-grey sky. Life is so quiet in this town studded with Gothic churches that it is as though I had been suddenly carried right back into the middle ages: the upthrusting lacework of stone creates a mystical atmosphere, and the slate roofs swim in so peaceful and so living a twilight that I feel rather like a fashionable young woman of former times who, touched by grace, is beginning a retreat in the peace of a nunnery.

It was only yesterday, in the din of the Paris streets, that Jeanne said to me, 'My poor Chantal, you are going to be horribly bored in the provinces.' Her pity was disagreeable, but I did not like to reject it. She was entirely mistaken in being sorry for me – one day was enough for me to realize the quantities of pleasant possibilities around me . . . This evening I revel in the knowledge that at last I am going to be able to savour all the wealth of experience that life brings me, to savour it to the full and at my leisure. At the teachers' college one lived only by stealth, in hurried, eager bursts. To be sure, because of their very rarity, the minutes stolen from preparing for the competitive examination had a special, exciting flavour, almost the taste of forbidden fruit (oh the slow moonlit strolls in the park, the sunsets over the Saint-Cloud wood, Lucile's clear laughter along the grey corridors), but they never satisfied my hunger. What happiness, now that I am here, to be able to devote all my energy just to this one thing – just to living.

Yesterday, as I sat comfortably in a corner-seat of the carriage, I felt my past slipping away from me: I had an impression of calm strength as I felt it go, while without stirring I let a new life come

49

towards me, a life whose shape I could not yet make out. Slowly Sèvres and Paris, the world I had lived in up until then, began to turn themselves into memories, to grow delightful. The little arguments, the little irritations, that had sometimes made our Italian journey disagreeable faded away and all I retained was the pure visions of Siena, 'that blood-red city', of the gilded domes of Florence, Lucile's light-coloured dress in the Palatine gardens, Jeanine's keen, intelligent face as we talked about aesthetics all along the Venetian canals.

When I left my luggage in a very ordinary hotel opposite the railway-station and stood there alone in the streets of an unknown town I had a moment of weakness. The shy, anxious Chantal I have not yet quite killed (the Chantal the real one does so detest) made a sudden reappearance. With some displeasure I thought that at this very moment Jeanine and Lucile would be listening to the Debussy quartet or the Ravel concerto without me, that they would be talking about me in pitying tones, and that because of these conversations, which my absence would make more frequent and more intimate, Jeanine would acquire a not altogether desirable influence over Lucile. Faced with the future I was a coward. And then all at once, as I reached the quays and the breeze wafted sea smells from the river, I was filled with an immense sense of adventure. I went into a café and lit a cigarette; and it came to me that I had no need of anyone to help me to live. It was a curious sort of café, looking as though it had been carved out of a solid block of nougat, so that it would all have been good to eat, like the witch's house in the tale of Hansel and Gretel. People stared at me: but careless of the common faces all round me, indifferent to friendship and forgetfulness, suddenly victorious and triumphant I plunged rapturously into solitude, as though into pure, icy water.

My pupils would indeed have been surprised if they had known how their future mistress spent her first evening in Rougemont.

When I woke this morning I thought happily that for me the days of book-based culture were over and that now I was to come into contact with reality: I was to find a room in which I could think and work, I was to make myself an environment, and I was to create just the right kind of relationship with my pupils. These are the concrete problems that life faces me with at present.

I began by going to a hairdresser: I do not like undertaking anything until I am physically as impeccable, as fully prepared, as I am psychologically: sitting obediently under the metal dome while I gave my hands over to the manicurist, I felt less like a young secondary-school teacher about to go to see her headmistress than an adventuress getting herself ready for battle.

Mlle Bidois was very agreeable: my duties and my timetable suit me perfectly. She gave me the addresses of several furnished rooms, and as soon as I left her I began my search. It was only in the evening, after I had looked at five dreary places – those characterless, impersonal rooms that cannot possibly count for anything much in one's life – that I found this old house, whose massive outer doors seem less to bar the entrance to a dwelling than the way into a soul. An exceedingly distinguished white-haired lady led me very graciously through the garden and then through her apartment: even before I had seen my room I was entirely won over. These walls contain all that is most touching in provincial France: the mellow surfaces of the old furniture, the books in their rare bindings, and the precious little ornaments and curiosities, handed down from generation to generation, retain some wavering, mysterious hint of the reflection of the eyes that have gazed at them: in every corner of this house the vanished past has left an impalpable scent – one that gives the present the rare and heady bouquet of a very old wine.

Now it is quite dark. I have arranged my beloved books in my cupboard, my dear and inseparable companions Proust, Rilke, Katherine Mansfield, *Dusty Answer*, *Le Grand Meaulnes* . . . I am not sure yet which of them I shall finish the day with. I look forward with amusement to beginning my life as a teacher tomorrow. I feel, more ardently than ever, that in spite of everything Life is wonderful.

3 October

I love this town with its faded colours, like those of an old tapestry: the houses look as though they were painted in pastel on a soft, dim blue sky: and this evening a delicate melancholy drifted about the streets. They have picturesque and charming names, these streets – la rue du Pré-aux-Marles, la rue du Pot-Cassé, la rue des Ecrouelles. On my way to the lycée at eight o'clock I felt as though I were walking through a Balzac novel, and I was almost surprised not to see old women in stringed bonnets and young housewives in mob-caps coming out of the sleepy houses. The spire of St Ruffien's can be seen from every part of the town; and this morning it soared up into the pale blue as clear and as vibrant as an angelus bell.

The lycée is an old sixteenth-century mansion, but I am quite certain that not a single one of my worthy colleagues ever pauses to relish the delicate blacks and yellows of its façade: I caught a glimpse of them in the teachers' common-room – withered old maids, all puffed up with their heavy, useless academic culture, who have never looked real life in the face. Fortunately I can absent myself from my immediate surroundings when I wish, and while they were gossiping I was wholly taken up with listening to the frail voice of a harpsichord singing away inside me, a harpsichord whose antiquated notes seemed to me an exact translation of the impressions created by my morning walk. As I walked into my classroom I was a little nervous. I felt I had such wealth to give these pupils, but what would they be capable of receiving from me? Could I take as much interest in them and like them as much as I wished? I was not disappointed. There is something charming and equivocal about these girls who are not yet women but who are no longer children. They are not all of them agreeable, but all that is needed to make me happy is that the charming forms of a few girls in blossom (as dear Proust would say) should stand out among those of the common kind.

There is Rosa, a fair-haired, blue-eyed daughter of the Vikings whose pearly complexion flushes at the slightest emotion with the scarlet she has inherited from her forefathers, those fierce, handsome giants. I can perfectly imagine her, shy and smiling in a long white dress, pouring out mead for huge red-headed warriors. There is Lydia, with a gazelle-like body, timid movements, and dreamy eyes; it seems that her grandmother was Greek, and her nose with its quivering nostrils has the purity of Praxiteles' statues. There is Monique, so like a Lippi virgin with her slender profile and her misty eyes: her graceful neck rising –as from a calyx – from a finely pleated flame-coloured collar, which she had spread out over her schoolgirl's pinafore with coquettish attention to detail.

I admit that I did my best to be charming, but without affect-ation, as naturally as I should have smiled at the beauty of a basket of flowers on a spring morning. The recollection of their freshness has scented my evening. I must get to know Lydia.

15 October
A blank day. But these hours of truce have their sweetness: when one looks back to the far horizon to see beautiful moments of the past, one finds that the clear, sharp memories are surrounded, magically surrounded, by a soft mauve halo.

Mme de Beauregard, my landlady, asked me to tea. We talked about music: she may not be very highly cultivated, but at least she has an unusually fine ear. She also told me a little about her husband, who seems to have been one of those enlightened amateurs who are perhaps no longer to be found anywhere but in the old provinces, one of those lovers of art who can add genuine erudition to an entirely disinterested curiosity. She told me some interesting archaeological details about Rougemont and lent me a pamphlet by M. de Beauregard on the Tour Saint-Romain that I shall be glad to look through. This conversation had the moving quality of certain antique shops, of certain novels by Dickens –something antiquated, faded, and precious. I particularly liked looking at Mme de Beauregard's face: a Madonna oval that age has delicately worn without destroying, as time erodes some stone Virgins in such a way that their beauty is enhanced, because their present imperfection suggests a pure and faultless image more dazzling than if it were directly shown.

I am going to write to Jeanine; I do not want her to think that I have sunk into a rut, living in the provinces – I have never felt so well-balanced, nor so strong, nor so enthusiastic.

20 October
Beside me I have laid the heap of logical analyses that I must give back to the fifth form tomorrow; but how can I bring myself to correct them when my room is filled with the scent of autumn roses? Yesterday Mme de Beauregard gave me an armful, and just now little Françoise, more like a Benozzo Gozzoli page than ever with her halo of curls, brought me this magnificent sheaf. These lovely flowers called for a little elegance round them, and that is why I put on my Japanese dressing-gown and my Turkish slippers. Dressed like this, in this bower of a room, I am more like an idle young woman than an austere schoolmistress.

When I reach the lycée with my hair well done, my face well made-up, and wearing a tawny blouse, the colour of chrysanthemums, it amuses me to feel the disapproving looks of my colleagues and the somewhat astonished, wonder-struck gaze of the pupils, who probably do not think that I am quite real. And I am very fond of running down the stairs under the scandalized eyes of the other mistresses.

I like Monique Fournier more and more. She carries her head high, like a young infanta, and there is an enchanting touch of insolence mixed with her obvious admiration for me. She knows that she and her companions belong to different races: hers is more fragile, but it is rarer. If I ask her to tea I shall have to ask Andrée Lacombe too, since they are bosom friends. For her part Andrée belongs to the heavy, graceless race of those who are good at their lessons: like her aunt, she will become a worthy member of the teaching profession. School-time values must indeed be very strong for a charming dunce like Monique to treat that graceless girl as an equal: no doubt Andrée's triumphs dazzle her.

As I touched the fragile roses I brushed a petal off, and it fell on the pile of essays: it is transparent, it is frivolous, and for me it symbolizes the easy, light-handed affection that my little pupils surround me with. I know that although I may retain a nostalgia for a pair of acid-green eyes or some particular childish, scornful pout, this affection will have faded long ago: but what does it matter? I do not ask these fleeting sympathies to fill my heart, but merely to encompass it with the graceful, aerial atmosphere of a Shakespearean fairyland, in which it can allow itself to be enchanted for a while.

6 November

Monique and Andrée have just left. They were rather shy at first, but Monique, with her feminine instinct already quite developed, soon found the right note. She has such an inherent grace that she would naïvely hit upon the right way of behaving in the most difficult situation.

She looked very pretty today, wearing her flame-coloured dress closed at the neck by a thick cord, like those bags they pass round for the collection at high Mass. She admired the pale tulips and the black-centred anemones that I had placed about my room: it was as though there were some subtle understanding between her and the flowers. Her childish grace made me think of the girls of Francis Jammes: it seemed to me that, called up from the remote past by the ancient, provincial scent of my room, a sister of Clara d'Ellébeuse and of Almaïde d'Etremont had come to sit quietly beside me. Under the softened light of my lamp her eyes were more mauve than ever.

Although she is of a coarser kind, Andrée did not spoil the picture's harmony: she is excellently designed for the role that seems to have fallen to her – that of the confidential friend, somewhat given to scolding and a little too reasonable, but intelligent and devoted. She is not bad-looking: a little retiring –just what is called for in those attendants who accompany kings' daughters throughout their splendid adventures.

I talked mostly with Monique. Any attempt at recording our lively, graceful to and fro would make it impossibly heavy: she has a delicate sense of humour, a fresh and discriminating vision of the world, and talking with this child seemed to me infinitely more precious than the intellectual conversations that Jeanine pities me for being deprived of. I am tired of the mere interplay of ideas. *Primum vivere* . . . By the grace of her youth and her artlessness alone, this fifteen-year-old schoolgirl goes deeper into the heart of Life than many austere thinkers. Today, and with a wonderful clarity, I understood the truth of certain pages of Bergson that have long been close to my heart: dissecting our fleeting impressions, shutting them up in words, and turning them into thoughts very often means coarsely destroying the impalpable shimmer that gives them all their value. Yes: what we must do is set our awareness in tune with the changing flow of life as this sincere, instinctive child does, and with a constantly renewed intuition grasp the world's perpetual freshness . . .

Since I began writing the anemones' centres have darkened, the scent of the night has changed, and all around me countless beauties that have just come into flower call for an affection adjusted precisely to them alone . . . I want no part of life to go by me without grasping it.

20 November

There are weightless, airy days that are born with a smile and that all through their light-filled hours shed a rain of little joys, as resonant and crystalline as the notes of chiming bells.

I had been rather low-spirited for some time, because of that letter of Jeanine's. I do not like life to go on without my being there. And then Jeanine's quietly superior tone irritates me: though really at present she does not seem to be leading so happy a life that there is any call to envy her. A little note from Anne dispelled the cloud. The comfort of knowing that I am missed: and of knowing that my presence could sometimes perfume other lives around me.

In my first year at Sèvres I would often repeat these lines of Baudelaire:

> Mainte fleur épanche à regret
> Son parfum doux comme un secret
> Dans la solitude profonde.[1]

Now I give Valéry's splendid reply:

> Calme, calme, reste calme
> Connais le poids d'une palme
> Portant sa profusion.[2]

I reached the lycée my heart high. I was expecting the inspector general's visit this morning, and I was a little uncomfortable when I began my lessons because I knew that L. was very favourably inclined towards me, that G. had spoken to him on my behalf, and that if I gave him a good idea of me, he would not refuse me his support. I do not want to moulder in this hole for years on end. Fortunately my explanation of Plato was really brilliant and the girls made a very good impression on L.: Andrée Lacombe answered in a really outstanding manner. L. made a little fun of 'my impetuous youth' but in fact he was delighted, quite charmed by the living, direct tone of my teaching. Tiny though it may be, this little victory has given me some confidence in myself.

Strolling in the streets of Rougemont in the evening: reading a few pages of Proust. No more is needed for life to seem to me as

[1] Many a flower grieves to spread/its scent, sweet as a secret,/in the depths of loneliness.
[2] Calm, calm, stay calm/know the weight of a palm/bearing its abundance.

easy and as charming as a Watteau picture. I feel so young, so gay
. . . I have the delightful impression that I vibrate with the least
breath of life and that I turn everything I touch into a delicious
honey that scents and strengthens my inner life.

It seems that Mme Fournier would like to know me. I saw her
once as she was getting out of a splendid car with Monique; she
was very well dressed indeed – her husband is one of the richest
manufacturers in these parts. It would be amusing to study that
stratum of society.

25 November
A grey day. I answered Jeanine, perhaps rather sharply; and now
that my letter is finished I feel empty and on edge. I mind other
people's opinons too much: I ought to have more pride. But this
evening I cannot help seeing myself as Jeanine sees me – alone,
withdrawn from life, buried in the provinces, without love,
without a future. How slowly these evenings creep by. I have not
even spirit enough to keep this diary when I am so downhearted.
I do not know exactly what it is that I want: I am bored; I am bored
to death. I want to be nearer Paris: I shall never be able to bear this
life for two years on end. What loneliness! I wish it were already
time to go to bed. And to think that I am reduced to sleeping
ten hours a night to kill time. The cinema programmes are
impossible: I do not even do my morning exercises any more,
everything seems so pointless. And tomorrow the lycée again,
homework to correct, an afternoon to kill. I am stifling: I have
the feeling of being buried alive.

II

When Chantal walked into the headmistress's office the meeting
had already begun: she sat down in a corner. Her colleagues were
gathered in a half-circle round Mlle Bidois' desk, and she looked
at them with amusement – 'How seriously they take themselves!'
On the wall there was a reproduction of the 'Victory of
Samothrace' and an etching of an old street in Rougemont: a
well-dressed, pretty woman must seem strangely out of place in
this conventional room and its context: Chantal crossed her legs

and smoothed the rich stuff of her skirt with an approving hand. That evening, for the first time, she was going to have dinner with Mme Fournier, Monique's mother, and she felt that her life was brilliant and varied: this dreary teachers' meeting was not really part of it.

'Fifth form,' said Mlle Bidois: she read out the names of the pupils who had been awarded a place on the roll of honour. 'The following fulfil the conditions required for the disciplinary council's congratulations: Renée Canu, Monique Fournier, Andrée Lacombe, Lydia Neveu, and Renée Poncet.' She paused. 'Who proposes Renée Canu?'

Several hands were raised. Chantal hesitated: 'She isn't very intelligent,' she said. 'She always seems to take her work so terribly seriously.' She smiled. She thought it daring to make such a paradoxical reproach in this pedantic gathering. 'But after all I let her pass.'

'Monique Fournier,' said Mlle Bidois. 'Who proposes her?'

'I do,' said Chantal.

There was a general outcry. 'She has a most undesirable attitude in class,' said Mlle Métral. 'She always looks as though she were making fun of people.'

Chantal stared ironically at the history teacher, a fat woman dressed in tawdry, garish clothes: she looked like . . . Chantal hesitated. Was it a Toulouse-Lautrec? Or rather a Daumier? In any case she was like a caricature.

'Her exercises are often very pretty,' said Mlle Lacombe. 'She writes quite well; but in view of her intelligence she could do much better.'

'She is well beyond Renée Canu,' said Chantal.

'It doesn't come so easy for Renée Canu.'

'Oh well, if stupidity is to be rewarded!'

The headmistress intervened. 'It is fair to make allowance for the effort,' she said curtly.

Mlle Normand, the English teacher, gave a mirthless laugh. 'Monique is absurdly affected: she does not behave like a girl.' Chantal looked at her scornfully. 'That Normand is typical,' she thought. 'Fit to be set up as an Aunt Sally.' Amused, she called to mind the cardboard heads that had made Lucile and her laugh when they were walking about the Foire du Trône: ever since Rimbaud had shown her the poetry of fairs she went once or twice a year. Mlle Normand went on, 'In a corridor the other day I heard her say, writing and wriggling as she said it, "Oh, I loathe Paul Bourget – it's just rose-water psychology." ' Laughter.

'I wonder whether her hair is real,' said Chantal to herself. 'I have a mind to pull it.' She smiled: 'This really is one of my witty days.'

'She scarcely acknowledges you when she meets you in the street,' said Mlle Métral.

Mlle Lacombe shrugged with a disillusioned air. 'They are all like that: they greet the year's new mistresses, and after that they no longer know you.'

Chantal drummed impatiently on her handbag. Monique and Andrée were to fetch her at half-past six; she would never have time to get dressed before they came; and she would take no pleasure in the evening if she felt that her hair or her make-up were not quite right. The Fourniers might introduce her to the society of Rougemont: she had to make a good impression on them. She gave her colleagues an irritated look; it was obvious they had no interest in life apart from their professional worries; nothing waited for them outside the lycée and they stayed there talking as though they were on a social visit. The reason they were so dead set against Monique was simply that she provided them with a subject of conversation. 'That was exactly her sister's way,' said the headmistress. 'Mariette was at the lycée for ten years without ever confiding in us at all; she did not even send us a wedding announcement when she was married.' She paused: 'It is no, then?'

'It is no,' said several voices.

'Then I refuse to let Renée Canu pass,' said Chantal. 'She is far behind Fournier.'

'It is not a question of comparison,' said the headmistress. 'There is no going back on a decision that has already been taken.'

Chantal half-formed a contemptuous grimace: how could these academics, shut up in their narrow school notions, distinguish the quality of an intelligence or a soul? They judged the children according to out-of-date values and without the slightest psychological insight. Chantal was the only person there capable of understanding those young beings' turn of mind and of valuing them at their real worth.

Congratulations were unanimously accorded to Andrée

Lacombe. 'She has made a great deal of progress this year,' said the headmistress; and everyone directed friendly looks towards Mlle Lacombe.

The hands of the clock pointed to half-past five. 'In any event I shan't have time for a bath,' thought Chantal. 'Particularly as the archaic water-heater takes ages to make the water even luke-warm.' Provincial women were dirty. Mme de Beauregard had found it very strange that Chantal should make her remove the books piled up in the bath – the bathroom must have been used as a study. 'Four francs a bath: I shan't pay it. If she thinks I will let myself be exploited, she is quite mistaken.'

Fortunately Chantal was not required to be there for the discussions about the two top forms, and she hurried home, almost running. It was cold in her room. 'When school starts again in January I shall look for somewhere else,' she said crossly: she was no longer on good terms with her landlady – arguments about the electricity and the central heating had put an end to their friendly relations. As she undressed and carefully put on new make-up, Chantal thought about Jeanine's apartment. Jeanine was lucky: she had succeeded very early. She must certainly have gone to bed with Delpierre; she could not possibly have managed without his help. And she took great care not to introduce me. Chantal put on her fine silk stockings and high-heeled shoes: her gloom vanished. Her black dress trimmed with green really looked as though it came from a very fashionable shop. For a year she and Jeanine had studied *Vogue*, *Femina* and *Votre Beauté* with great attention and they had retained these basic principles – that black is always elegant, and that being well dressed depends in a large degree upon the shoes one wears. Looking in the glass, Chantal thought that this evening no one could take her for a schoolmistress: a gratifying reflection.

As she was finishing her hair there was a knock on the door. 'Come in,' she said.

Monique and Andrée had come from the library: their cheeks were red and they were in high spirits.

'Papa will come and fetch us in the car at about eight,' said Monique. 'I do hope this dinner is not too much of a bore for you?'

'Not at all,' said Chantal indulgently. 'I saw your Mama in the visitors' room once: she looked charming.'

She filled three glasses with port, and leaned back on the divan: what a perfect example of free, intelligent, happy life she must represent for these children! To begin with they were rather awkward together, but Chantal soon made the girls understand that she was on their side and that she could be spoken to with perfect freedom. She lit a gold-tipped English cigarette.

'Do you know the latest thing that Mlle Lalorie has done?' asked Monique. 'She refused to let Suzanne come into class because she was wearing woollen socks with a fancy pattern. Mama was absolutely furious.'

'It doesn't surprise me,' said Chantal. 'If they had been ugly stockings, well . . . but I'm sure they were very pretty.'

'Very pretty. What a vile hole! We're forbidden to wear boots, too: though boots are a very good thing on rainy days.'

'Yet Mlle Lalorie wears some very odd clothes herself,' said Chantal. 'With her gilt metal earrings and her frizzed hair she looks like a gypsy.'

'From what they say, she's no puritan,' said Andrée. 'But she wants us to do the lycée honour. It mustn't be said in the town that we don't behave as well as the girls in the church and private schools.'

'Yes, and she spies on us in an utterly disgusting way: she goes through our bags, you know. And when her friends meet us outside they go and tell her how we were behaving.'

'It's ridiculous,' said Chantal. 'All it does is either create hypocrisy or a silly prudishness. Just imagine it – in the third form yesterday Simone Boilly put on a shocked expression because I translated *femora* by *thighs*.'

'And the Lord knows Simone Boilly . . .' said Monique.

'You mean she knows all about it?'

'As for that,' said Andrée, 'everybody does. The only reading my worthy aunt allows us is Desgranges' *Morceaux choisis*, but if she had a suspicion of what kind of books are handed about among the boarders . . .'

'From the first form on there ought to be classes in sex education for girls as well as for boys, and without any false modesty,' said Chantal. 'That would be the best way of putting an end to unwholesome curiosity.'

'Yes,' said Andrée doubtfully. 'But that would not stop them passing on dirty magazines or collecting photos of actors – they are disgustingly romantic.'

Chantal shook her head. 'And to think that the task of teaching you how to live is entrusted to women who have never learnt anything about life,' she said pensively. 'How can they possibly understand you? Most of them have never been young themselves!' She looked feelingly at the two childish faces turned towards her: suddenly they seemed to her almost tragic. Youth is a grace that is hard to bear. She thought of the young Rimbaud, of Raymond Radiguet, of *Le Grand Meaulnes*. 'Being young,' she said, her gaze following the cigarette smoke, 'is a great and splendid thing: but often very difficult, isn't it?'

Andrée's eye lit up. 'Oh yes!' she said impulsively. 'It's not at all agreeable.'

For the first time since she had made her acquaintance, Chantal thought she could make out something secret and romantic in Andrée's expression. 'What makes you unhappy, Andrée?' she asked in an almost tender voice.

Andrée made a vague movement. 'We do none of the things we want to do, and we don't even understand why our life is like that. We understand nothing.'

The answer disappointed Chantal: still, she said 'If ever you need any help or if you want anything explained, don't forget that I am your friend.'

There was a rather embarrassed silence. Monique was the first to break it. 'They are beginning to hate you in our form: they are furious because you are so kind to us.' She smiled at Chantal with a slightly provocative archness. 'It's not everyone who likes you, you know.'

'I'm sure you're right,' said Chantal, carelessly flicking off her cigarette ash; but she felt a little stab at her heart – she hated being disliked. 'What do they have against me?'

'Oh, it's just that they are jealous, as jealous as small-minded women,' said Andrée.

'But you really have started something in the fourth form!' said Monique gaily. 'Your name is carved on all the desks. You've noticed it, Andrée – whenever Mlle Plattard goes along the corridor there's always one of those girls looming up behind her. I'm sure they write poems in your honour.'

Chantal smiled. 'Some do.' She hesitated. 'Indeed, it can be very awkward – you promise not to tell?'

'Of course, mademoiselle,' said Monique.

'Well, yesterday I had a parcel from the little Caro: she's quite seriously ill and she will not be coming back to the lycée for a long while. She sent me a very pretty necklace that her mother had given her for her birthday and a photograph, and in a touching little note she begged me to accept the present. I'm not sure what to do.'

'You wouldn't like to keep it?' asked Monique.

'That would be impossible. In the end her mother would certainly notice that Ginette no longer had her necklace, and if the child admitted giving it to me, she would have the right to be thoroughly displeased. I think I shall give it back to Mme Caro.'

'Ginette will be scolded,' said Andrée, 'and in any case it would wound her horribly to have her parents mixed up with it.'

'I'll try to persuade Mme Caro to say nothing to Ginette.'

Andrée put on a doubting expression. 'You know what parents are like.'

Chantal's face darkened. 'Well, you find a solution yourself,' she said curtly. Andrée often irritated her: either from bumptiousness or a desire to assert her independence of mind in front of Monique, she was very apt to contradict Chantal. Chantal treated her on a footing of equality, of course; but it was a want of tact on Andrée's part to assume that footing herself.

There was the sound of a car's horn. 'That's Papa,' cried Monique. 'He said he'd wait below.'

They put on their coats. Chantal locked her bedroom door and walked smiling downstairs. M. Fournier had on a fine greatcoat and the ribbon of the Légion d'Honneur in his button-hole; Chantal thought his expression shrewd and energetic. The conversation, mostly about the beauty of Rougemont and its surroundings, ran smoothly. Chantal felt that she had easily adopted the right fashionable tone, light and quick, and she walked confidently into the big lit-up villa. 'I can be charming when I want to.' Mme Fournier was wearing a midnight-blue dress relieved by a rope of pearls. She looked very imposing. 'All dark colours are distinguished,' said Chantal to herself. 'Blue would suit me very well.' She looked covetously at every detail of the furnishing. 'How beautiful genuine luxury is! If one is at all artistic, it's unbearable living among vulgar objects. When all is said and done, Jeanine's apartment looks poor. I should like rich things all round me: I would know how to spend money really well!' And all at once she felt it was blindingly obvious that she would not always be a mere teacher.

'Do you like it at Rougemont?' asked Mme Fournier as they went into the dining-room. 'I remember that I took a great while to get used to it. When one has lived much of one's life in Paris, the provincial state of mind seems so narrow.'

Chantal was rather disappointed to find that apart from Andrée she was the only guest. 'I must tell you that I lead a very secluded life: I should not have the courage to mingle with the society of Rougemont – it must be deadly boring.'

'It is really hard to imagine how low the intellectual level is here. For my own part I do not complain, since we have delightful friends of our own; but the dyed-in-the-wool, thoroughbred member of Rougemont society is appallingly mean and petty. Still, we do have some acquaintances among them; and do you know, for them it is a downright scandal that I send Monique to the lycée.'

'Yet now that Mlle Bidois is headmistress, there is no longer anything objectionable about the conduct of the lycée,' said M. Fournier. 'She is an outstanding woman – most unusually capable.'

Chantal was uncomfortably aware of the two girls' eyes fixed upon her. 'She puts her whole heart into her work,' she said, 'and hers is certainly a very heavy responsibility. I imagine it must be a relief to her when the holidays come round,' she added. It would be better not to talk about the lycée too much.

'You will not be staying in Rougemont for Christmas, of course?' said Mme Fournier.

'No. I shall certainly go off for winter sports, either to Switzerland or the Tyrol. I am not sure which.' Chantal heard herself say this with the utmost pleasure. 'I took up skiing last year, and I really long to be at it again.'

'How lucky you are to be young and to be free,' said Mme Fournier with a kindly smile. 'I love the snow, but I am never able to get away in the winter.'

'It gives one a wonderful sense of overcoming difficulty, of danger, of solitude . . .' said Chantal, and she eagerly described the joys of tobogganing and skiing. No strikingly original points of view or profound thoughts were exchanged during the rest of the evening; but Chantal did not make the mistake of preferring intelligence to all other qualities. She valued elegance and charm, and she inwardly vowed that she would neglect no opportunity of frequenting these tasteful, artistic people who had so graciously received her. Some days later she sent flowers to Mme Fournier and ordered a blue marocain frock at a good dressmaker's. From time to time Mme Fournier sent her informal invitations, and Chantal congratulated herself on combining the pleasures of seclusion with the charms of fashionable society. When she succeeded in seeing her life from this point of view, her exile in Rougemont became almost bearable.

III

Mlle Lacombe was the moral conscience of the girls' lycée. She presided over the teachers' association. Her opinion carried most weight at the meetings of the society of incorporated teachers and at the disciplinary council. Every year her colleagues entrusted her with the management of the circulating library. She was always asked to collect the subscriptions whenever there was a death, a marriage, or a retirement. Her brother was also a teacher and he was very active at the boys' lycée on behalf of the League against Prostitution! He was a member of the Society for the Protection of the Birthrate and of Children. He had lost his wife after two years of marriage, and since then he had lived with his sister, who dedicated herself entirely to the bringing up of Andrée.

Andrée Lacombe had indeed been brought up very carefully. As soon as she could read, Lacombe had inscribed edifying maxims from the best authors on pieces of cardboard and decorated his daughter's bedroom with them. Andrée was neither frivolous nor inattentive; she accepted reproof politely; she did not chatter in class; and she had an excellent reputation in the lycée. Every New Year's day her companions chose her to present the whole form's best wishes to the headmistress; and for the lycée's fiftieth anniversary it was she who handed the Minister of Public Education a basket of saffron-yellow roses in the name of all her fellow-pupils.

That was one of the most painful memories in Andrée's life. When she recalled the scene – her cream-coloured tulle dress, her crimped hair, and all those faces turning in her direction – she blushed for shame. The whole lycée knew she was Mlle Lacombe's niece: her mistresses were unobtrusively favourable to her and her companions slightly mistrustful. Andrée loathed her aunt, and the lycée. She was not a lazy girl; on the contrary, she was intensely eager for knowledge; but in class no subject of any interest to her was ever raised, and in any case she looked upon the opinions of Mlle Lacombe and her colleagues as totally unimportant. She knew these people too well; she was acquainted with their domestic difficulties, their intimate ailments and their family troubles, and her one wish was never to be like them in any way. Her father wanted to make a teacher of her, and with great distress she wondered whether she too would be a schoolmistress in a provincial town just like Rougemont. Andrée lived in a neighbourhood devoid of surprises, where all the streets led straight from one familiar place to another and where all the passers-by looked as though they were related: when she left her bedroom and its edifying maxims she knew that nothing, absolutely nothing, was waiting for her outside. There were no trees in the streets; the sky was always overcast; no colours, nothing but grey and from time to time the insipid pink of a corset-shop; and to find so much as a smell in this rain-soaked, washed-out town one had to go down to the river-side. 'When shall I get out of here?' Andrée wondered despairingly. 'Is there anything else in other places? And if so what? And where?' She could not see so much as a glimpse of an answer to these questions: in the books Monique lent her she read accounts of lives unlike her own, but she knew very well that hers would not be spent in the spheres described by Loti or Farrère. The reason why Plattard had fascinated her right away was that the young woman seemed to come from a world that was infinitely rich and yet accessible.

That day Andrée was to spend the afternoon alone with Plattard, and the street that she took to go to the lycée, the rue de l'Hôtel-de-Ville, seemed to her less dreary than usual. As she approached the library she walked faster: in the middle of the group of boys from their lycée and of girls from hers she had caught sight of Monique. Monique was wearing a green suit and a big orange scarf that made her hair look bright yellow: she was talking to Serge. 'It's five to two,' said Andrée, giving her companions a disgusted look. For this meeting they had hastily powdered their noses and rouged their lips the moment they left their homes: their shining eyes, their laughter and their shrill voices shamelessly betrayed their pleasure. The youths received these tributes with a rather superior air. 'I'm coming,' said Monique, leaving her hand in Serge's for a long moment. The group broke up. The girls ran across the square, rubbing their lips with their handkerchiefs – make-up was forbidden at the lycée –and rushed into the cloakroom. 'In two hours I shall see her,' thought Andrée with joy, and she set off cheerfully for the history class.

'Monique, pull down the sleeves of your overall,' called the vice-principal. 'You look as though you were about to do the washing: there is nothing elegant about that.'

Monique plucked at her pink cotton smock. 'You know what would be fun?' she said. 'Suppose we persuaded Plattard to come to the dance-hall with us?'

'All you have to do is to ask her,' said Andrée. She sat down next to Monique right at the back of the class. This evening Monique was to introduce Serge to Plattard, and Andrée did not look forward to it with much pleasure: she disliked Serge and she would have preferred always seeing Plattard alone.

'I only hope we don't meet anyone we know at the Royal,' said Monique. 'They would go and tell my parents straight away. Imagine the uproar!'

'Aunt Jeanne would have a fit,' said Andrée, and she began to laugh rather unsteadily.

'Andrée Lacombe, you have a black mark,' said Mlle Métral. Andrée stared curiously at the history teacher's puffy face: Métral was conscious of being immensely superior to her pupils, and in class she would often burst into laughter at the very notion of being fifteen years old, of not being an agrégée, an incorporated teacher, and of not knowing the exact area of the United States; yet behind her arrogance Andrée thought she could make out a kind of timorous hatred. When she handed out black marks she always seemed to be working off an old grudge.

'Perhaps Plattard will tell me why,' thought Andrée. She gave a start: Métral was saying, 'Will you show me the notes you have taken?' Without speaking Andrée held out her book. 'You will have a zero.'

'What a bitch!' said Monique in something more than an undertone.

Métral gazed absently at the ceiling and carried on with her lesson: coarse insults put her out of countenance – she preferred not to hear them. No mistress filled Andrée with a greater repulsion. Métral was wearing a black velvet dress down to her ankles: its low bib-top displayed a red pullover with horizontal white stripes. 'When she looks into a mirror, what does she see?' Andrée often asked herself. She felt that perhaps Métral did not possess the same perceptions as herself: it was rather frightening.

At four the bell rang. Andrée washed her ink-stained hands and asked Monique for a little of her powder: then she went and knocked at the door of the teachers' common-room. It was empty. She walked in and stood with her back to the radiator. Andrée was well acquainted with this long, dismal room, because she was always the one Mlle Lacombe sent to find a scarf or a forgotten book in her locker: she would have liked to open each one of this line of cupboards along the wall, a visiting-card showing the name of its owner, but she did not dare. She contented herself with leafing through the publications that strewed the table – *Les Amis de la Pologne, La Quinzaine Universitaire, Le Bulletin des Agrégés*. There were papers pinned to a board by the french window: notifications of funerals or of marriages, requests for charity, a list of the books in the circulating library, the programme of an Educational Conference, the minutes of the last meeting of the union. Andrée leant her forehead against the window-pane. Far away the cathedral spire thrust up into the sky: it could be seen from everywhere, and at every moment the stone lacework pitilessly reminded her that she was a prisoner in Rougemont. She sighed. If only she could catch a glimpse of a way out, of a goal to aim at, she would be able to resign herself; but she remembered that during these rare talks with Plattard she had not managed to awaken her interest, nor had she found the questions she ought to have asked in order to get the answers she needed. Plattard had provided her with no revelation. 'It will be the same as the other times,' she thought despairingly. The wait was becoming endless.

'Forgive me,' said Plattard, coming in. 'A pupil's mother came to tell me all about her daughter's character. I thought she would never stop.'

She went to the wash-basin, turned the tap and up-ended a glass ball that parsimoniously emitted a few drops of pink soap. A handwritten card over the basin read 'The ladies of the staff are asked not to put flowers in the wash-basins.'

Andrée looked round the room. 'How funny it is that you should be a teacher,' she said. Plattard's smile had restored her confidence: all she had to do was to talk without being shy, as she did with Monique, and then Plattard would talk too.

'Mademoiselle, have you seen Mlle Métral's latest dress?' asked Andrée as they left the lycée.

'Yes, it's appalling,' said Plattard. 'They wear any old thing.'

'This particular dress is the result of careful study,' said Andrée. 'I'm sure she pondered over it a great while, you know, and that she thinks it charming.'

Plattard smiled. 'There's a fine collection of fossils in this lycée,' she said.

'It's strange that women so much older than we are and who think themselves so superior can hate us: they really do hate us. Why?'

Plattard shrugged. 'These creatures don't interest me in the least, you know, Andrée.'

'I'd love to be hidden under the table the days of the roll of honour meeting. Sometimes it must be very amusing.'

'I must admit that on those occasions I take no notice of what is happening around me,' said Plattard. 'As far as I am concerned, it's as though my colleagues did not exist. You attribute too much importance to them.'

'They exist all right for me, alas,' said Andrée.

'It is so useless, letting our thoughts be taken up with things that can bring neither richness nor beauty into our lives.'

Andrée smiled sweetly. 'Oh, but you – it's quite different for you. You must know so many interesting people.'

'That's true,' said Plattard thoughtfully. 'I have been lucky: I've had such . . . such wonderful friends.'

She pushed open a tea-shop door, a place with long mirrors showing countless reflections of the green walls and cut-glass chandelier: she found an unoccupied table in a corner, ordered tea for two, and went to choose the cakes herself, bringing them back on a small plate.

'I think the reason you find your life barren, Andrée,' she said, plunging her spoon into the yellow unctiousness of a cream horn, 'is that you do not distinguish between what is wonderful and what is extraordinary. You liked that English novel I lent you, *Dusty Answer*? Well, nothing very unusual happens in Judy's life, yet nevertheless . . .'

'Of course: if I were to meet Judy or Jennifer I should be very happy,' said Andrée. 'But look . . .' she said, nodding towards the next table.

'You have Monique,' said Plattard, 'and she is a most uncommon person. With her mauve eyes and her spun-gold hair she is like a little princess in a stained-glass window.'

Andrée laughed. 'I see her eyes as blue,' she said. 'I am very, very fond of her; but she is so much part of my everyday life.'

'Yes. It's a pity that one cannot have perpetually fresh impressions of the world, like those of children. You know Monique so well you can no longer see her.'

Andrée sipped her tea: the rattle of spoons, the hum of conversation and the warmth prevented her from gathering her thoughts. She liked looking at Monique and talking to her: she thought she understood her thoroughly. Although Monique led a more sociable life than her friend she too was stifling in Rougemont: she was trying at all costs to give herself the illusion of a free and well-filled life; and it was to escape from her environment and from the lycée that she hung about in cafés and flirted with Serge: her attempts, clumsy at times, were often generous and brave. But even though Andrée called up her image with all possible affection, she still could not feel overwhelmed.

'I'm trying to understand what it is that you find so precious in Monique,' she said.

Plattard lit a gold-tipped English cigarette. 'The conditions of human life are too brutish for such beings,' she said. 'One would like to comfort her for being born.'

Andrée smiled rather awkwardly. The conversation was not going very well: she realized that her worries and her opinions were too childish to interest Plattard, but at least she would have liked to understand what Plattard said to her right away. Instead, she only felt nonplussed.

They left the Poussin Bleu and, having crossed the cathedral square, they walked along a cobbled street lined with houses as clean and grey as a nun's habit. 'Do you feel the charm of this place?' asked Plattard. Andrée could scarcely prevent herself from crying out: she had paid so many calls with her aunt in this neighbourhood that she could not read the names on the brass plates under the bells without repulsion. Summoning up her better feelings she said 'When I was small I was very fond of these little men,' and she pointed out one of the moulded hooks that held the shutters back against the wall – shutters with heart-shaped holes cut in them.

'Why, I had never noticed them,' said Plattard. 'It's as though we were walking about in a Balzac novel, don't you think?'

'That's true,' said Andrée without conviction: she added, 'I should have expected you to loathe Rougemont.'

'Oh, I do loathe the stupid provincial prejudices; but seen from the contemplative point of view, everything is so perfectly typical here!' And as Andrée gave her a questioning look she went on, 'You must certainly have noticed that a vulgar or hateful character in a novel can interest or charm us as much as a spotless hero: well, what is there to prevent us from carrying out the novelist's aesthetic transposition in our own lives? Take the old beggar by the lycée, for example, the one who is always there selling shoe laces and fumigating paper: if I look upon him as the incarnation of one of Goya's prodigious freaks he no longer seems to me repulsive but beautiful.'

'At that rate everything would always be fine, everything would be beautiful,' said Andrée in a sceptical voice. 'I see quite well that my aunt is typical and that she could be described in a novel, but that doesn't get me much further.'

Plattard carried on with that flow of words which always astonished Andrée in class. 'There were people in the last century – Ruskin for example – who maintained that the only moral law was to live beautifully; and in a way there is a certain amount of truth in that. Only they had a preconceived and very conventional idea of beauty. I do not in fact say that everything is beautiful, as you claim, but only that all things can be looked at from an aesthetic point of view. It is the same as in painting: nowadays it is acknowledged that the subject does not matter, and that what counts is the manner in which the picture is handled.'

'But that is not the same thing,' said Andrée, almost in spite of herself.

Plattard smiled. 'Where does the difference lie?'

Andrée blushed. 'I don't know,' she confessed. Plattard would have had to help her to express herself; but Plattard took no notice of Andrée's objections – she wanted the girl to take her word for everything. Rather sadly Andrée fell silent.

The street changed character: the middle-class buildings gave way to dilapidated houses: a stream ran beneath the pavement on the left-hand side and from time to time its dirty, imprisoned waters could be seen through a grating. Andrée watched two ragged men as they went into a fried-fish shop. She had not the least notion of what their lives or their thoughts might be: for that she would have to sit down with them at one of the wooden tables every evening, eating the white beans that filled a tureen to the brim and the fried fish laid out on the false marble counter. What fun that would be!

'These streets exude a sorrowful poetry that I love beyond words,' said Plattard. 'You meet strange characters who do not seem quite real and the most unlikely happenings seem possible, don't you find?'

Andrée was happy to be in agreement with her at last. 'Oh yes! If I were free, that is where I'd live,' she said, pointing at the blue façade of an hotel that stood with its feet in the stream. Children were playing hopscotch in the street and washing fluttered at the windows; one could almost forget that one was in Rougemont.

'You would be devoured by bugs,' said Plattard, laughing.

'Never mind; I'd buy disinfectant,' said Andrée, looking at Plattard with some surprise. Had she been Plattard, this is where she would have lived, far from the whitewashed houses, the lacework churches and the corset shops. 'Mademoiselle,' she said, 'would it bore you to go into this little café, just for a moment?' Deep red curtains covered the glass door half way up and inside big varnished barrels rose in tiers against the wall.

'Aren't you afraid it might be very dirty?' said Plattard. 'It's better not to get too close – the charm might fade.'

Andrée did not press the point and all at once her happiness died away. She saw that their harmony had been false: it was not for the same reasons that they liked these streets. They went back to the middle-class town almost in silence; Andrée felt that Plattard found her dull and somewhat irritating. It was natural enough that she should; Andrée had never thought herself particularly interesting. Yet she did think that if Plattard had talked to her about her pursuits, her friends, her travels, she would have listened intelligently; and if Plattard had questioned her with a little care she would have found things to say. 'I only have two hours left,' thought Andrée sadly as she walked into Plattard's room: there were fully open tulips in a copper jug and a faint scent of English tobacco floated in the air. 'I love that smell,' said Andrée. Perhaps, sitting side by side in this peaceful room, they would at last have a moment of genuine intimacy.

'You wouldn't mind if I were to correct these Latin exercises, Andrée?' said Plattard. 'I absolutely have to give them back tomorrow.' She took the papers and began to examine them: from time to time she looked up and asked a question; but she did not listen to the reply. When dinner was brought she opened a newspaper and suggested that Andrée should help her solve the crossword puzzle. It was all over: the last half-hour dragged along, empty and endless, like a kind of lingering death; it was almost with relief that Andrée saw Monique and Serge come in.

Curled up at the far end of the divan, Andrée took no part in the conversation. She could not bear Serge: he was handsome, he was thought to be very charming, and he had already had several amorous successes. Andrée disliked him for having deserted Gilberte Viard, a first-form girl he had made his mistress the year before, when she was scarcely fourteen: Gilberte was pretty, and her recklessness was more respectable than her comrades' sly, underhand prudence. Andrée suspected that Serge now preferred Monique to Gilberte not because she was more attractive but because she was richer . . . 'I only hope she won't be so silly as to marry him,' she thought, looking anxiously at her friend's shining face. Monique was laughing a little too eagerly as Serge made quite witty fun of the mean and antiquated notions of the provinces. Andrée noticed with displeasure that Plattard was putting herself out to please him.

'What a pity that you can't come with us, Mademoiselle,' said Monique, when she said good-bye at about eleven o'clock. 'Compared with the places where you dance in Paris, the Royal

73

is obviously nothing at all,' said Serge. 'I can see that it would not tempt you much.'

'If I were not so tired, I'd come with pleasure,' said Plattard. 'Have a good time: it's agreed that you left me very late.'

'What do you think of her, Serge?' asked Monique rather anxiously, when the door was closed.

'She's a woman who understands life,' said Serge. 'She's emancipated.'

'Yes, she's splendid. At the lycée they think she's a revolutionary, she's so broad-minded.'

There was no one about: almost all the cafés were already shut, all the windows dark. Only in the rue des Vergetiers were there a few signs that shone with a gentle glow – a pink windmill, a black cat standing out against a pale-green background, a star with red and mauve rays. Old women wrapped in shawls sat in the doorways knitting, their feet on foot-warmers. The houses were newly done-up, as clean and trim as those in the middle-class districts, but their light colours and the wafts of music that came through their closed shutters gave them a welcoming aspect.

'If I were a man, I'd go to a brothel very often,' said Andrée.

Serge shrugged. 'You don't know what you are talking about: those places are absolutely vile.'

'At least they are different from the rest,' said Andrée.

'For this evening, just you put up with the Royal,' said Monique cheerfully. She opened the door with its pleated silk curtain. 'Where shall we sit?'

Serge walked confidently to a table next to the bar and sat down opposite Monique and Andrée. 'Three gin fizzes,' he ordered, without asking them what they would like.

The place was fairly big: knots of ribbon and faded artificial flowers hung from the ceiling, which was itself covered with a green trellis: the walls were painted with scenes of Venetian life in blue and vermillion.

'Will you dance?' said Serge to Andrée.

'No,' she replied. 'I don't know how.'

He stood up, took Monique's arm without a word and led her to the dance-floor. The band was playing a slow foxtrot: Andrée had never heard jazz, and now she listened, deeply moved – would she ever experience hope or sadness that had just the feeling of this music? What was there that could be hoped for, what was there that could be regretted with such piercing sweetness? It was like a scent that came from a great way off and that one could delight in, but without seeing the country it came from, nor the faces of the people there, nor the shapes of the houses.

'Do you like it?' asked Monique. Her eyes were shining: the dance had made her pant a little, and as she looked at Serge her parted lips seemed to offer themselves. Serge began stroking her bare arm and Monique's faced glowed red. Only last year she and Andrée had made fun of loving couples and their swooning attitudes: now she herself was caught in the trap.

For more than an hour, and with scarcely a pause, Monique and Serge danced cheek to cheek. Andrée did not find the time long, she amused herself watching the dance-hostesses sitting with ribbon-wrapped bottles in front of them that nobody asked them to drink. Their low-cut dresses set them off from the other women like a uniform. She tried to imagine their lives; and meanwhile the jazz awakened hopes in her that she could not define.

'I'm tired, Serge,' said Monique at last, in an apologetic tone, as he stood up for another foxtrot.

'Tired? Dancing will cure that,' said Serge, and he pulled her up, putting his arm round her with a commanding air. Andrée looked after him with angry eyes. When Monique came back her face was quite drawn. 'Monique, you are worn out,' said Andrée. 'We must go home.'

Serge shrugged his shoulders. 'So early? It's absurd.'

'My head is going round and round,' said Monique. 'It's the gin.'

'If you can't stand alcohol you shouldn't drink it,' said Serge crossly.

Monique's lips quivered. Andrée darted an indignant look at Serge: how sure he must be of Monique's love to dare speak to her like that. 'It was you who ordered the gin fizzes,' she said, 'and in any case it's high time we left.'

Monique was to sleep at Andrée's house, as she often did when she spent the evening in Rougemont. While Serge was escorting them back to their door, Andrée wondered whether Monique would confide in her; she would like to know the exact nature of Monique's feelings and to beg her not to commit her life rashly. But she could not take it upon herself to speak first. When they were alone Andrée only said 'You're not ill, Monique?'

'Not at all,' said Monique, who still looked weary. 'I think I'm just sleepy.'

The other nights they spent together they talked in low voices until dawn. But this time Monique turned to the wall straight away: she was beginning to grow acquainted with those joys and those anxieties that are not to be shared. Andrée gazed at her rather sadly for a moment, then put out the light and snuggled down between the sheets. There was nothing she could do for her friend. The only person who could influence Monique's decision and stop her before it was too late was Plattard. But Plattard saw neither Monique nor Serge with the same eyes as Andrée. 'I shall never, never be able to persuade her,' thought Andrée sorrowfully. In any case she no longer hoped for anything from Plattard: and after this wearisome day she hardly even wanted to see her again.

IV Chantal's diary, continued

10 April

There is something depressing about the time I spend with Andrée. By the end of today I was drained of life. She has a literal mind, absolutely devoid of any sense of the wonderful. In her eyes I read a dumb worship that touches me; but it paralyses her and gives her strange complexes. By some kind of instinct of self-defence she takes the opposite view of everything I say; and after a while this irritates me. She did not choose to understand that an impartial attitude towards the world allows one to find beauty in the humblest object. I feel that so strongly. When I see my life as a novel of which I am the heroine, the hours of sadness are transformed into touching passages – pages from which I can draw pleasure. It is the same with everything . . . Fortunately the arrival of Monique and Serge at once restored me to a state of grace. What an adorable child-couple! They might have escaped from a chapter of *Le Grand Meaulnes*: I was irresistibly reminded of young Frantz and his fifteen-year-old fiancée the moment I saw them.

By odd words here and there Monique has told me their story, so beautiful in its simplicity. They grew up very far from one another, both of them lonely beings in this monastic, youthless town. Serge belongs to the old landowning middle class: his mother's estate is quite far from Rougemont and in term-time he lives with relations who do not mix with the new bourgeoisie: they only met last year, but long before that, long before they met, they had dreamed of belonging to each other. A friend had told Monique of this handsome, proud and often cruel boy who seemed to have made a vow to keep his heart whole, untouched, for a being of his own race: but all that was needed was that one day Serge should catch sight of Monique to understand that her conquering beauty could move him at last. From the moment their eyes met their destinies have been wonderfully fulfilled. Serge is like that Raphael portrait of a young cardinal upon which Stendhal is said to have based his description of Fabrice del Dongo. There is a steely gleam in his grey velvet eyes: I love that mixture of tenderness and rigour. The day her friend Gilberte took Monique to his house he was wearing a kind of black Russian shirt embroidered with gold and he was sitting in a corner of his room – a room quite by itself, in a little building at the far end of a garden – playing an accordion. They had scarcely exchanged more than a few words before their only wish was to see one another again. The word 'love' is too fierce and violent a word to describe what unites them. They both shine with youth; they are both pure and beautiful; and they know that it is only together that they can escape from the dim regions in which they were brought up and fly far away towards those light-filled worlds whose keys each holds for the other. It is a feeling almost tragic in its grandeur; and a mere nothing would be enough to flaw this direct and solemn matter whose weight they bear with such a carefree lack of concern.

It would have hurt me if Monique's choice had not been worthy of her, but Serge quite won me over with his artless fervour. He is carried away by the breath of revolt. He finds the hypocritical morality taught in the lycées and the life of a small landowner that his mother would like to force upon him unacceptable. He sketched some witty and thoroughly amusing portraits of the people of Rougemont: this put me in form myself and together we drew a positive gallery of monsters, a fantastic picture in the style of Hieronymus Bosch. He also told me in confidence that it was his ambition to become a film director and to make Monique a star. Childish dreams, as pretty and as fragile as soap bubbles. But who knows? Neither the one nor the other is cut out for a minor role, and I believe that our fate models itself upon our souls. How beautiful it is to see them travelling towards life, hand in hand, their heads held high, trusting in their star. Nothing mawkish or insipid in either of them. Only a blaze of light in Monique's eyes and a look of serious, quiet certainty on Serge's face.

There was something sad about being left alone in my room (but it would have been too dangerous to go to the dance-hall with them: if I want to help them try to escape I must not run the risk of being discredited). When their shining presence vanished, something like a phosphorescent glow remained behind; but now everything has grown dim again. What of it? All that matters is that from time to time the path of my life should cross the road of dreams. In the darkness there are red dots shining like little lamps under a cathedral dome: the mysteries of youth and love are being celebrated on an unseen altar and earnestly, fervently I bow my head. – Andrée's ambiguous attitude: was she at one time in love with Serge? Is she still?

23 April
So many things to write about my journey to Paris: what a great deal of good it did me, swimming in that vivid atmosphere again for a fortnight! I am happy to have brought Anne and Pascal together at last. 'I like the way he is so spontaneous and so serious, both at the same time,' said Anne as early as their second meeting. It is true that Pascal has some charming qualities: my individualism and his mysticism often clash, and the kind of holding-back that exists both in his conversation and in his life irritates me; but I have a great deal of friendship for him.

Long wandering discussions in the Champs-Elysées: affection: Anne's face aglow under her pink felt hat. Her eyes filled with tears when she spoke of her mother – this persecution is odious. She is criticized for her ideas, for the books she reads and for her friendship with me as though they were so many sins. It is only with Pascal that she could be happy without remorse and remain a Christian without growing stupid. For my part, I am too far from Catholicism: although she trusts me I frighten her. 'Become what thou art,' said Nietzsche, and that is just what I am trying to help her to do – to become what she is. Sometimes she struggles, but I know very well that it is life and truth that will win in the end. The pleasure of reflecting that it is thanks to me that this victory will be won.

20 May
Monique has just left me. I have promised to tell Mme Fournier that she spent the whole evening with me: if some kind fairy did not watch over youth and love, men's coarse hands would soon shatter these fragile blossoms. I like to think that thanks to me the world will have been filled for a moment with the scent of a little more beauty, a little more happiness.

There is so much vulgarity, even in people with quite discriminating minds like Mme Fournier. It would be impossible to make her understand what is exceptional in a feeling like that between Monique and Serge.

I walked a little way with Monique. The cathedral garden looked fantastic, almost unreal, in the moonlight: a black cat was yowling among the tormented stones. We talked about Serge. I told Monique his intransigence and his eagerness made me think of that Pisanello Saint George which is so very beautiful: his only armour is the brilliant whiteness of his linen garment – a hard simplicity, an unbending purity. She did not answer; she only smiled – a rather grave, a rather mysterious smile: the beautiful smile of a woman not yet accustomed to the heavy burden she carries in her heart.

The other day Andrée asked me whether for some time now I had not found Monique less cheerful. But happiness – a happiness that does not choose to be either easy or middle-class –is not a cheerful thing: I was quite sure that Monique would react with this mixture of ecstasy and dread. In my last letter to Jeanine I tried to convey the almost *holy* character of this poem of love and youth that is unfolding before my eyes.

V

After a rainy month of May, a close and heavy summer suddenly descended upon Rougemont. Andrée loathed this time of the year: the sun awoke no colour in the burning streets, and the only strong contrasts on the white pavement were made by the black clothes of the passers-by. When she left school Andrée hurried to get home. The narrow alleys were full of stagnant shadow, like the bottom of a well; all shutters were closed; and under the hard blue sky the silence seemed unusual, almost oppressive.

Andrée shut herself up in her room, but a warm wind wafted over the table she worked at and she could not prevent herself from dreaming of forbidden pleasures – boats gliding along a stream, a bottle of fizzy cider in the groves of a pleasure-garden. All she could see from her window was grey roofs and the cathedral spire.

It was above all Sundays and Thursdays that passed so slowly. Monique was always with Serge and Andrée scarcely ever saw her except at school: she had read all Plattard's books. By way of distraction she ate slices of bread and jam or bread and cheese almost without stopping; she would have preferred smoking, but her aunt would not allow it; she put on weight. She did not even wish for the end of this school year – the next would be even less agreeable. Plattard expected to be sent to a post nearer Paris, at Chartres or Beauvais. Andrée felt that Plattard would leave without having enriched her in any way: Andrée did not even have the impression that she knew her, and when she could no longer see her face, nothing of Plattard would be left to her at all.

At the lycée the atmosphere was stormy; like the girls, the teachers were all on edge with the heat and the coming of the holidays, and black marks were handed out in great quantities. The monthly visit of the headmistress was expected with a certain amount of amusement and a certain amount of anxiety.

'She will be here in ten minutes,' said Andrée, nodding towards Mlle Bidois as she crossed the courtyard, a blue exercise-book under her arm. 'We are in for it, all right!'

Monique gave an indifferent shrug. Nothing seemed to matter to her these days; she had grown plain; her blouse was not properly buttoned and her untidy hair straggled over her pasty face. Serge was not always pleasant, and although she was too proud to admit it, no doubt his conduct wounded her.

Mlle Lacombe tapped on her desk and Andrée resumed her attentive expression. *Britannicus* was being explained. Mlle Lacombe had a pile of square-cut, closely-written papers beside her: she had compiled a portable dossier on each of the authors of the set books, a file that contained an account of the author's life and an appreciation of his works based on the most approved critics; and every year, without changing a line, she read these notes out to her pupils, who submissively copied them into their exercise-books. This method produced excellent results in the examinations and Mlle Lacombe was a respected teacher. Yet, even after fifteen years of teaching, she still felt ill at ease when giving a lesson, and her face was always somewhat red.

The door opened: Mlle Lacombe and the pupils stood up; the headmistress walked in. She had done her hair carefully, and the blue frock she was wearing no doubt came from Lestrange's, the best dressmaker in Rougemont; but on her lumpish person the elegant clothes seemed barely decent. She sat down next to Mlle Lacombe.

'Before giving you your rolls of honour,' she said, 'I wish to tell you that at present I am thoroughly displeased with your behaviour and with the way you dress.' There was a great silence. 'You know that you are not to come to school in short sleeves,' she went on, 'and that you are not merely to throw your coats over your shoulders: I wish them to be put on properly, with your arms in the sleeves – offences against this rule are reported to me from all over the town. There are even some among you who take their hats off the moment they turn the corner of the street. And there are some, whom I do not choose to name but who will know they are meant, who have been caught bare-headed and bare-armed on café terraces. This unrestrained conduct is deeply improper: it reveals both a want of self-discipline and of dignity. How can you hope to be respected if you do not respect yourselves?'

Her tone was strained, unnatural, uncertain: Mlle Bidois might have been reciting a lesson; yet she took what she was saying seriously. On the other hand, her indignation always remained abstract. Andrée had something in the nature of a revelation. 'But she's nothing more than an outward show,' she thought with sudden pleasure. Nothing real: never a joy, a dislike, an affection, a thought – nothing but the intention of feeling this joy, of believing in this idea: and the words to express them. A massive body in which the heart always beats at a steady pace; a meticulous concern for behaviour; and a vast emptiness.

Now the headmistress was giving out the rolls of honour. 'Monique Fournier, no roll of honour: six propositions, four abstentions, one opposition for bad behaviour. For a big girl like you to lose your roll of honour for bad behaviour, that really is a shame.'

Monique had stood up and she was staring at Mlle Bidois with a vacant look: on her lips there was a ghost of a smile which Andrée did not understand. It was not an insolent smile, but the headmistress interpreted it wrongly. 'I must ask you to stop sniggering,' she said. 'You give yourself the airs of a young woman and you have less notion of the consequence of your acts than a child of four.'

For a moment the smile remained fixed on Monique's lips; then suddenly she burst into tears. All eyes turned in her direction: no one had ever seen her cry before.

'If you are sorry for your behaviour, that is already something,' said Mlle Bidois, embarrassed by the violence of these tears. Standing there, her face buried in her hands, Monique sobbed and choked. Andrée looked at her anxiously: no mere reprimand could upset her to this degree.

When Mlle Bidois had gone the class remained deeply silent. All that could be heard was Mlle Lacombe's luke-warm voice and the scratching of pens. Monique had dried her eyes; she was leaning her face on her hand, a hard though childish face framed in the absurd setting of the Watteau reproductions on the walls, the ink-stained desks and the blackboard.

'Where will you be this evening?' asked Andrée, when the four o'clock bell rang.

'At the Brasserie François with Serge, I dare say,' said Monique.

'If I'm lucky enough to get away for an hour, can I come and join you?'

A gleam showed in Monique's eye. 'Oh yes! Do try to come,' she said eagerly.

That day Mlle Lacombe was giving a tea-party: it was Andrée's duty to open the door and then hand round the tea. 'If only she will let me go out,' she thought as she passed her aunt the sugar-bowl – an aunt whose visage was enlivened by a decent gaiety. Mlle Lacombe had embellished her dark dress with a white collar, but her hair was rather greasy and her skin somewhat shiny – she never looked altogether clean. 'You may go back to your work, Andrée,' she said after a while. 'I don't need you any more.'

Andrée left the tea-party and stepped into the dining-room: there, lying flat on her stomach on the carpet, she could either listen to the conversation or follow her own thoughts, whichever she preferred. She had often gathered amusing information in this way. When these good ladies greeted one another they asked for news of their more private illnesses, and gave highly detailed accounts of their own little feminine troubles. Andrée knew that on her first day of menstruation Métral suffered pains 'as violent as those of childbirth' and that Mme Thomas, the physics mistress, had had two miscarriages; sometimes when she overheard their confidences, Andrée's palms went damp with disgust. For the moment they were talking about the coming marriage of Mlle Lanthenoy, a stout young woman of thirty, whose fiancé was an art-master at Lyons, said to be somewhat lame. 'Lyons: that's a great way off,' said Mlle Lacombe compassionately.

'It's so sad, having no home,' said Mme Thomas. 'When my husband comes to see me we have to sit in a café: we get bored. It's appalling!' She was pregnant again. Her face was blotched with yellow, and she was very thin with a large protuberance in the middle of her belly.

'We shall see one another during the holidays,' said Lanthenoy placidly. For eight years she had been saving so as to be able to treat herself to a husband: she had bought some shares and taken out life-insurance. With a thrill of horror Andrée reflected that it was this kind of future that her father and her aunt, in their simplicity, wanted for her. 'Nowadays a salary is safer than a dowry,' Mlle Lacombe had said to her brother one day. Wearing the same dress all year long, lunching at school for six francs, never travelling, never going out – this would allow one to be married some day to a little civil servant anxious to improve his standard of living. Monique would have a right to a more charming husband, a more spacious flat; she would be able to look down on her daughters' teachers from a certain height. 'Oh, I do want to help her,' said Andrée passionately: it appeared to her that she had never so clearly understood the lack of real occupation, the disorder and confusion of mind that had thrown Monique into this affair with Serge. Their childhood toys no longer amused them and no one would undertake to introduce them to the adult world: in any case no one was capable of doing so, except for Plattard, and she had not troubled herself about it. Andrée got up: she opened the door. 'Excuse me, Aunt Jeanne,' she said, 'I wanted to ask whether I might go and study at the library.'

'Go along, but be back in time for dinner,' said Mlle Lacombe.

Almost every evening before going home, Monique went to have a drink with Serge at the Brasserie François: it was the most dismal of all the Rougemont cafés. Andrée pushed her way through the revolving doors and walked down the long thin room, never touched by the light of day: whores were sitting under mirrors that reflected a yellowish light endlessly to and fro, Andrée did not see Monique, but in the room at the far end of the gallery she caught sight of Serge, who was playing billiards with some friends. She walked on. Monique was sitting a little way off, leafing through a copy of *La Vie Parisienne* without reading it.

'Serge is a cad,' thought Andrée angrily. She smiled at Monique. 'May I sit down?' she asked.

'Do,' said Monique. 'I'm glad you've come.'

'Suppose we go for a little walk, rather than sit down,' suggested Andrée. 'Since Serge is playing billiards . . .'

Monique hesitated, then she firmly closed *La Vie Parisienne* and stood up. 'That's a good idea,' she said. 'Let's go for a walk. This place is utterly dreary.' She went over to the billiard-table. 'Serge, I'm going. See you tomorrow?'

Serge shook Andrée's hand, giving her an unfriendly look. 'You might have waited for me,' he said to Monique in an almost threatening tone.

'Yes, I might have,' she said. She took Andrée's arm. 'Come on, Andrée. Let's go.'

When they were in the street once more there was a short silence.

'Serge is cross because I came for you,' said Andrée.

Monique did not answer: her face was hard. 'I don't give a damn,' she burst out suddenly. 'I don't give a damn what he thinks, or what he says or does.'

'Monique,' said Andrée, 'what's the matter? Are you unhappy?'

'I hate him,' said Monique. She looked at Andrée fiercely, adding nothing more: Andrée did not know what to say. 'I hate him,' Monique went on. 'When I'm there he takes no more notice of me than if I were a block of wood; but yesterday, when I ventured to be late for a meeting . . .' Her voice died away.

'What did he do?' asked Andrée.

'He slapped my face.'

Andrée dropped her friend's arm. 'And yet you came back today? It's just not possible. Are you afraid of him?'

They had reached the embankment; the air was full of the smell of tar and of dust. Without replying Monique walked down the steps leading to the river. Andrée stared at her. Then, speaking very fast, almost in a whisper, 'You aren't his mistress, Monique?'

Monique walked on, her head bowed, doggedly pushing a piece of coal along with her foot. Andrée grasped her shoulder. 'Answer me. What's happening, Monique? I must know.'

Monique looked up. 'I went to bed with him three months ago and I'm pregnant. I don't know what will happen to me.'

Andrée gazed at her friend with horror, though she could not yet quite believe her. It seemed impossible that a mysterious rot should be spreading in that slim, graceful body. 'Are you sure, Monique?' she asked.

'Certain,' said Monique. 'It's the second month.' She stopped: her face fell to pieces. 'Andrée, I don't want to have a baby. I don't want to marry Serge.'

All at once Andrée knew that it was true. She could not cry out 'It's only a game: let's not go on,' as she could in her dreams. Her head began to swim and she let herself drop onto the dirty grass of the bank. 'Does Serge know?' she asked.

'Yes. He says I must tell my parents right away and that we must marry.'

Andrée shivered. She looked at Monique's familiar face but without being able to overcome an immense disgust. Under the blue silk dress, under her belly's satiny skin there was something shapeless, something living, that grew and swelled with every minute. 'Something must be done,' she said.

In seven months! Monique's waist was going to thicken; her belly would grow drum-tight: already her features were drawn and her eyes had rings under them. Caresses had made her body faint with pleasure: soon it would be torn by the pangs of childbirth. Andrée looked away. A train crossed the iron bridge, making a great din; then everything fell silent again. It was a warm, calm evening. Sometimes a woman's voice or the cry of a child floated up from the barges with their painted sides. The cathedral spire could be seen, far away and slightly misty.

'Serge did it on purpose,' said Monique in a brooding voice. 'He wanted to force my parents' hand. But I can't tell them that, Andrée.'

'There is certainly something to be done,' repeated Andrée, making an effort to shake off the weariness of mind that had come over her.

'He doesn't love me; he's not capable of loving anyone. All he's good for is playing billiards or cards from morning till night: he's a stupid egoist.'

'Is it long that you've stopped loving him?'

'Yes. Ever since . . .' She bowed her head a little. 'How could I have brought myself to go to bed with him? Oh, I was so taken in! If only you knew how all that disgusts me now.' She grasped Andrée's hand. 'I'd rather die than live with him.'

Andrée considered for a while. 'Plattard promised to help us if ever we needed her,' she said at last.

'Plattard? But what could she do about it, Andrée?' said Monique. Her mouth twisted. 'I don't want her to know: I don't want anyone to know!'

'Let me tell her; she'll understand,' said Andrée, gently stroking Monique's hot, feverish hand. 'She has no prejudices. She will be able to advise us – tell us about something you can take, the address of a midwife. They say it's easy: all you have to know is what to do.'

Monique gripped Andrée's hand with all her strength. 'Would it be possible?'

'I'm sure of it, Monique. You'll get out of this.'

'Oh Andrée, I must.' She gave a kind of sob. 'I've been through two horrible months . . . horrible.'

Andrée helped her up. 'I'll speak to Plattard tomorrow,' she said.

Andrée was quite sure that Plattard would find a way of saving Monique: but even so she was in a very nervous state the next evening when she sat down at a little round table on the terrace of a café by the quays, and to give herself courage she ordered a glass of calvados. The black waters of the river could be made out on the other side of the road, behind piles of barrels and crates. The breeze had a tidal smell, and on the far shore a great blue light shone in the darkness. Nowadays, when Andrée spent an evening with Plattard she was satisfied with gazing at her, almost without speaking and quite without expecting anything from her: there was a melancholy sweetness about these moments that pleased her. But today she would have to speak: and what would be Plattard's reply? What could she do? It was Monique's happiness that would be at stake. Andrée took a sip, and the spirit brought tears to her eyes. Gypsy musicians in scarlet shirts were tuning their instruments. Andrée drank another mouthful and started: Plattard was coming towards her, smiling under a broad-brimmed straw hat.

'I'm quite dazed with sun and fresh air,' she said. 'I spent the afternoon in a boat.' She sat down, gently rocking her wicker chair to and fro.

'Monique and I tried last year,' said Andrée. 'But the water is dirty and then you are always among the barges.'

'You don't attach enough importance to the physical side of life,' said Plattard. 'Yet the body is a beautiful thing. You've never read Lawrence? No, of course not: you're too young.' She spoke without expecting any answer and Andrée stared at her in silence: Plattard was very pretty in her summer dress. The orchestra began Schubert's Unfinished Symphony.

'Always great music,' said Plattard, smiling.

'Yes,' said Andrée: there was a lump in her throat, and to gain time she said 'The people who come here understand music: next door there are more of them, but they are more mixed.'

The orchestra's pianissimos were drowned by the echoes of the jazz coming from the neighbouring terrace. Men in caps and bare-headed women stood on the edge of the pavement, listening to both at once.

'Have you noticed how artificial the leaves look in the light of the street-lamps?' said Plattard. 'They might be cut out of metal.'

Andrée gathered all her courage, 'Mademoiselle,' she said. 'I have something to talk to you about, something very serious.'

Plattard gave her an inquiring look. 'Tell me, my dear Andrée. What has happened to you?'

'A disaster has happened to Monique,' said Andrée in a very low voice.

'Disaster? What disaster?' Plattard seemed deeply interested.

'She told me yesterday that she had gone to bed with Serge.' Andrée gazed at Plattard with imploring eyes. 'She is pregnant and now she loathes him.' Her cheeks flushed scarlet. 'He's a swine: he did it on purpose to force her to marry him.'

Plattard seemed overwhelmed; she looked quickly round and said in a troubled voice 'I can't believe what you tell me, Andrée. We had better go. We cannot talk about it here.' She paid quickly and stood up. 'I had such a different picture of Monique. So she is Serge's mistress? I can't get over it. What will her parents say? There will be the most appalling scandal.'

The trouble and the look of reprobation that Andrée saw in Plattard's eye froze her heart; in a hesitant voice she said, 'But isn't there a way of not having babies? Don't you know any? Or people who could tell us?'

Plattard looked at her with a kind of horror. 'God, what filth!' she said in a deeply shocked tone. 'To think that such an idea can have come into Monique's head, and into yours, Andrée. It's unbelievable!'

Andrée went white. She did not understand what Plattard said; all that she understood was that she had been completely mistaken and that there was no hope of saving Monique. Yet she wanted to make one last attempt. 'But why?' she cried passionately. 'Why is it wicked? Monique can't have her whole life ruined because of this nonsense.'

Plattard's features grew sharp. 'Who has been influencing you? Have you no moral sense at all? It's monstrous!'

'Oh God,' said Andrée. 'So you won't help us?'

Plattard's face was hard. 'Certainly not. All Monique has to do is to marry as soon as possible; and if her parents have their wits about them the story will never be known.'

A great wave of anger flowed over Andrée. 'But I tell you she hates Serge,' she cried violently. 'She's said she'd kill herself rather than marry him!'

'She won't kill herself,' said Plattard curtly, 'and no doubt she won't hate him long. She will be a good wife and mother. I find it rather disappointing, but for her it is better than dragging wretchedly about with men. Believe me, you don't understand life, Andrée.' Andrée choked back her tears and stammered some unintelligible words. 'What?' said Plattard. 'Don't you agree?'

'I should never, never have believed this of you,' said Andrée. Plattard bristled. 'Upon my word,' she cried, 'It's I who should never have expected behaviour like this from Monique or from you. Monique has betrayed my trust. If I had known the nature of her relations with Serge I should never have encouraged them. She should never have mixed me up in this affair.' She was ready to cry. 'Oh, how disgusting it all is,' she said, stamping her foot.

Andrée came to an abrupt halt. 'Very well,' she said. 'I had better go home. I shall warn Monique.' She turned her back and ran.

VI

Every year the lycée Sévigné's prize-giving took place in the main hall of the Circus, and the teachers gathered in a kind of anteroom until the ceremony began. Chantal arrived last. There were several members of the Parents' Association, two generals, the treasurer-paymaster-general, M. Lacombe and some of his colleagues. The headmistress, in black satin, was talking to the Prefect. Métral, wearing gold lamé, hurried from group to group. Chantal felt that it might be amusing to describe the scene in her diary that evening, but she was in no mood to set down humorous observations. She had not opened her plum-coloured notebook since her last conversation with Andrée. She had only one wish and that was to forget Rougemont as soon as possible.

The band of the Garde républicaine began the 'Marseillaise' and the important people paced towards the dais in solemn procession. Chantal saw her name on a little card pinned to the back of a chair and sat down behind Mlle Lacombe, whose transparent dress revealed a pink corset. The treasurer had kindly consented to preside over the ceremony and while Mlle Bidois pronounced a few words of thanks, Chantal looked over the audience. She could hardly recognize these girls in muslin or taffeta frocks as the same pupils she had taught: even their faces had changed under all the curls and ringlets and moiré ribbons that adorned their heads today. 'There they are, completely reabsorbed by their families,' said Chantal to herself in a melancholy tone. 'They no longer think of anything but the holidays.' For a short while she meditated sadly upon the ingratitude of the young. The treasurer-paymaster-general was speaking about the economic situation in France.

Monique was not in the hall. Her engagement had been announced ten days before and she had gone to stay in the country with her future mother-in-law and her family. She had not even sent Chantal a note to say good-bye. Andrée was sitting in the fourth row: she was tastelessly dressed in a pale blue frock. Chantal looked away; everything was over between them.

'Tomorrow I shall be far away from here,' thought Chantal with relief. 'What a ridiculous affair!' She shivered with disgust. She remembered the letters she had written to her friends about Monique and Serge; there were phrases in them that had been haunting her this past fortnight. Monique's mauve eyes; the ingenuous mouth that recalled Clare d'Ellébeuse's, that childish love, so tragic and so pure. Nothing was true. Monique had made game of her; she had abused her kindness and her confidence. 'What an adorable child-couple! They might have escaped from a chapter of *Le Grand Meaulnes*.' Chantal blushed with shame: perhaps they had come to see her that very evening, straight from their bed. Serge must indeed have laughed, hearing her approve of his revolt and his unyielding firmness. 'They might have compromised me,' thought Chantal angrily. 'All this filth!' 'Upper sixth form class prize, Andrée Lacombe.' The vice-principal, standing and wearing white gloves, read out the list of awards: she had uttered these words with particular warmth, and there was general applause. Mlle Lacombe swelled with satisfaction; it was the first time that Andrée had won this prize – she owed it chiefly to her marks in Latin and Greek. All the teachers smiled at the prize-winner's father and aunt with a conspiratorial air.

Andrée stood up: she walked forward without shyness but without smiling: an assistant-mistress handed her a pile of books and pushed her towards the dais. 'Go and kiss your Papa,' whispered Mlle Bidois. Obediently Andrée pushed her way through; M. Lacombe clasped her with a theatrical gesture and then she moved on to her aunt, who kissed her on the forehead. Andrée passed quite close to Plattard: she turned her head slightly aside so that she should not meet her eyes.

'She will be a little pedant, like the rest of her family,' thought Chantal angrily; she knew that this child, with absurd self-conceit, presumed to judge her, and she could not bear it. If she had not had a letter in her handbag confirming her appointment to Chartres – a letter from Ramonet, a former teacher at Sèvres –she would have wept with nervous irritation. It was oppressively hot and she seemed no longer to possess any spirit or sense of the comic.

At last the ceremony came to an end. The teachers stepped down from the dais, and the pupils and their parents pushed their chairs back in a general din: girls and smiling fathers and mothers crowded round Chantal; she shook outstretched hands; she replied gracefully to thanks; ardent faces turned towards her and she saw tears in a pair of dark eyes. All at once her sadness vanished. At the dawn of these young lives her form would stand out forever, her slim form, so well set off in a tailored suit – a somewhat enigmatic, paradoxical form, whose appearance in an old provincial lycée had been so dazzling. In a flash she saw herself again, walking briskly along a provincial street in the morning, strolling dreamily in the evening shade of the cathedral, wittily carrying on a fashionable conversation, listening to the confidences of an old lady in an archaic drawing-room. 'How varied my life has been,' she said to herself. And for a heart enamoured of the wonderful, seeing her own image already becoming legendary in the depths of two dark eyes was the sweetest of rewards.

For a moment Andrée stood motionless in the doorway. Among the jumbled chairs and in a great noise of talking and laughter groups formed and dispersed and fresh groups came into being.

Plattard was smiling, her hand on a girl's shoulder, as though she were drunk with kindness. This was the last picture of her that Andrée would carry away. Everything was completely finished: admiration, hope, and even regret.

'Are you coming, Andrée?' called Mlle Lacombe. M. and Mlle Lacombe walked home, very dignified in their best clothes, and Andrée fell into step with them. Her arms were loaded with books; her dress and the ribbon in her big wide-brimmed hat glowed in the sun; it was so hot that the silk stuck to her skin. Many eyes turned in her direction. 'I wish I were dead,' she thought.

Dying was not so easy. Monique had not killed herself. She had confessed everything to her parents and she would marry Serge in a month's time. M. Fournier had refused to give her a dowry and she would live with her husband in a house belonging to her mother-in-law, far away out in the country. She would knit; in the evening she would listen to the radio; and to console herself she would try to love her child. Andrée would see her perhaps twice a year; and soon they would no longer have anything to say to one another.

Andrée closed her bedroom door, took off her dress and lay down in her underclothes. There was a buzzing in her head: she would have liked to stay like that, lying flat and half asleep, but soon her aunt would come in and reproach her for being idle. 'Nothing great is ever accomplished without enthusiasm' said one of the cards on the wall. She would have to get up: sadness was an immoral luxury.

Andrée put on a linen dress. 'May I go and say good-bye to Mlle Plattard?' she asked.

'Yes, do, my dear, and thank her very much from us,' said Mlle Lacombe. She did not much care for Plattard, but she was grateful for Andrée's success.

Andrée walked along the rue de l'Hôtel-de-Ville and came to the cathedral square: in the rue des Petites-Eaux a drunkard was asleep by the underground stream, a bottle of red wine between his knees. A heavy stench came up from the filthy water and children were spitting into it. Andrée went down to the embankment and followed it as far as the end of the town: she walked for a long while; she was not running away, she was not looking for anything, and the scene around her did not change –

it was the same empty sky everywhere, the same stifling heat. It would be so for all eternity and from now on no one would share this horrible boredom with her; she was alone and she was afraid.

She did not want to go home: the mere thought of the blue carpet in the corridor made her feel sick. When she was back in the town she walked in the direction of the Brasserie François: the long gallery was almost empty and she sat down on the leather bench and ordered coffee.

Some way off, on her left, two commercial travellers were drinking Pernod; she looked at them for a moment and then her gaze shifted to the wallpaper. It was red, and in places broad patches of yellow had eaten into it: if you looked at them for a long time you found that they had the shapes of animals, of plants. It was almost cool.

For a long while Andrée sat there motionless, fascinated by the patches: she did not want to think of what would happen later – the corridor carpet, the holidays in the company of her father and aunt, the return to school in this town where from now onwards she would be entirely alone. Two years of the lycée; then she would study for the teachers' college – Sèvres or the Ecole Normale. The patches on the wall grew indistinct and merged into one another: at the far end of the gallery of mirrors there was a girl sitting in front of a cup of black coffee. Andrée smiled at the image, and the image sent her back her own smile exactly. She thought, 'In spite of everything, one day I shall certainly end up not being young any more.'

❦ ❦ ❦ ❦ LISA ❦ ❦ ❦ ❦

L ISA NARDEC was a boarder at the Institution Saint-Ange. The Institution Saint-Ange, run by Mme Leroy, a fervent Catholic, was both a money-making and a charitable concern; needy students were given board, lodging, and a superior education in exchange for providing the daughters of the well-to-do and pious middle-class inhabitants of the district of Auteuil with lively and modern schooling; and since the maintenance of these students was not costly, while on the other hand a thoroughgoing education coupled with an incomparable religious training deserved a certain financial sacrifice on the part of Christian parents, Mme Leroy profited by the fortunate conjunction. She was helped in her task by former boarders who wished to turn their knowledge into love and self-sacrifice and who stayed on as volunteers after they had taken their degrees: they formed a kind of teaching community, which was run with gentle firmness by Mlle Lambert, an agrégée* of philosophy whom Providence had placed in Mme Leroy's path. In the college it was said that Mlle Lambert had renounced the world because an adored fiancé had betrayed her, and the students detected a tragic sweetness in her smile: passionate attachments sprang up around her. If they ever touched her heart, no one ever knew it. She dismissed some very foolish young women who, in their conversation and their private papers, overdid their praise of her pale, severe eyes and the austere fringe of black hair covering her beautiful forehead; but with the really gifted students she did not discourage the religious vocations aroused by her ardent voice, her deep and soulful eyes.

Every morning Mlle Lambert worked on her thesis on Duns Scotus in her office; yet, because she felt that spiritual matters should come before private research, the students were allowed to knock at her door if they needed moral help, educational advice, or leave to go out apart from the usual holidays. But unless Mlle Lambert particularly encouraged them to come and

* One who has passed the *agrégation*, a competitive state examination for admission to the teaching staff of lycées and universities.

97

tell her about the evolution of their minds or the state of their hearts, they scrupulously respected her privacy. She was therefore rather surprised when Lisa Nardec came in one morning: there had not been any intimacy between them for a long while.

'What do you want, my dear Lisa?' she said in a kindly voice: she smiled at the young woman, and once again she was struck by her thinness and her pallor. When she first came to Paris she had been a fine, healthy girl, and Mlle Lambert, who had coached her for her degree in philosophy, had had great hopes of her; she liked the unusual turn and the acuity of her replies and she had followed her progress with particular interest. At that time she had thought that if Lisa were touched by grace she might be of great value to the establishment; and it was with sorrow that during these last four years she had seen the girl sink gradually into a sterile, wasting scepticism. Lisa had not succeeded in bringing her unusual qualities of scrupulous sincerity and penetrating accuracy to maturity and in making them bear fruit: they had turned against her, eating into her like an acid. Intellectual work had undermined her body, and far from enriching this thin and unproductive soil, cultivation had made it barren: nowadays there was something spare, frail, and un-giving in both her looks and in what she said. She would never pass an *agrégation:* she would never write a book.

Lisa took a few steps forward. 'I should like to spend the afternoon in Paris, mademoiselle,' she said. 'I have to go to the Bibliothèque Nationale for my diploma work, and I have an appointment with the dentist.'

Mlle Lambert brushed the full-blown roses in a blue faience jar with her fingertips. 'Weren't you at the library on Tuesday?' she asked.

'Yes,' said Lisa. 'But I could not get the book I needed.'

Never once during her stay at Auteuil had Lisa yet asked any of those particular favours that were so readily granted to well-thought-of students. What powerful motive had got the better of her pride today? Mlle Lambert adopted her most impersonal tone. 'You have been provided with all the books that are of use to you,' she said. 'And you know that it is against the rules to spend more than one day a week away from the Institution.' She looked at Lisa. 'What is it that you wish to consult?'

Lisa hesitated for a second. 'There is a comparison to be made between Leibnitz and Hobbes,' she said, 'and I do not have Hobbes' works here.' She stared at the blue-curtained windows with an expressionless gaze – impossible ever to meet those stubborn eyes under that hard Breton forehead.

'Does your subject interest you?' asked Mlle Lambert.

'It is fairly interesting,' said Lisa. She felt how suspicious this request must seem after her usual reserve; and hastily, awkwardly, she added, 'As far as Hobbes is concerned I can wait until next week: but must I put off the dentist?' At once she saw how clumsy this manoeuvre was: by withdrawing her request so easily she did not diminish its importance at all but rather accentuated its strangeness. There was an endless silence. Mlle Lambert looked absently at the ceiling; Lisa waited, her face devoid of expression, her body motionless.

'These questions of form are not of the least importance,' said Mlle Lambert at last in her beautiful mellow voice. 'Do as you wish, my dear Lisa.'

'Thank you very much, mademoiselle,' murmured Lisa in a guarded tone: she went towards the door without looking up.

'Come and see me sometimes, when you have a moment,' said Mlle Lambert with a kind of interest. 'I should like it.'

'Thank you, mademoiselle,' said Lisa again. She felt no pleasure; and when she had closed the door behind her she leant against the wall for a long moment, drained of strength, her heart empty.

At whatever time Lisa went to the Bibliothèque Nationale, she always found Marguerite sitting in chair 243 with a pile of books in front of her, taking notes with a disagreeable expression: it was concentration alone that could distort her round face like this, for neither anger nor anxiety ever made her look unpleasant. That day Wanda, a young green-eyed Pole, was sitting next to her. Lisa settled in number 241. 'How are you, Lisa?' asked Marguerite affectionately: she pointed to the books. 'As soon as I have finished we'll go out and have some coffee, shall we?' She plunged back into her work.

'What an ox!' thought Lisa resentfully. Marguerite really might have guessed that Lisa needed certainty right away: how limited even the most intelligent people were! Stupid and insensitive. As she filled out her book-slip Lisa looked at her friend with a kind of despair: every day Marguerite stayed there, clamped to her chair from nine in the morning until six in the evening, breaking off only for a few moments to eat a sandwich: without the least concern she wore a purplish-red dress that was threadbare at the elbows and sweat-stained under the arms.

'I shall never be able to reach the level of the *agrégation*,' said Lisa to herself: yet it was the only chance she had of earning a little money one day.

She got up and took her slip to the central desk: the librarian was a grey-faced young woman with plaits coiled over her ears: she spent hours receiving and stamping the yellow forms passed her by the readers, of whom she never saw anything but their fingertips. She had passed a competitive examination to get this sterile job. 'My head will have burst before ever I carve out a place in the world for myself.'

Lisa drew up her heavy caned chair and spread out her diploma sheets on the table. Half past two. How long would she still have to wait before knowing?

Library assistants moved about among the tables, their arms loaded with books: another employee paced slowly along the central alley, carrying a spraycan: every two seconds, with a slight hiss, it emitted a cloud of droplets smelling of turpentine. Lisa pressed her hands to her head: she did not want to ask the question that was burning in her, yet she knew that after an hour of torment she would end by interrogating Marguerite. All around her the learned men, the students, the cranks and the respectable tramps – the usual frequenters of the library – quietly turned the pages of their books; nothing could be heard but the rustle of paper and a few stifled coughs. In this studious atmosphere Lisa felt the blood rise to her cheeks even before she had begun her work: what a barbarous activity it was, using one's brain as though it were a machine for grinding knowledge that had nothing to do with life itself. Nevertheless it was a comfort to have Marguerite by her: she was a strong, reliable girl, thoroughly alive, and the only friend Lisa had ever had. She alone had understood Lisa, appreciating her fragile gifts at their true worth; she grasped the finest shades of a feeling; and when one expressed an idea she found that it had a greater depth than one had supposed. When she listened to Lisa recounting them, the happenings of the past week became important, like the life of a heroine in a novel. There was nothing conventional or affected about Marguerite: indeed, although the freedom of her words and thoughts delighted Lisa, they sometimes shocked her too.

'She is my friend,' thought Lisa, with sudden joy. At that moment Wanda leant over towards Marguerite, who began to laugh; then with her coat over her shoulders Wanda walked to the main door. Lisa could see nothing attractive about her: she was surprised that Marguerite should let herself be taken in by a pretty, meaningless laugh and a caressing voice; Marguerite lacked discrimination. With exasperation rising in her, Lisa watched Marguerite's eyes running along the lines of print: she looked stupid.

Lisa touched her arm: she could not sit there in a state of doubt any longer. 'Come on, do stop reading,' she said impatiently. Marguerite smiled, and in her good-natured way she followed Lisa to the flagstoned hall outside the reading-room. 'We're going to have coffee, aren't we?' she said.

'No,' said Lisa irritably. 'Let's stay here: I don't feel like coffee . . .' She only had one franc fifty on her, just enough to go to the dentist and then back to Auteuil, and she could not have accepted a cup of coffee even from her best friend without feeling like a poor relation. In any case she loathed Marguerite's eagerness to plunge into noisy places as soon as they were alone together.

'Wanda has made another conquest,' began Marguerite in a lively tone.

Lisa interrupted her. 'I'm not interested in Wanda. Is your brother coming to fetch you today?'

'He'll come when he leaves the Ecole des Chartes,' said Marguerite. 'He'll take the A1, and be here about half-past five.'

'He was supposed to come on Tuesday too,' said Lisa. 'He doesn't know I'm here?'

'I did not mention you,' said Marguerite.

Lisa reflected. 'Why does that young man run away from me?' she said slowly. 'You noticed, last time? He barely shook my hand and then leapt into a taxi with you.'

'But we really were in a great hurry,' said Marguerite. With a helpless gesture she added, 'I can't talk to Pascal about such things.'

Lisa paced the icy hall in silence for a moment. 'Sometimes I wonder whether you don't know more about it than you say,' she said in a suspicious voice. She did not utter all that was in her mind. Could she be certain that Marguerite had not passed on her confidences to Pascal? If he had not been on his guard against her, Lisa might have won his friendship, with patience: perhaps it was because of Marguerite that he avoided her – avoided her out of scrupulousness, out of virtue. She gave her friend a hard, inimical look.

'But I would tell you,' said Marguerite, quite taken aback. 'You know very well that I only want to help you: only there's so little intimacy beween Pascal and me.'

She had often helped Lisa, that was true. But how could one know that she was not playing a double game? After all, Lisa knew nothing whatsoever about Marguerite; she had never encouraged her confidences.

'Perhaps he has felt . . .' began Marguerite, and then she hesitated.

'Believe me, I have never flung myself at his head,' said Lisa, irritated. 'I don't mean to eat him up.'

A dark-complexioned man came through the revolving doors from the courtyard to the hall and gave his umbrella to the woman in the cloakroom. On approaching Marguerite he greeted her and his eyes lit up. 'Is Mlle Wanda here?' he asked. You would think it happened on purpose: every time Lisa managed to get Marguerite on to the only subject that really mattered to her, someone appeared. Marguerite had such a wide acquaintance! One might really have loathed her for the careless way she spent herself on so many people.

'My only friend,' thought Lisa with great distress: she wept when Marguerite did not turn up at a rendezvous: she desperately needed the warmth of her smile and the gaiety of her voice. Yet she could not prevent herself from poisoning this friendship with doubt, envy, and sometimes a kind of hatred. – 'I have never been able to make an act of faith.' – The man went on into the reading-room.

'That's the Roumanian Wanda was such friends with last month,' said Marguerite, looking amused; and she seemed to find relief in this diversion! Lisa listened with only half an ear to the tale of Wanda's loves.

'How can she bring such a powerful intelligence to bear on such trivial stories and people?' she wondered. 'Maybe this trifling talk is a way of getting rid of me.' Marguerite came to a fairly abrupt halt of her own accord. 'Is Anne better?' asked Lisa. She had been anxious, deeply anxious for news of her for a long while, but she had been afraid that Marguerite might suspect her of ulterior motives. She had a real affection for Anne, and she felt grateful to her: Anne had a depth of soul and a delicacy that Lisa had never met with in anyone else. Pascal's judgment was unerring.

Marguerite's face grew very sad. 'Since Tuesday she has been so delirious that they have had to move her into a ward quite by itself: she took her violin: no one is allowed to see her. It seems that all yesterday she did nothing but call out, perpetually asking for Pascal, Chantal, and a glass of sherry. Pascal learnt that from a nurse.' Her thick lips quivered.

'What appalling treatment!' said Lisa. It was indeed very sad: there were so few beings whom it was a joy to think about. How Pascal would suffer if Anne were to die. 'But there is hope?' she said.

Marguerite shrugged her shoulders without replying. 'Oh, how I should try to ease his sorrow,' thought Lisa: the corners of her mouth moved in an almost imperceptible smile. 'If he is very unhappy, he will accept my affection.' She said, speaking sincerely, 'It's monstrous, all these worthless creatures bursting with health while Anne. . . ! Such a rare being . . .'

They walked to and fro in silence for a while, their metal-tipped heels echoing on the flagstones of the bare, empty hall.

'I must go and do some work,' said Marguerite in a low voice.

Lisa gave a start: yes, Marguerite did find her presence wearisome. 'You have plenty of time!' she said, and she went straight on in an eager voice, speaking very fast, 'I thought Mlle Lambert would not let me out: she quite understood that I was not asking for a day off just to study Leibnitz, and she began by giving herself great airs of importance.'

'You are still not friends?' asked Marguerite rather absently.

'Mlle Lambert no longer takes any interest in me now that she has realized that I shall never be an outstanding scholar,' said Lisa, with an unpleasant laugh. She had been well received at the Institution Saint-Ange, but it had soon become apparent that she was by no means a professional examination-passer nor a likely recruit for the establishment, and Mlle Lambert had stopped appreciating qualities that could not be turned to account: this had wounded Lisa deeply. The other boarders had so little in the way of talent that, in spite of everything, she might still have been preferred if only she had been equally obsequious; but her independent and critical mind made her detested. 'To begin with I liked her,' said Lisa resentfully. 'For a while you let yourself be taken in by her fine phrases and her soulful eyes.'

'It was quite kind of her to let you go if she had guessed you were lying,' said Marguerite.

'She would let a soul go to perdition rather than appear openly tyrannical,' said Lisa; and abruptly she added, 'I shall go and wait for Pascal at the A1 bus-stop in the Place du Palais-Royal: don't tell him you've seen me. It's my only chance of having five minutes' talk with him.'

Marguerite nodded.

The Place du Palais-Royal clock said five o'clock when Lisa reached the corner of the rue de Richelieu. With a quick glance she examined the immediate surroundings: there were a few people gathered at the bus-stops and, leaning against one of the pillars of the Théâtre Français, a middle-aged woman was reading a paper.

Lisa stopped. Two bare-headed women, each holding one handle of a basket of violets came running down the avenue de l'Opéra: a dwarf was hopping very fast in front of them, waving a long stick with a bunch of flowers fixed to its end. Any woman coming out of a library that smelt of dust and turpentine – any woman with a little kindness towards herself – would have indulged in a franc's worth of scent and living freshness. They came closer; and as the dwarf passed before Lisa he held out the bouquet so that it almost touched her mouth, making a derisive face as he did so. She drew back with a slight start.

'A little bunch, young lady,' said one of the women in a gasping voice. Lisa's hand moved down her black, rather threadbare coat. 'I am young,' she thought with anguish. She had no wish for the flowers and she had no wish to give herself a little treat; but she did have a need to do something that would contradict this cruel indifference.

'I shall walk to the dentist's,' she decided. She took one of the bunches, mauve-petalled, tightly wrapped in its ivy. The middle-aged woman had folded up her paper and it seemed to Lisa that she was watching her with a malignant eye.

Lisa felt her coat, then her blouse: she needed a pin to fasten the violets. She searched in her handbag, but when she had taken out her handkerchief, her powder-compact, her lipstick and her key she saw nothing but the lining, stained with rust and make-up. Holding the flowers in her hand, no longer knowing what to do with this sad, useless purchase, she walked slowly towards the statue of Alfred de Musset. The flowers had taken on the ivy's bitter smell: all the scent of violets was gone.

The woman with the newspaper took a few steps by her side, staring at her with a fixed, hostile look. The streets of Paris and the passers-by always had this inimical expression. 'Today it takes all the strength of my desire for me to expose myself to these contacts that so wound my heart – to expose myself without a defence.'

Unclean streets: the hour was heavy with obscenity: not the least breath of tenderness. Lisa hated the shattering din of the hooters, the buses with their enormous wheels, and above all the pedestrians, who rushed from the pavement across the roadway in serried ranks at the policeman's whistle: if she were to fall under their feet, how heavily they would trample on her body! A flashily dressed woman went by, pressing an elderly man close to her side. Lisa looked at them with disgust. These closed-in, shut-away faces would never produce a single word nor even a human smile to save her from despair. 'My little body is aweary of this great world': it seemed that Shakespeare might have written the words for her.

'My belt,' she thought suddenly. She undid the pin that fastened the plastic buckle to the black suède and put the belt away in her bag; then, with considerable difficulty, she pinned the fragile, dripping stems, wound about with greyish wire, to her lapel. 'Spending one's last sous to buy violets,' she whispered in a dreamy tone: but who would care about such a moving gesture? The world was filled only with coarse, vulgar beings. She stood behind the statue, her head bowed, waiting for the A1 bus to come. All at once the inimical-looking woman was there in front of her: she was quite stout and her face was beginning to grow blotchy. 'I am Mme Legris,' she said in a flat voice. Lisa looked at her, astonished: for a moment they stared in silence.

'It's no good waiting any longer,' said the woman in the same neutral tone. 'He's seen me: he won't come.'

Lisa flushed: she did not understand, but she was ashamed of being caught in this humiliating attitude of waiting. 'Who are you talking about?' she said. 'What do you mean?'

'About my husband,' said Mme Legris. 'You are my husband's mistress: you meet him here every Saturday and you both go to the flat he has taken in the rue Sainte-Anne. No use lying. I know all about it.'

Lisa's heartbeat returned to normal. This was an amusing adventure, the only one that had ever happened to her. 'You are mistaken, madame,' she said politely, and hesitated: 'I am waiting for a young man, but he is not your husband.'

'A queer way to wait, hiding like that,' said Mme Legris, inspecting her with a critical eye. 'And in any case the description fits.' She remained standing there in front of Lisa, looking determined. She pointed at the bunch of violets: 'The flowers are no use.'

'Wait: you'll see,' said Lisa impatiently. She was growing cross. If Pascal did not come, this fat woman was capable of dogging her the whole evening. How puny Lisa felt, compared with her! She had always envied those strapping wenches whose toes no one ever dared tread upon.

'I'll wait, never you fear,' said Mme Legris with a sneer. A bus pulled in and, as Lisa came some way out from behind the statue to watch the passengers, so the woman moved a corresponding distance, as if she were her shadow. From the middle of the square Pascal could not fail to notice this purplish mass of a woman and at the same time to recognize Lisa: she jerked back, tears of resentment coming into her eyes.

'I am not your husband's mistress. Leave me alone,' she cried in a choking voice. The woman moved a few steps away, muttering. Pascal was not among the people who got off the bus.

'Your husband's mistress . . .' repeated Lisa automatically. It was curious to see how the slightly old-fashioned, slightly ridiculous expression took on an obscene taste when it became a living word: it had a strange, completely fresh ring. 'I am not the mistress . . . I am the mistress . . .'

The woman was no longer on the pavement. Lisa glanced around, and on either side of one of the pillars she saw the plum-coloured stuff of her coat. Lisa's thin body quivered with anger: she could do nothing against this great fat creature and she did not want to run the risk of a public scene breaking out just at the moment of Pascal's arrival: if he guessed that she had been waiting for him, she would die of shame.

She left her post: maybe Pascal had already gone by without her seeing him. Slowly she made her way towards the rue de Richelieu. The woman followed her, gliding from pillar to pillar. Lisa took a few more steps. She could no longer bear this presence, and she whipped round suddenly. Pascal was there behind her, and he was smiling at her kindly. 'Oh, it's you,' she said with an edgy laugh. 'It felt as though there were someone following me ever since I left the métro. Are you going to call for Marguerite?'

'Yes. I did not recognize you until you turned round. Have you seen my sister?'

'I've only just arrived from Auteuil. I wanted to say hello to her before going to the dentist,' said Lisa. What had he seen? Was he really taken in? Emotion and anxiety made Lisa's temples throb, and, as it happened at every meeting, they drove all thoughts out of her head: with every step that brought them closer to the library she felt herself sink deeper into stupidity. How to find the words that would pin his interest – find them in five minutes? How to give him some faint notion of a sensitivity and an intelligence whose existence he did not even suspect? 'Leaving me so little time is unfair too. Even examiners are less barbarous.'

As she was searching for the decisive phrase in silence they passed a newspaper-stand. Pascal glanced at the headlines of *L'Intransigeant*. 'It's really interesting and often quite unexpected to see how people react to what is happening in Germany,' he said in an encouraging tone. 'Have you read Romain Rolland's letter in *Europe*?'

'No,' she said. He had offered her a subject, and they would have reached the library before they had exhausted the question. She could not bear it, and she burst out 'Does all this political stuff amuse you?'

Pascal's face darkened slightly. Then he smiled. 'I was forgetting that you never read the papers.'

'Do you think I ought to pay more attention to politics?' she asked eagerly.

'Well, if it doesn't interest you . . .' he said. There was a little pause, then, with an appearance of concern he said, 'And how is your work coming along?'

She shook her head. 'I am less and less capable of working,' she said. And with a contained violence she added, 'I think it's horrible that one can be reduced to using one's brain as a means of earning a living: it's . . . it's inhuman.' She clapped the flat of her hand to her forehead. 'My whole future – the bread that I eat, my coal, my shoes – I must look to my brain for everything. And a brain is fragile: it's so fragile.'

'There is something hateful about this system of exams and competitions,' he said.

They were at the entrance of the library and this was all he had found to say to her: he walked into the reading-room to fetch his sister.

In former times it had been very different. Once again she could see that look which had seemed to search for her heart at their first encounter: straight away Lisa had known that there was nothing commonplace or trifling about this young man; the least thing he said was so exactly right and so directly to the point that one felt like crying 'Touché'. She had spoken without shyness; and he had explained her to herself better than she could ever have done. Why had his behaviour suddenly changed after three or four meetings? It was before she had confided in Marguerite.

Pascal came back with his sister. 'We shall have to take a taxi,' he said. 'Perhaps we can drop you somewhere?'

'Near the Gare Saint-Lazare if you like,' said Lisa. It was not far. When she got out they gave her friendly smiles through the window. But she knew that as soon as she was out of sight they would tell the taxi to stop and they would go into some warm café ablaze with lights. She waved with a sad smile. He had not noticed the flowers, of course.

Lisa was at her dentist's. Thick carpets deadened the sound of footsteps and the doors opened and closed silently: the whole house seemed numbed by the smell of iodine and chloroform that wafted along the corridors. What an oasis of luxury and peace! In the waiting-room there was only one young woman, muffled in furs.

Lisa sank into a deep easy-chair: she did not even reach out towards the magazines that strewed the table: she was thoroughly comfortable. This was the only moment in the week when she could allow herself to sit motionless in an armchair without trying to force her mind to produce ideas or without darning her stockings. The half-open pink damask curtains with gold fringes showed two broad windows veiled with wide-meshed tulle: a radiator emitted an even, slightly heady warmth.

To be sitting in a warm bedroom, wordlessly stroking that archangel's head, laid at last in her lap: no kisses: but the possession of his strength, and forever: no longer having to rely on oneself for everything. No eye would ever dull the purity of this refuge, where he would shine and gleam, hard and clear like a beautiful crystal. Lisa choked with tender feelings: how she would love him, when at last he lay against her heart in surrender; how she would love him when he was away; for when he was there it was no longer him that her eyes saw but a virtuous hateful young man who prevented her from coming close and touching her beloved. Dark flower of my passion.

'Mademoiselle Nardec.' Lisa stood up and followed the young woman in an overall and a flat cap that hid her hair: Dr Desvignes' inner room was a dazzling, almost gaudy white. 'How are you, mademoiselle?' said a strong, kindly voice. 'Thank you, Doctor, I have had no pain all this week,' said Lisa, giving him her hand.

'Why, you are springtime in person, all covered with flowers,' said Dr Desvignes, pointing to the violets, which were beginning to fade. 'Someone has been spoiling you,' he added in a meaningful tone. He was thirty-five or forty and he had a face as pale as an abcess, devoid of form; Lisa smiled a little bitter, flattered smile and sat in the chair. The nurse spread a fresh piece of tissue-paper on the leather headrest; Dr Desvignes washed his hands. As though she were fascinated Lisa watched the motion of these froth-covered hands, the one kneading the other, their ritual grasping, separating, coming together.

The dentist sat beside Lisa on a high stool with an adjustable seat: with his foot he made the chair rise a little. 'Open,' he said. 'Open wide.' For a moment Lisa, with her head leaning right back, focused on the frosted glass of the window; but the electric lamp, reflected by the countless facets of the projector, so dazzled her that she shut her eyes. She was not afraid: Dr Desvignes never hurt.

'Still deep in philosophy, mademoiselle?' asked the dentist. 'If you allow a mere layman to utter his thoughts on the matter, I am surprised that the people at your Sorbonne are not more concerned with the Hindu philosophy. Do you know that they have found a way of detaching the soul from the body and sending it into the astral world?'

He scraped the sick tooth with a steel instrument: Lisa, half-lying in the chair, was wholly in his power; she thought of nothing, she felt nothing apart from a gentle touch at the corner of her mouth, the pressure of a soft palm against her cheek. The dentist was talking: he described the various stages of the initiation that allows man to free himself from his body, but she scarcely listened – nothing existed apart from his hands, his skilful hands. She half opened her eyes: they were plump, translucent hands with carefully cut nails, over-washed hands that smelt of almonds and that had the pallor of dead tissues preserved in a jar of spirit.

'You have to take care,' said the dentist. 'If you try the experiment without having enough strength of will you will never manage to call your soul back, and it will remain a wanderer forever.' He broke off. 'Rinse, if you please,' he said. Lisa filled her mouth and spat a pink liquid and pieces of stopping into a glass bowl: she wiped her lips. 'Do you believe in the existence of another world, Doctor?' she asked. 'For my part, I don't know: I should call myself a sceptic.' She opened her mouth again. The dentist brought a sharp point into contact with the tooth and pressed a lever with his foot. Lisa's head was filled with a disagreeable hum. 'It is years now that I have been going into this science they call theosophy,' said the dentist. 'To begin with I too was a doubter: I read a few books and went to meetings merely out of curiosity. But I do assure you I have been the witness of really very strange and disturbing events. I must lend you Annie Besant's book, a most unusual piece of work. That woman reached such a degree of purification that it was granted to her to see exact pictures of her former existence.'

He rang and said a few words to the nurse, who laid out a blue glass slab and some ingredients. 'We are going to fill this tooth,' he said. 'Rinse, mademoiselle.' Lisa spat and watched the doctor kneading a white substance: the tooth was healed: presently she would have to leave. A little while ago it was drizzling in the streets: she lay flatter still in the chair. What well-being! Inwardly she repeated a phrase that tickled her strangely: 'You are my husband's mistress.' How amusing. So my virginity is not written on my forehead, then.

The dentist put a saliva-pump into Lisa's mouth and stuffed her cheeks with cotton-wool. 'I cannot believe that you accept that philosophy which claims that all the phenomena of life can be reduced to simple mechanisms: don't you feel that your whole being reaches out for something that this crass materialism cannot give you?'

Lisa tried to give a signal of agreement, but her movements were paralysed. The dentist fell silent.

Once again the plump, supple hand brushed her lips and her chin: under this caress, and in this warm air heavy with pharmaceutical odours, Lisa felt her body relax. Most of the time she loathed her sharp-featured face and her thin, frail body – an absolute grasshopper – but now all at once it seemed to her that her flesh had become soft to the touch, yielding and rich. Could I really be taken for a middle-aged man's mistress? The tissue paper crinkled against the nape of her neck.

'You will lose all your teeth if you go on working so hard, Mademoiselle Nardec,' said the dentist. 'It is not philosophy that a young lady like you is in need of.' He spread the white paste with a spatula: it made a little creaking sound when she bit on it.

'This fat lump is the only man who has ever talked sweet nothings to me.' A mischievous idea darted into her mind. 'What if I asked him to lend me the fare home?'

The doctor removed the saliva-pump and took out the cotton-wool with pincers. 'How do you suppose I should live?' asked Lisa with a little laugh in which there was both coquetry and bitterness. She got up from the chair: Dr Desvignes walked over to the handbasin.

'Pretty women should not be allowed to study,' he said in a bantering tone. Lisa put on her hat in front of the mirror. She was not without elegance: if she were well made up and if some wealthy man bought her expensive clothes she too could strut about giving herself the airs of a princess. 'I am too proud, too reticent: I daren't even borrow five francs from this man.'

'Good-bye, Doctor,' said Lisa.

'Good-bye, mademoiselle. Avoid eating on the right side until tomorrow morning.' He held on to her hand. 'My Saturdays will be quite sad from now on.' Lisa gave an embarrassed laugh. He let her hand go, saying, 'I will send you the book I was telling you about.'

'Forgive me, Doctor,' said Lisa. 'It's absurd, but I have no change on me.'

How easy it was! Going down the steps into the métro Lisa reflected proudly that she was not the timid hare, the trembling creature people supposed: she could look at men with bold eyes, and failing love she could make life yield luxury and pleasure. 'What a fatuous ass of an archangel, to be afraid of breaking my heart.' – 'Perhaps one day I shall get some man to keep me,' she murmured defiantly. 'That really would amaze them! – My husband's mistress.' She sighed: her soul was not base enough for that, alas. Lisa experienced the pleasure of being able to regard her poverty as the choice of a proud nature and no longer merely as the fate of a girl devoid of beauty.

Dinner was over when Lisa reached Auteuil. She slipped quietly along the corridors. A ray of light showed under Mlle Lambert's door: there was a meeting of the Sisterhood of Saint Ange. The students who did not belong to it (for everyone was free, merely being in greater favour or in less) had tea in their bedrooms, gathering in little groups. In the dimly lit library only Marthe and Françoise bent their fat peasant faces over works on philology.

Lisa went upstairs: the air was heavy with all the weariness that had piled up during the day: voices with no gaiety in them could be heard the other side of the doors, and the clink of spoons and cups. All day long nothing had happened to anyone and no one had anything to say: nothing was sought but a pretext for waiting until one could decently go to bed.

A door opened. 'Lisa, will you come and have a cup of tea?' Usually Lisa said no: there was nothing in common between her and these resigned young women who accumulated pieces of information as others threaded loops on to knitting-needles. They never had an idea of their own; they never opened a book that was not required reading for their course; they submitted to a fate imposed on them by chance. A few of them dreamt of being

farmers' wives or mothers of families; most never desired anything at all. But Lisa disliked the company of Thérèse less than
that of the others because she and her friends called themselves
'independents', that is to say they did not admire Mlle Lambert:
and in any case this evening Lisa wanted to hear the sound of her
own voice. She walked in, threw her little black hat onto the
divan and sat down on the floor between Jeanne and Hélène.

Thérèse handed her a cup of tea. 'What lovely flowers, Lisa!'
she said in an admiring voice. She was thirty, and in her eyes Lisa
was the incarnation of youth and grace. With one finger Lisa
stroked the violets, which were beginning to give off a mawkish
smell of decay: there was a great deal of weariness in her, and a
kind of gaiety. 'I bought them from some very strange flower-
sellers,' she said dreamily. 'Weird people like those that Rilke
speaks of, you know . . .' No one here cared about Rilke: she
stopped, then added, 'I only had the price of a métro ticket in my
bag, but I could not resist.'

'A cigarette?' said Hélène. Lisa accepted one and then took a
tangerine from the basket.

'Were you out all day?' asked Thérèse.

'I went to the Nationale and then to my dentist,' said Lisa. With
her nail she took the skin off the scented tangerine and smiled.
'The dentist almost made a declaration – a big fat man of forty.
How I laughed! A little more and he would have suggested
making me a kept woman.'

'A forty-year-old dentist: that's a fine beginning,' said
Thérèse with a pert look. Lisa laughed cheerfully: she felt as
though she possessed the scornful heart of an entirely satisfied
woman. 'Perhaps he thinks his compliments please me,' she said
in a mocking voice. 'He wants me to go and see him so that he can
tell me about the astral world: he's a theosophist.'

Jeanne and Hélène smiled faintly. 'I knew a dentist who
went in for spiritualism,' said Jeanne.

'Dentists and teachers of German are very fond of entering into
contact with the other world,' said Hélène. 'It's well known.'

For a while they smoked in silence. Lisa squeezed a piece of
golden skin between her fingers so that she would be permeated
with that odour of tangerine and tobacco which scented the
bedrooms of the Institution in the evenings. There was no more
to be said about this dentist.

'Lisa, do you know that there's still a party going on at Mme Leroy's?' said Thérèse. 'All the windows in the pavilion are lit.'

'She wants to marry Elizabeth off,' said Hélène. 'She doesn't want her daughter to be like us. It's understandable.'

'She's carefully guarded her against Mlle Lambert's influence,' said Jeanne with a sneer that emphasized her face's lack of symmetry.

'That Circe!' said Lisa.

'Don't laugh about it,' said Thérèse. 'Do you know that Geneviève Neveu has joined the Sisterhood? She's on the right road. When will your turn come, Lisa?'

'A side parting doesn't suit me,' said Lisa.

'After three years you are allowed to have it in the middle,' said Hélène.

'Silence and discretion,' said Thérèse, putting her finger to her lips with an exaggerated gesture like a clown.

There was a heavy silence. Lisa made an effort. 'These flowers brought me a very amusing adventure,' she said, looking cheerful. 'As I was waiting for a bus in the Place du Palais-Royal, there was a woman who took me for her husband's mistress. Just imagine that!'

'Did she really?' cried Hélène.

Their faces turned towards Lisa with a vague interest: she hesitated.

'It once happened to me too,' said Thérèse after a short pause. 'One day I was accosted by a woman who maintained that my name was Mlle Gontran . . .'

A great weariness came over Lisa: she could no longer see what had given the trifling events of the day their value, and nothing was important any more. Nothing that happened to her could seem important for long. If Marguerite had been there, perhaps, in spite of everything, it might have made a story.

Lisa stood up. 'I must go and do some work,' she said in an unenthusiastic voice. Not a single one of these sick creatures was even capable of feeling sad at her going.

Ten o'clock. Now all the students were alone, each in her cell. The last light in the library had been put out. Mlle Lambert was praying in the chapel, her face buried in her hands: and what thoughts, what memories preyed on her? Did the woman even believe in God? At the foot of their beds, the members of the Sisterhood of Saint-Ange ran through their rosaries; Marthe and Françoise doggedly pored over the philology books that they had carried to their bedrooms; and the more particular students washed their collars and underwear with a great rushing of water, or darned their stockings. These dismal little tasks would have been the only pleasure of the day for their housewifely souls.

Sleep was better. Lisa undressed: with a modesty learnt in her childhood she put on her pyjama trousers before she took off her slip, and when she put on the flowered jacket she averted her eyes from her breasts. When she was in bed she lit a cigarette: the lampshade made a round, indented shadow on the ceiling, like a sunflower.

'You are my husband's mistress.' The dentist's soft, transparent hands. Soft, downy grass brushing one's lips. Dark flower of my passion. A light shower of petals on one's cheeks. One petal crinkling like tissue-paper behind her neck. Pascal's hands, long and pure, chastely touching the hollow of her shoulder. An archangel dressed in shining white with a fiery sword in his chaste hands: sweet breath. The warm breeze melting the pure crystal. Warm hands, lily-soft hands still damp with moss. You are the rain of light caresses, the shower of snow-flakes on a tender body where the dark flower shines, the velvety flower of passion. Pascal's hands stroking hair and neck, the lovely crystal melting away, warm breath, hands moving over the secret flesh, archangel's hands gliding slowly down a tender victim, your hand quivering flesh, your dear archangel's hand beloved: beloved, beloved.

Lisa's hand dropped the cigarette into the ashtray and slipped under the pyjama's silk: she no longer felt her arm – her hand was no longer hers and it was under the caress of these stranger's fingers that the soft moist inner tissues thrilled and quivered.

Your dear archangel's hand beloved, well-beloved.

ANNE

*L*ORD, *I return Thee thanks for having descended upon me, the hum-*
blest of Thy servants. Behold me prostrate at Thy feet and accept
the worship and the love of Thy most unworthy child. I give myself up
entirely to Thy guidance, oh God: Thou hast entrusted me with the care of
these souls and one day Thou wilt call me to account. Help me, protect me.
I am so uncertain, so anxious: there is no question but it is a man's
writing, no doubt one of those youths at the Sorbonne – no young man of
our world would presume to write to a daughter of mine. The third letter
since the beginning of the holidays. I wonder whether she replies – she is
never to be seen writing. How fervently she prays! All through Mass she
kept her face buried in her hands. Enlighten, oh Lord, this straying
conscience; she is letting herself be carried away by weakness; inspire her
to make a sincere confession. I prefer not to ask the question directly:
Mama never got anything out of me in that way when I was young. I
believe she writes at night; that is why there is a light under her door: her
face is drawn in the morning – a mother's eye is never mistaken in these
matters – and she is not well. She drinks too much tea: I shall take her to
see the doctor at the beginning of term. This is the first time she has ever
had a secret from her mother. What can he have to say to her, in those fat
envelopes? When it is a question of her daughter's soul, a mother has the
right to commit an impropriety; but even using steam it is hard not to
leave a trace: I have never opened my children's letters – it is an abuse of
authority and it is so clumsy. It is absurd that she has not yet spoken to me
of her own free will: I have been too weak with her: Lord, give me the
strength to be hard. Thou didst not spare Thy own Son! One should not
have a preference for any particular child, but she is so sensitive, so
affectionate. I am punished for my love. I should never have allowed her to
continue her studies; that was my first mistake. They have not changed
her heart, but they have warped her mind: see the pitch things have
reached at present, my daughter secretly corresponding with a man! She
should have been made to break with Chantal long ago: I hate these
intellectuals. I had kept her so pure for Thee, oh Lord! She had in her the
makings of a saint and for a while I thought that Thou wouldst do us the
great honour of reserving her for Thyself; now she is the prey of an
unbeliever and a stranger. Save her from them! For twenty years I have

watched jealously over her soul, and I shall not allow the first comer to endanger her salvation. Marry her off as soon as possible: I have done enough for Lucette; I have spared nothing and she has already cost me dear in interviews: this is her last chance. Bless the day the marriage is performed, I beseech Thee! In any case he is a young man worthy of all praise, with the highest moral standards, and we have known his family forever. She can make a good impression if she chooses to be agreeable; her smile is really pleasant, and she has a very good mind; she would be a positive treasure for a husband. It is sad that the young men of today should be so afraid of life: obviously I had looked forward to something better for her: but with this crisis they have not the spirit to found a home. Fortunately Pierre is good at mathematics. Lord! I could not have borne having dunces for sons; that must be dreadful for a mother: to begin with they will just have to live with us, and Robert will find him a job; I will put the twins on a divan in the little drawing-room and give them the big bedroom – they will be on their own. At twenty-five you no longer have the right to be ambitious. Then perhaps I shall send Anne abroad for a year, to a convent where she will be supervised and where she can perfect her English, it might always come in useful. Lord, Thou seest that I talk to Thee as a child talks to its father: I entrust myself to Thee, oh God, and all I wish is to be the instrument of Thy holy will. More will be asked of us than of others because more has been given us; we do not belong among those wretched souls who struggle in the darkness, for we have the happiness of living in Thy light: render us worthy of this very great favour. Anne is weak; she is too sensitive, as I was at her age; it is my duty to be strong for her: I shall not let her be contaminated by contact with the ungodly. Chantal shall not set foot in the house this year: an unbeliever, an adventuress. She was nice when she was young, but Mme Plattard did not know how to bring her up, poor little woman – she was overwhelmed. I distrusted her for a long while, and I struggled, but Anne is so fond of her; yet she has quantities of charming friends – she is surrounded with affection on every side. All the difficulties come from this pretentious little intellectual, a girl who hangs about cafés with men, who has no family, and who does not believe in God or the Devil, and who has lost her social position: it was at her place that Anne got to know him: she blushed and she could not meet my eye when I handed her the letter: I expected her to say something, but she walked off without a word. This is the first time. Never, never have my children had anything to hide from me. In Anne's case it was unbelievable: at home I always found her so obedient, so kind, so affectionate that I was not firm enough. All that was just to soothe me and set her conscience at rest; but I shall no longer be imposed upon: her soul must submit to guidance again. And the books that I found on her shelves yesterday! What reading for a Christian girl! I should prefer downright obscenity. I have never wished my daughters to be ignorant of the facts of life, and I think I give them quite broad-minded information – it is the best way of dealing with unhealthy curiosity – but I detest these morbid, twisted minds: to have the face to call yourself a Catholic when you write such horrors about the family! What times we live in! All these false teachers, all these false prophets: Robert ought to have supervised her more – I have not had time to open a book for years and years, so the titles mean nothing to me and I cannot guide her, in any case it is a waste of effort: in spite of my keeping her busy and active she always finds some time to read and dream. She reads when she ought to be asleep; and I must say it is not very intelligent, after that, to complain of having a headache. How did she dare to take Communion this morning with that letter in her handbag? She lies to herself. Open her eyes for her, appeal to her honesty, her straightforwardness, compel her to keep to a single confessor – this last year she has been going to confession here, there and everywhere. It is absurdly presumptious, and in October I shall send her to Father Chiboure; he knows how to deal with young people and he is not one of these modern priests whose great idea is to show that they are broad-minded. I think it must be this Pascal Drouffe she has sometimes told me about; quite a good family, it seems, but I shall never give my daughter to a friend of Chantal's – I am not one of those women who want to marry off their girls whatever the cost; thanks be to God, I can ensure my children's future as far as money is concerned and I shall not allow one of those sudden impulsive marriages that people regret for the rest of their lives. In any event I doubt that he thinks of marrying her – it can't be serious – young men have lost their respect for girls, quite understandably. These so-called pure relationships between men and women, it's the promiscuity of savages and wild animals. Anne believes that they like being with Chantal because of her intellectual qualities, poor child: unless Thy grace sanctify them, Lord, men are only filthy beasts. I am sure Chantal is no longer a virgin; she has no principles; she looks like a woman used to dissipation. I shall not let them sully my little Anne, my pure treasure. My God! The day I opened Mme Ernoult's eyes for her, I never imagined that one of my daughters could behave like Paulette! You gave me such beautiful children, with healthy bodies and such clean souls that perhaps I have been a presumptuous mother. Lord, Lord, do not punish me too severely: Thy will be done; but if it is possible, take this cup from me. Speak, oh God: I shall obey. Yes, stop this correspondence immediately. I should have preferred to avoid a direct confrontation, but the situation is very serious: force a confession and make use of my authority: she knows her duty as a Christian and she will obey. Lucette has never given me any of these anxieties, I must admit. Anne is so romantic: there was that childhood love of hers – it broke my heart – and for a year she was only a shadow of herself. Of course, I spoilt her a little in those days, but I was never unjust and this jealousy is perfectly odious – I am sick of seeing that great idle, gloomy, argumentative girl dragging about the house; no one can bear her any more; she is so cross and so domineering with the little ones. She is growing sour, and it's her own fault: let her become a nun: but being an old maid is not a vocation. Oh, Mama's ironic voice yesterday evening: 'Another interview for Lucette? Let's hope it's the right one this time.' They look as if they thought I was responsible: an astonishing notion, upon my word. I too am eager to be rid of her. They might hide their feelings – very charming to hear, I'm sure. I shall shake her up a little, tell her that at the present time her civic duties are those of a wife and mother and this refusal to fulfil her mission as a woman is immoral. It's vanity that is her undoing; she can't bring herself to lower her sights – a poor hanger-on, a wretched failure, like Cousin Marie, that's what she will become, a pretty sight in a family. Jesus cursed the barren fig-tree: I shall know how to compel her to accept her role in society and to fulfil the destiny Thou hast allotted her – all her friends are married. I shall take Anne. It would be more decent and in any case I should rather she drove; I am not at my ease with Lucette. A pâté, a tart, and a bottle of wine will do very well. Lord, forgive me: my mind wanders: I have too many things to think of to be able to concentrate – and now here is Jacques kicking his prie-dieu. I do not want to force the little ones to make too long a thanksgiving: how I envy those women who serve Thee in cloistered silence, Lord. But Thou hast decided otherwise; Thou hast reserved me for the world, blessed by Thy holy will. In the name of the Father and of the Son and of the Holy Ghost, Amen.

Mme Vignon stood up and made a deep genuflexion. 'We will go straight home, Anne,' she said. 'We just have time.' Anne took the wheel while the children bundled into the back of the car; it was eleven o'clock and already the sun was overpowering. On the road the car raised clouds of hot dust. 'You must go and change, Lucette,' said Mme Vignon. 'Your blue dress suits you better.' She looked at her younger daughter out of the corner of her eye. Anne's face was drawn, but she seemed radiantly happy. 'That letter has transformed her,' thought Mme Vignon bitterly: in earlier days all Anne's childish joys and sorrows had depended upon her alone.

The car stopped in front of the house: Anne got out first and gave her mother a hand to help her from her seat. 'Dear Mama,' she said affectionately, 'you look perfectly lovely in that hat: you will dazzle the whole countryside.'

Mme Vignon stroked the girl's black hair. 'What a baby you are,' she said, smiling. 'Be very kind, Anne, and get the picnic ready for us, will you?' She paused at the foot of the steps for a moment, breathing in the scent of the wistaria and the phlox: Simone and Pierre went towards the kitchen, carrying loaves of bread, the three little ones ran across the lawn and vanished under the branches of the weeping elm that they had made their own. Suddenly the twins' piercing voices rang out. 'Simone, Anne, come and see! Mama has given us a carpet for our house!' Mme Vignon smiled and began to climb the steps.

'That carpet was still perfectly good,' said Lucette rather sharply.

'It gives them such pleasure,' said her mother in an indulgent tone.

'You spoil them too much,' said Lucette. 'There's no holding them.'

'My dear,' said Mme Vignon, 'you can carry out your ideas of bringing up children on your own offspring.' She followed Lucette into her bedroom and sat firmly down in an armchair.

Lucette began to undress in silence. 'In short, this young man has no job,' she said abruptly.

Mme Vignon put her hand to the heavy gold clasp of the black velvet ribbon round her neck. 'Your father will help you both,' she said in a conciliating voice.

Over her silk slip, her best Sunday slip, Lucette put on her blue dress. 'As far as brilliant matches go, it isn't much of one.' Her voice was full of resentment.

Mme Vignon stared inimically at her elder daughter's gloomy face. 'If you had a slightly better understanding of what marriage ought to be for a Christian woman, you would not let questions of vain pride enter into it.' She shrugged her shoulders. 'Believe me,' she added harshly, 'if I had only thought about *my* pleasure, you would never have come into the world.'

Lucette shook her powder-puff. 'I can't see why you want Anne to go with us,' she said after a moment.

'She has never done you any harm that I know of,' began Mme Vignon and then she stopped. In the silence there were sudden shouts and cries. 'It sounds like Grandmama,' said Lucette. Mme Vignon stood up. 'Now what's happening?' she said: she would have liked to carry on with the conversation. 'Go and see, Mama,' said Lucette. 'They are sure to have done something silly again.'

The shouts were coming from the garden: Mme Vignon went downstairs without hurrying. At the door of the woodshed she saw Mme Boyer, purple in the face, waving her arms. The twins were looking at her with a mocking expression: their hair and pinafores were covered with sawdust. 'Look!' cried Mme Boyer, pointing at Suzette's bleeding knee and grasping her by the shoulder. 'I thought I should have a fit. I heard them shouting, and when I reached them I saw them struggling for the axe, the big axe!'

'We only wanted to cut sticks, Mama,' cried Suzon in his shrill voice, 'and Suzette fell on the axe, but she has not hurt herself much. Grandmama is always afraid of everything.'

'An axe bigger than you are: you might perfectly well have killed yourselves,' said Mme Boyer, shaking her grand-daughter angrily.

Mme Vignon dabbed the wounded knee with her handkerchief; she was not a woman to make a fuss over the incident. 'It's not serious, Mama,' she said. 'Go and ask Anne to bandage you, you silly little thing.' Suzette limped off and Mme Vignon went to give Simone and Pierre her last instructions; when she came back to the car she saw Jacques and Suzon skipping round Lucette and laughing. 'Look how her hair is curled,' they shouted. 'She's going for an interview, she's going for an interview!'

'Little fools,' said Lucette.

'She's as curly as a sheep,' said Jacques again, bursting with laughter.

'This is no sort of life,' muttered Mme Vignon crossly; she knew that in the kitchen there were sneers and whispered gossip, that in the library Pierre and Simone were betting on the issue, and that throughout the house there would be a little fever of hope and anxiety until the evening. 'Come on,' she said brusquely, slamming the car-door to.

These picnics on the banks of the Vézère were an honoured tradition for the local families: the children settled at the water's edge under the poplars and the parents sat rather farther back, on great blocks of stone. Each had a paper napkin and cardboard plates and a mug, and the girls passed round the huge dishes of pâté, cold fish, braised beef and chicken in aspic that invariably formed the meal.

'Your little Anne is a positive sunbeam,' said old M. de Castillanne, helping himself to a piece of turbot with mayonnaise. Mme Vignon smiled indulgently: old men always liked Anne. 'She is a dear child,' she said, 'but she lacks her elder sister's balance and sense of measure: she takes after me,' she added with a faint sigh. 'It is Lucette who has inherited her father's brain. I do not say so because she is my daughter, but she is much cleverer than I am – she makes all her sisters' dresses, and she is a wonderful cook. She draws and plays music, and with all that she still finds time to read and cultivate her mind.'

'All your children are splendid,' said Mme de Castillanne with enthusiasm.

'Oh, they have their faults,' said Mme Vignon modestly, looking about for her daughters. Anne was really striking in her simple white dress; she was laughing, and as usual there were many people round her. In spite of her habitual reserve there was a gay, affectionate spontaneity in her voice and her laugh that won all hearts. Lucette was talking to André Naville, Mme de Castillanne's nephew: Mme Vignon heard her say, 'No doubt people from the north are less brilliant, but you can rely on them.' She was looking pleasant, but then Lucette always looked pleasant at a party: that proved nothing. The young man was rather quiet, but when he spoke he had a cultivated voice: he was not bad looking. 'It might work,' thought Mme Vignon.

'You ought to send me your girls for a few days,' said Mme de Castillanne. 'Mariette and Line would be so happy, poor little things: they are all by themselves.' She gave Mme Vignon a significant look. 'They could come by the morning train tomorrow, for example: André would fetch them at the station. He is leaving us soon, alas: he brings such cheerfulness into the house.'

'My dear Jeanne, you are too kind,' said Mme Vignon.

The meal came to an end: conversation began to die away. Mme Vignon turned a severe eye upon the sleepy bodies half-lying under the poplars: the Rungis girl's hair was almost touching Pierre d'Alassac's shoulder; Nicole Duflos had linked her hands behind her neck; and Suzanne's skirt showed her legs as far as the knee. Mme Vignon observed with satisfaction that Lucette, always opposed to free-and-easy ways, was still sitting with her back against a tree and talking in a calm, steady voice: as for Anne, she could not see her. Anne often used to vanish like this when she was a child: she would desert her friends in the dining-room, and she would be discovered in her father's study, reading or talking to Chantal. Mme Vignon scolded her for the sake of appearances, although these spontaneous impulses amused her; but now Anne was too old for such behaviour. Without showing her displeasure Mme Vignon turned to M. d'Alassac: 'Yes, it was a crime to have built that saw-mill,' she said. 'As it is, the young peasants are only too inclined to leave the land.'

M. d'Alassac nodded. 'In twenty years the countryside will be completely deserted,' he said.

Still Anne did not come back: after a moment Mme Vignon got up. 'Lucette, have you seen your sister?' she asked.

'Anne? I think she went that way,' said Lucette, pointing to the path along the Vézère.

Mme Vignon felt anger rising in her. She strode off looking for Anne. The sun-filled meadows were empty, but at the foot of a tree she saw a pair of shoes and a little heap of clothes; and a vague form was splashing about in the water. 'Anne, are you mad? Come out this minute,' cried Mme Vignon.

A head rose from the river, its hair streaming, flattened by the current. 'If only you knew how lovely it is in the water! Doesn't it tempt you, Mama dear?'

This time Mme Vignon was in no mood to smile at her daughter's childish nonsense. 'Come out immediately. What utter folly, on top of your lunch!' Anne swam slowly to the bank. 'You are behaving like a baby: you have no right to play with your health,' went on Mme Vignon.

Anne came out of the water. She was wrapped in an old overcoat she had taken out of the boot of the car: she shook herself, laughing, then began to dress, looking cheerful. This increased

Mme Vignon's anger. 'You might at least do your duty in the way of good manners,' she said icily. 'It is not a great deal to ask when I beg you to keep up something like outward appearances.'

Anne looked at her with surprise, and then blushed violently. 'What appearances?' she murmured.

'Yes. You are living in the most total anarchy; if your conscience can put up with it, that's your business: but in public, try to behave properly.' Anne bowed her head and buttoned her dress without replying. 'I inspected your books yesterday evening, and I chanced across some pages that made me blush,' said Mme Vignon.

'You never look at my books except to find something that may be shocking,' said Anne.

'And you, what do you look for in them? It is something worse than levity; it is unwholesome curiosity. If you want to enrich your mind, read the Fathers of the Church or Saint Theresa. In any case saving your soul does not call for all that amount of knowledge.' Anne stared into the middle distance and made no answer. Mme Vignon went on: 'I warn you that Chantal will not set foot in my house this year.' The blow went home: Anne gave a start. 'You had let me hope that she would come, Mama; you had agreed . . .' 'I have been only too willing to give you pleasure, and now I am sorry for it: I will not have a ruined girl in my house.'

'Mama,' said Anne in a voice full of pain, 'you are unfair to Chantal. It does not seem to me that losing one's faith is a sin: it is a trial, and we have no right to judge.'

'I do not judge anyone,' said Mme Vignon sharply. 'Every night I pray for souls who have lost their way; but first and foremost we must preserve ourselves from sin and not allow scabbed sheep to contaminate us. Believe me, it wounds me to feel that you are soiled by unclean books, by associating with young men who have no scruples, and with puffed-up, immodest women. Only God knows what point you may have reached by now.'

Anne had gone very pale, 'Mama, you know perfectly well that I have the same beliefs and the same moral code as you,' she cried. 'How you do hurt me.'

Mme Vignon stared at her in silence. The appeal moved her, but hitherto she had been only too easily tempted to trust in

Anne. She hardened her heart. 'I know nothing,' she said wearily. 'My own daughter is a stranger to me.'

Anne looked at her with a tormented expression on her face: there was a long silence. 'You are talking about those letters?' she said at last, getting the words out with great difficulty. 'Pascal Drouffe asked if he might write to me during the holidays: there is nothing in that to worry you.'

'What point have you reached with him? Does he want to marry you?' asked Mme Vignon in an urgent voice.

Anne stiffened. 'It's not a question of that,' she said. 'We like one another; we are friends – it's simple enough. Does it really make so much difference if I wear a skirt and he wears trousers?'

'Anne, my poor child, you don't know anything about life,' said Mme Vignon. 'Listen: I shall never allow one of my daughters to have a friendship with a man who is not intended to be her husband. I know what men are: they talk about ideals, but they are full of base desires. The fine theories of Chantal and her friends are only good for justifying the lowest instincts. I am sorry to be forced to tell you these harsh truths, but that is how things are.'

Anne opened her handbag. 'Would you like to see them?' she asked abruptly, holding out one of the letters.

'No,' said Mme Vignon. 'I'm quite sure they are full of nothing but fine phrases and noble sentiments; but those who start as angels finish up as brutes, my poor Anne. What absurd pride to imagine that you can expose yourself to temptation without being harmed! You know quite well that there is no worse crime in God's eyes than pride. Not running away from temptation is in itself a sin.'

'I am sorry to have caused you so much anxiety,' said Anne faintly.

'Don't think about me, Anne: think about your soul. It's quite plain and straightforward – you will give up this correspondence.'

'Mama!'

'You will stop having any contact with this young man,' said Mme Vignon, growing more heated. 'If he wants to marry you, let him ask for your hand: we will make enquiries and go into the matter more thoroughly. But meanwhile I don't want any of these shady relationships: an honourable man does not write to a girl in secret.'

Anne's face had lost all its composure; even her lips were white. It was atrocious, torturing this child; but it was her salvation, not her happiness, that must be thought of. Mme Vignon uttered a brief inward prayer that God would harden her heart.

'But why?' cried Anne. 'Why?' She looked drawn and haggard. 'My decision is irrevocable. I wish you to break with that whole intellectual circle. When term begins, you will leave for England and you will stay there for a year. It will do you a great deal of good to be alone with your conscience.'

'A year . . .' said Anne.

Mme Vignon put her hand on the girl's shoulder. 'We must go along now,' she said. 'We have already been away too long.'

Anne recoiled. 'Go back to all those people?' she said wildly.

'We must do what we have to do without taking our feelings into consideration, Anne,' said Mme Vignon. She shrugged. 'I used to be like you: but one learns not to pay attention to oneself.'

They walked along the bank of the Vézère in silence. Mme Vignon put on her cheerful face again. 'This stupid girl had taken it into her head to bathe,' she said to Mme de Castillanne with a pleased, mock-scolding look. 'She will never learn sense.' Anne sat down a few paces from her sister. 'Well, Anne, you fickle thing,' called her cousin Maurice, 'are you coming to play hunt the slipper?'

Anne gave a ghost of a smile. 'It was a delightful bathe,' she said, taking her place in the ring: she knew how to behave.

'He is a pleasant young man, isn't he?' said Mme Vignon to Lucette in an inviting tone, as they were driving home two hours later. She was sitting in the back of the car next to her elder daughter; Anne was at the wheel, looking grim, desperate.

Lucette gave a little laugh. 'He has no conversation, Mama, and no culture; I really can't see myself spending a whole lifetime with him.'

'It always seems strange, bringing a stranger into one's life,' said Mme Vignon. 'One gets used to it.'

'But you don't know how boring he is,' said Lucette with some distress.

'What I do know is that I've given you your last chance: the next will be for your sister. She can't be kept waiting for you all her life.'

'Of course not,' said Lucette. 'But is it my fault that none of the matches suggested for me has ever been acceptable?'

'No doubt you will have a better opinion of M. Naville when you know more of him,' said Mme Vignon in an authoritative voice. 'I am sure you will learn to appreciate him during the two days that you two are going to spend at the Castillannes.'

Anne looked round. 'I don't have to go with Lucette, do I?'

'Of course you do. I told you so just now, only you never listen. The Castillanne girls will be delighted to see you.'

'I'm so tired, Mama,' said Anne.

Her tone irritated Mme Vignon – Anne paid too much attention to her whims. 'Don't argue.'

'Mama, I beg of you,' said Anne. Mme Vignon made no reply.

When the car stopped in front of the house, inquisitive faces appeared at the windows. 'Did you have a good time?' asked Simone with a knowing grin.

'A very good time; the weather was perfect,' said Mme Vignon, going rapidly up the stairs after her elder daughter. She walked into her bedroom and took off her hat and gloves. 'I meant to warn you this morning,' she said. 'If you don't marry M. Naville, from now on you will live at Fargeas all the year round. I leave you the choice: think it over carefully.'

Lucette seemed taken aback. 'I can't make up my mind before I know him,' she said with something like good grace.

'Naturally,' said Mme Vignon in a conciliatory tone. 'Though I do assure you he made a really good impression on me.' She sought the arguments Lucette would find most persuasive: André Naville was quiet, earnest and hard-working; with M. Vignon's backing he would certainly make his way quickly; in two years at the outside Lucette would be able to set up house on her own, and with the dowry her father would give her she would be quite comfortably off; and she would live in Paris, which would have many advantages. Lucette made an objection from time to time, but her resistance was weakening. 'I knew the idea of being buried alive here would frighten her,' thought Mme Vignon, and she began tracing the Navilles' family tree in order to show her daughter that in spite of their having no *de* to their name they were very well connected.

The afternoon was coming to an end; the shadow of the blue cedar now touched the first of the steps in front of the house; a gentle breeze made the leaves of the poplars tremble; and from time to time the clear voice of a child could be heard in the silence. Mme Vignon smiled: how peaceful it was now! The worries that had tormented her that morning had vanished. Once again God had listened to her prayer: Lucette was going to marry; and of her own accord Anne had confessed her fault, a fault that was perhaps no more than a piece of foolishness – she was dutiful and obedient after all, and a year would cure her. The smell of caramel custard rose from the kitchen: the wistaria flowers were full of the hum of bees.

All at once a great cry rang out. It came from the wood-shed as it had done in the morning but this time Mme Vignon recognized Anne's voice: she ran downstairs.

'She has cut her foot with the axe,' shouted Mme Boyer from afar. 'The clumsy girl. I told you so: that wood-shed ought to be locked.'

Anne lay there unconscious, with the twins and old Maria bending over her. 'She said she would cut sticks for our fire,' said Suzette, bursting into tears.

'It's nothing, madame,' said Maria. She had taken off Anne's shoe and stocking: the foot was bleeding profusely. Mme Vignon took Anne under the arms. 'Help me to carry her, Maria.'

Maria lifted the limp body and carefully they made their way up the stairs, Mme Boyer following them and repeating 'What a disaster! What a disaster!'

Mme Vignon was all on edge: 'Crying does no good,' she said to Suzette, who was still sobbing. In spite of her habitual self-possession, she felt a stab at her heart that was very like remorse.

They laid Anne on the bed. The wound was not very deep, and as Mme Vignon finished dressing it Anne opened her eyes. 'I meant to cut sticks for the children,' she said in a faint voice, 'I don't know how I did it.'

'I wonder too,' said Mme Vignon. For a few seconds she stood there motionless, staring at her daughter's closed face: Anne would have to spend at least a week on a couch. She could not go to the Castillannes. 'But no one would have the courage to cut herself with an axe like that on purpose,' said Mme Vignon to herself.

She went down to the kitchen to make a soothing drink.

II

The train thundered across the bridge over the Gour Noir.
Chantal took her toiletry bag out of her suitcase and began to
attend to her make-up with great care. She remembered her first
stay at Fargeas – the lisle stockings, the summer frock with
patches where the sun had bleached it, the dresses Anne had
been obliged to lend her when people came, and the little girls'
sniggering. With a feeling of self-satisfaction she polished her
shining nails and renewed her lipstick: in the Vignons' circle
women did not make up apart from the barely tolerated powder,
but she liked deliberately shocking people who had never spared
her a single humiliation in earlier days. In her flared, light-
coloured overcoat, her soft felt hat and her peccary gloves she
looked like a rich woman on her travels.

She had received Anne's letter at San Sebastian three weeks
before. 'It hurt me so to see Mama worried and even suspicious
that in the end I told her. The result is that I can no longer write to
Pascal, and Mama insists that until further notice I should not see
him again: by way of taking my mind off it she gives me
permission to have you to stay, but I don't like to urge you to
come – I should be wretched company. I am so exhausted by all
these discussions that I should like to bury myself in a convent
and never speak to anyone again.'

Chantal had found the note waiting for her when she came
back from a walk with Jeanine and Paul Baron: she had talked to
them a great deal about Anne and about the place she filled in her
friend's life, and the three of them had agreed that Chantal
should answer this signal of distress as early as possible; but on
reflection she had decided to spend only the last days of
September at Fargeas. She did not choose to give Jeanine the
advantage of staying so long with Paul by herself.

Chantal leant back in her corner-seat. She was fully aware of
the gravity of her task. Anne had too much submissiveness and
Christian resignation to ensure her own happiness, and Chantal
had always had to fight for her; it was Chantal who had
persuaded her to carry on with her studies, who had lent her
books, and who had introduced Pascal Drouffe. Ever since she
had realized that life was more important than books and

concrete action than thought, Chantal had undertaken the mission of plucking Anne from her environment, of doing away with her prejudices, and of making her an emancipated, happy woman. It was not easy. Anne adored her mother and she was deeply religious; yet Chantal believed that she had already succeeded fairly well, and now she was happy to take up the fight once more. Anne must have been brought very low for her mother to have reversed her decision: it was a real stepping-down on the part of Mme Vignon. Chantal felt quite moved at the notion that she was bringing her friend treasures of hope and joy and happiness.

'Uzerche,' called a railwayman. Anne was standing there on the platform, hatless; Chantal jumped out of the train and ran towards her.

'Did you have a pleasant journey, Chantal?' asked Anne, taking the heavy pigskin suitcase.

'Fine, thank you,' said Chantal. She had been drawing up her plan of campaign all the way, and now she was completely taken aback by meeting a cheerful eye that asked nothing of her.

'You will find masses of people in the house,' said Anne, 'the Castillannes and my Delatouche cousins – you remember them?' She put on her leather gloves and took the wheel. She did not seem unwell: indeed, she was in form. 'If she gave up that prim and proper style, she would be really pretty,' reflected Chantal: there was a careful modesty about Anne's way of dressing that reminded her of the women coming out of St Thomas Aquinas's after Mass, but it would be no good trying to reform her on that point until she was married.

'What a lovely coat,' said Anne affectionately.

'Yes, I like it,' said Chantal. She had not imagined an arrival like this: Anne was welcoming her as a very dear friend, but not as a saviour.

The car stopped behind the house and Anne opened a french window that led into the library. Chantal's heart beat a little faster at the idea of once more facing these people who had known and despised her in the days when she was a penniless little student: she mastered herself and walked towards Mme Vignon with a charming smile. Mme Vignon returned the smile, inspecting her with a malignant look that Chantal bore without flinching – she knew that she was impeccable.

'Take Chantal to her room, darling,' said Mme Vignon to Anne. Lucette, Maria and Jeanne de Castillanne, and Nadine and Zette Delatouche went upstairs with them. They had not changed these last three years; they were dressed with the neatness that Chantal had envied in former days, but without taste; and it was clear that they waved their hair themselves with curling-tongs every morning.

When Chantal laid out light silk slips on her bed and well-cut summer outfits, their looks clearly expressed a mixture of disapproval and envy. Nadine was the first to stop pretending not to take any notice. 'What is this pullover made of?' she asked. 'How pretty it is!' Full of curiosity, she felt the soft material; and then the others, forgetting their wearisome reserve, passed the frocks from hand to hand. For the first time since she had stepped out of the train Chantal smiled with genuine pleasure: nobody here suspected that at San Sebastian she had found these clothes quite inadequate. She was bringing something like a scent of luxury and adventure into these austere surroundings: her arrival was a real triumph.

Throughout dinner Chantal took a keen pleasure in this revenge, a revenge that she had promised herself with tears of rage in earlier days. After the tormenting doubts that she had harboured in Spain, it was delightful to recover a little self-confidence. The two months that Chantal had just spent with Jeanine had been exhausting: Jeanine led a very active life in Paris and she described it brilliantly; the inner wealth Chantal had amassed in Rougemont could not so easily be made fascinating, and when she tried to tell the story of her year she often felt a depressing sensation of emptiness. She had let herself be outdone in their arguments, and when they looked at pictures or landscapes together it was always Jeanine who first thought of some clever insight. For Chantal it was a relief to feel that she was now in a world that belonged to her alone, among people and things that were entirely outside Jeanine's influence.

They went into the drawing-room. M. Vignon organized a foursome of bridge with the Delatouches and the elder Castillanne girl; Mme Vignon sat down at the piano and began playing old French songs that Anne and the children took up in chorus; at the fireside Mme Boyer turned her rosary. As she exchanged a few words with Lucette, Chantal looked around her: she would describe this old drawing-room with its faded furniture in her first letter to Paul Baron, and through their correspondence he would perhaps learn to know her better. She would tell him about all these dead things that were slowly coming to the end of a second death – the stuffed birds were losing their feathers, the shells were crumbling away, the butterflies pinned in glass-topped cases were disintegrating, old women in mob-caps and men with side-whiskers smiled out of crackled canvases. This vine-covered house was filled with a poetic, old-fashioned atmosphere like the beginning of an old English novel.

Chantal smiled: she no longer had the uncompromising rigour of youth; she had grown more supple; and she was capable of appreciating the beauty of tradition and of looking with an artistic eye upon this peaceful scene of which Anne was the heroine. By the wavering light of the candles that lit the yellow keyboard Anne was very beautiful: no surroundings could have been better designed to enhance that fleeting and perpetual youth of which she was such a brilliant incarnation: her character would have to be presented with great care. Chantal called up the image of the little girl with the irregular, mocking face she had so much admired in her childhood. In those days Anne was always unkempt; she fought with urchins round the fountains in the Luxembourg, and she walked on her hands and turned cart-wheels like a boy. Her mother allowed her a great deal of independence and Anne was most uncommonly daring. She shocked the old maids who ran the Notre-Dame private school: one day, when there was a public piano performance, she successfully played a difficult passage that she had often stumbled over, looked defiantly at her mother and then, in front of twenty rows of little girls with their hair carefully curled, in front of the chaplain, the headmistress and all the old maids in their new gloves, and in front of the impressive gallery of parents, she stuck out her tongue. Later she had sobered down. 'If I had not stepped in,' thought Chantal, 'she would be exactly what she seems to be at this moment – a girl in a white dress singing while she waits to become a loving wife and mother.'

Mme Vignon played a last chord and stood up. 'How pretty they are, those old songs,' said Chantal. Before her she saw a somewhat fleshy, coarsened face, but one in which there shone two lively eyes; and the mouth had a look of youth. 'At last she has grasped that she has me to reckon with,' thought Chantal with satisfaction: now that she was elegant and well dressed and had friends, it pleased Chantal to know that she was hated. She was rootless, without tradition, the stranger who comes into houses like a thief to lead over-cherished children off, to take them along the harsh highways of the world – she was the enemy, and she accepted the role proudly, a role that grew all the finer as the prison in which Anne was shut up seemed to increase in charm.

'I really should like to see her alone,' thought Chantal with some impatience; she had rather forgotten that Anne did not always submissively follow her, and she was abruptly reminded of it by seeing her sit gaily on her grandmother's knee. 'I have plunged into a positive idyll,' thought Chantal crossly. Had Anne really written the desperate letter that Chantal now repeated to reassure herself? However carefully it was scanned, her face betrayed no misery; her happiness seemed complete.

Anne had not yet made up her mind to choose between her mother and her friend: she could not accept the prejudices of her own circle or the life that Mme Vignon intended for her, but she did not yet posess the strength to throw off all restraint. 'She is constitutionally pagan,' said Chantal to herself again, 'but Christian in her sensitivity.' This marriage with Pascal was necessary, at least as a first stage, so that Anne should be able to free herself from the beliefs and the code that were stifling her. Apart from faith, Pascal had all the Christian qualities: he had a keener appreciation of religious feeling than if he had himself been a believer, and his mystical tendencies and lofty spiritual view of things had allowed Anne to love him without remorse. For a long time now Chantal had decided that he had an important part to play in her friend's destiny.

In her turn Anne sat down at the piano. She began playing and all at once a kind of uneasiness came over Chantal; all she could see of Anne was the back of her neck, leaning over, and a profile that had grown hard, almost ugly. Anne was no longer anything like the white-clothed figure that had been shining in the dim old drawing-room a few minutes ago; nor was she a child in distress willing to let herself be saved; she was a fierce, solitary, frightening being unknown to Chantal. When the piece was finished Anne went and sat on a low chair near the door; her face remained closed and grave and she hardly moved at all, though from time to time she touched her coral necklace. At one moment her black eyes met Chantal's and she made a faint attempt at a smile. 'She is not happy,' thought Chantal, and a feeling of triumph flooded into her: she would find the right words to arouse rebellion and hope in Anne. For a long pause she kept her eyes fixed on a corner of the carpet. She needed Anne's admiration and gratitude to restore a sense of her own worth: during the holidays she had often had unpleasant dreams in which the faces of Andrée and Monique appeared again – appeared too insistently: defence was scarcely possible at night, and in order to forget Rougemont completely she required a brilliant success.

She looked up: Anne's chair was empty. Chantal slipped quietly out of the drawing-room. The front door was ajar and she walked out; she was sure that Anne had escaped into the garden to be alone, to be sad, and to wait for her. She began running along the alleys, calling 'Anne', and the gravel crunched under her feet; she would take Anne in her arms, comfort her, and endow her with all the wealth of feeling that welled up so strongly in her heart. At last, for the first time in months, she felt happy, freed from Jeanine, freed from doubt; and she let tears of affection come into her eyes.

But Anne was not in the garden. Chantal returned to the house, waiting for quite a while in the darkness of the hall before going into the drawing-room. 'I have been ridiculous,' she thought angrily. 'Suppose someone had seen me running along those paths!' All at once she heard the stairs creak: it was Anne, carrying a dozen oil-lamps on a large tray. Her face was happy and unclouded. Chantal followed her into the drawing-room without speaking: she was well acquainted with this stab at her heart – often, when she expected Anne to call out for help, she had seen the same calm, cheerful expression. Anne said good-night to her friends and relations, looking round with smiles that did not appear at all forced; and each smile pierced Chantal like a betrayal. 'She's only a devout little prig, with no strength of character,' she thought resentfully: Chantal would never have resigned herself like this. She kissed Anne coldly and went up to her room to begin her letter to Paul Baron.

Chantal wrote for quite a while and then got into the big red-quilted bed: in the middle of the night she woke with a start and sat up – somebody had come into the room. It was Anne, wearing a long, high-necked nightgown that came down to her feet.

'Speak quietly,' whispered Anne. 'We must not wake Mama. Are you too sleepy to come for a walk with me?'

'Do you go for walks at this time of night?' said Chantal. She threw back the blanket and put on a pair of sandals. This kind of wildness amused her – Anne had always been charmingly original. With relief Chantal found reasons to be interested in her again.

'I hardly have any other free time,' said Anne. 'You'll see what a splendid sky there is tonight.'

They went downstairs on tiptoe, stopping anxiously at the slightest creak: the whole house was deeply asleep and they reached the front door without mishap. Anne carefully opened it. 'What a lovely night,' she said with intense feeling. She was wearing felt slippers and the hem of her nightgown dragged on the wet sand. 'The scent of the phlox is as fresh and pure as moonlight,' said Chantal: she envied the deep pleasure that showed in Anne's face – envied it with a certain resentment.

'I wanted to see you alone,' said Anne. She opened the creaking white garden gate. 'What have you been doing, Chantal? You write so seldom.'

'I had a very pleasant journey,' said Chantal. 'I met some remarkably interesting people; and I had a perfectly lovely time at San Sebastian.'

'It suits you so well, being happy,' said Anne tenderly. Chantal looked away: she was very fond of thinking about her friend's immense affection for her, but she always found it embarrassing to read it on Anne's face. 'I am so glad that you have been given a post near Paris,' said Anne, sitting down under a chestnut-tree and carefully spreading out the folds of her white nightdress. The moment of action had come. Chantal was full of anxiety: she had thought about the role she would have to play in connection with Anne for a long while, and now she was required to prove to herself that she was capable of fulfilling it.

'But let's talk about you, Anne,' she said rather abruptly. 'Just how do things stand between you and your mother and between you and Pascal?'

Anne was silent for a moment. 'Well,' she said, 'it's over.'

'Over?'

Anne twisted the curling end of a fern round her finger. 'Mama did not insist on a complete break; but from what she said I foresaw so many difficulties and so much struggling that I preferred giving him up.'

Chantal gave a violent start. 'But how can you possibly let yourself be managed like this?' she cried indignantly. 'And to begin with, what objections has your mother against this marriage?'

'He is not a believer; and it was you who introduced him to me. That would be enough,' said Anne sadly. 'And then Pascal has reasons that I thoroughly approve of for not wanting an engagement right away; so you can imagine all the thoughts that occur to Mama.'

'But it's not a hopeless situation,' said Chantal more gently –vehemence never worked with Anne: one had to reason. 'You said you were not forced to break it off, didn't you?'

'I struggled,' said Anne. 'You'd never believe how I struggled. Mama said such things to me . . .' Her face twisted with pain. 'Sometimes Mama's ideas are appalling, Chantal.' There was a silence: Chantal thought for a while – the position was more serious than she had supposed. Beside her Anne fiddled with a piece of bracken, nibbling at it.

'So you really and truly envisage not marrying Pascal! And what will become of you?'

'I don't envisage anything,' said Anne. 'I've made my sacrifice, that's all. And I'm at peace, Chantal: indeed, I'm almost happy, and it's a long time since I have been able to say that.' Her voice grew softer. 'Now nothing matters to me: if I were told that I was going to die, I should not feel any regret. You can't imagine how easy that makes life for me at last.'

'Peace,' thought Chantal with disgust. It was not to reach this point that she had communicated all the best of her reflections to Anne for three years on end. 'Yes. But after all, let's speak practically – what are you going to do this year?' she said.

'Mama wants to send me to England so that I may break with the Sorbonne and with you. Until then I shall stay at Fargeas: in Paris I should be too tempted to see Pascal again.'

'I should never have believed that you would resign yourself so soon,' said Chantal tartly.

'It was not easy, to begin with,' said Anne. 'These holidays have been very wearisome: you know the kind of life one leads here, obliged to be busy or to have fun from dawn till dusk. To write to you or Pascal I had to get up at night.' She smiled. 'Once I so needed to be alone that I cut my foot open with an axe. It meant ten days on a couch, and during that time they left me in peace.'

'You did that?' cried Chantal. Anne would never cease to astonish her. For a moment she sat there speechless, vaguely overwhelmed; it seemed to Chantal that Anne was escaping from her.

'I hope that Pascal will forgive me,' said Anne. 'You must explain everything to him. You must tell him that I shall never again be entirely unhappy, now that I know him.'

Chantal took a grip on herself. She knew very well that Anne was capable of wasting treasures of heroism in the most ridiculous way – using them up in suffering, in self-denial. She must be taught to direct them towards happiness. 'But you will tell him yourself,' she said rather harshly. 'I don't take your decision seriously. You will come out of this fatalistic crisis; you have come through plenty of others.'

'This is not fatalism,' said Anne. 'It is resignation. God will do what He wishes with me.'

'Even from the Christian point of view passiveness and inertia have never been virtues,' said Chantal. 'You have told me yourself that this total submission to the divine will is often only a cover for laziness and cowardice. Your resignation is in fact a definite choice: you choose peace. How do you know that God does not require of you the very thing that is hardest, not renouncement but resistance, not refusing to live but life itself?'

'Don't torment me,' said Anne in an agonized voice. She hid her face in her hands and remained silent for a long while; the blow had gone home. 'How can one tell?' she said unsteadily. 'I've never stopped struggling these last three years; I've struggled for every book, for every thought, for every time I wanted to go out. I swore I should never, never hurt Mama and I have never stopped torturing her. When I gave way to her I felt contemptible: when I resisted I hated myself. And I've never known how God wanted me to behave. I can't bear it any longer, Chantal.' There was a beseeching note in her voice.

140

Chantal was perfectly aware that Anne was unhappy: Anne was torn between tendencies and ways of thought that were all equally vigorous and that could not possibly be reconciled: this division was a source of moral uncertainty and emotional conflict that made her suffer a great deal. But Chantal was of the opinion that this was a stage required in any evolution: she went on calmly, 'Remember those words of Claudel that you liked: "Lord, preserve us from staying too long in any port of call and from the illusion that in any place at all we have reached the end of our journey." Your submission seems to me no more than a sham; the truth is that you want to put into port and have peace.'

Anne looked into the distance. 'Peace. Yes, peace,' she said in an undertone. 'Neither my life nor my happiness is so very important, after all.' After a moment she added, 'Sometimes I don't even care about my salvation.'

Chantal felt embarrassed. She was certain that she was pleading on the side of virtue, but after Anne's last words all argument seemed rather trifling. All at once she had an inspiration. 'Have you thought about Pascal's sufferings?' she asked. Anne did not reply. 'Remember, it was you alone who gave him back some confidence in the goodness of the world; he is quite unable to live without you; sometimes, before he knew you, mankind's ugliness made him weep with disgust and pain. Do you recall the beggar in the Petit Luxembourg?'

'Yes,' said Anne.

'Pascal said to you "You are here: that makes all the difference." If you were to leave him, and that by your own weakness, it would be . . . a betrayal.'

Anne threw back the hair hanging over her face. 'I know all that. I've said it to myself a hundred times.' Her expression showed a violent inner conflict: she seemed deeply moved. 'It's true. I have no right to do it,' she murmured. She turned towards Chantal looking weary and submissive. 'What would you like me to do?'

With a feeling of victory Chantal went on. 'You should go back to Paris and not speak of a break any more: begin by accepting Mme Vignon's conditions, however distressing they may be – with a little cleverness you will be able to improve upon them in time.' She thought for a while. 'Is an engagement really impossible for Pascal?'

'I think so,' said Anne. 'Otherwise everything would no doubt be much simpler.'

'You couldn't try to influence him?'

'I won't discuss it with him,' said Anne vehemently. 'I don't want to be a source of torture for everyone I come near.'

'Anne! You must know what happiness you give to those who love you,' said Chantal.

Anne stood up. 'Sometimes I'd rather that nobody loved me,' she said fiercely. But immediately after, she took Chantal's arm and smiled. 'You mustn't be cross with me. I know very well that if ever I amount to anything I shall owe it to you. You have given me back all my courage.'

Chantal pressed her arm without replying. She was proud of having handled things so cleverly. They walked slowly back to the house.

'Why,' said Anne, 'the door is closed.' She pushed at the unmoving wood without any real hope. 'Who can possibly have shut it? Grandmama must have come down to make herself a hot drink, and she would have thought it had been left open by mistake.' She seemed quite upset.

'They will take us for two lunatics,' said Chantal. The adventure amused her: all that could be heard was the song of crickets and the splashing of the fountain: the Great Bear was shining overhead. Chantal felt a sudden strong affection for Anne; she looked charming, standing there in her long white nightgown with its red border, anxiously gazing at the front of the house. Well directed, she would become a worth-while person.

'I'm going to get in by your room,' said Anne in a determined voice.

The wing of the house was built of cut stone, and there were narrow bands between the blocks as they rose: Anne set her foot on one of these and seized a knotted ivy-trunk with her right hand.

'You're not going up to the second floor,' said Chantal, alarmed.

'Everything's shut on the first,' said Anne. She let her heavy slippers drop one after the other and began to climb. Her long nightgown hampered her, and she came steadily down again. 'Give me the string of your pyjamas,' she said to Chantal.

Chantal held it out. 'But do let's ring, Anne, or softly call one of the children.'

Anne tied the cord round her waist and began her sure-footed climb again. Half way up she stopped, held on to the window-sill and, flattening herself against the wall, she looked at the sky. 'It's lovely up here,' she called cheerfully.

Chantal watched with a mixture of fear and envy; it humiliated her to stay behind, but she could not bring herself to follow her friend. On the second floor, quite far over on the left, Chantal's window was open: Anne reached out. As she caught hold of the parapet her foot slipped and for a moment she hung there with the sheer drop below her. Chantal uttered a stifled cry, but Anne had already swung over the window-sill – she had always been good at gymnastics. 'I'll come down and open the door,' she called in a low voice.

Chantal was trembling. 'I didn't say I wanted to die *tonight*,' said Anne in a bantering tone. They went cautiously up the stairs. 'I've done an excellent job,' thought Chantal as she got into her bed; but she no longer felt any joy.

In one way it was a pleasure to take Anne's interests in hand. Sometimes she resisted for a long while, being stupidly obstinate, but when she had been persuaded to act, then she acted. At the beginning of October she went back to Paris and obtained permission to see Pascal. No doubt it called for a great deal of persistence and tenacity: Chantal did not know the details of the arguments she had had with her mother, but Anne had always been able to deal with Mme Vignon. She was capable of listening to her reproaches without growing angry; she remained gentle and respectful and she reasoned so soundly that Mme Vignon could find no answer – she was forced to yield, so that it should not look as though she were exercising an arbitrary tyranny. Naturally, once Anne was with Pascal again she no longer thought of giving him up: as far as that was concerned, Chantal's mind was easy – Anne would defend her happiness. So it was without misgivings that Chantal saw her friend less often; she was almost always in Paris, but her relationship with Paul Baron took up all her time. It was not that he was very demanding, but she wanted to become indispensable to him: she learnt the games he liked, she took dancing lessons in order to be able to dance with him, and she avidly read the newspapers so that he should consult her on political matters; it was a prodigious task.

Anne was not offended: Anne was intelligent, she understood things – she was never offended. Sometimes her letters and her telephone-calls sounded a little pressing, but she always accepted Chantal's excuses with the sweetest candour; and she was far too tactful ever to force herself on anyone. 'She knows that if she needs me, I should come running,' said Chantal to herself. Friendship was not to be measured by hours of attendance; and often, in the train that was taking her back to Chartres, great waves of affection for Anne came over Chantal. She felt capable of making immense sacrifices for her.

Chantal had no more than a pied-à-terre at Chartres: she had taken a little apartment in Paris and furnished it with much care according to her own personal taste. Anne liked being there very much, and it was almost always at the apartment that she saw Chantal; but she never ventured to come without being invited. Chantal was therefore very much surprised when, one evening towards the end of October, a quite unexpected Anne rang at the door.

'Anne! How sweet of you to come,' she said a little awkwardly. Paul might appear from one moment to the next, and she did not want him to meet Anne. 'Come in. It's so long since I've seen you; I was just about to telephone.' Then she saw that Anne's eyes were red and that her lips were trembling. 'What's the matter, Anne dear?' she asked with a kind of avidity.

Anne plucked off her hat and let herself drop into an armchair. 'A week from today I leave for England,' she said. 'Mama made all the arrangements without telling me.'

Chantal gave a great start. 'But you must refuse to go,' she said. 'After all, you're of age. And to think I supposed everything was going quite well now!'

'I can't disobey Mama,' said Anne. 'All I can do is argue; and on this point the argument is closed. Mama feels I need a change.'

'So what are you going to do?'

'I've sent Pascal an express letter asking him to telephone here. I must see him: it's my last hope.'

'Indeed, I do think that if he were formally to ask for your hand, it would put things right.'

'Maybe. But even that's not certain,' said Anne despondently. 'And I don't know whether Pascal will want to.' She looked at the clock. 'He's not telephoned yet? I've just come from a wedding reception – I was so afraid of being late.'

'We must make him come to a decision,' said Chantal impatiently. 'After all, Mme Vignon cannot have any valid objection to this marriage.'

Anne shrugged her shoulders. 'That's not how marriages are arranged with us: and Mama would never like Pascal.'

'I dare say she wouldn't: but at least she has to have an excuse to separate you. She wouldn't dare, would she, if he didn't provide any sort of a pretext?'

'That's what I hope,' said Anne. 'But what if he doesn't agree?'

'Yet your mother trusts you!' said Chantal.

'It all depends: it's not my virtue she's afraid for but my reputation. What they look upon as the very worst sort of misconduct at home is laying oneself open to suspicion.'

Chantal smiled: she liked this bitter way of speaking. For a long while now Anne had found it astonishing that for her the path of salvation should be strewn with jazz tunes, cups of tea, and trying on clothes; she found it difficult to eat petits fours with the same fervour that she brought to the Communion; and it was in vain that her mother quoted Saint François de Sales to set her mind at rest. Now she was beginning to understand how much middle-class prudence was mixed with Mme Vignon's care for her soul; and when this hypocrisy had thoroughly sickened her, thought Chantal, the game would be almost won.

'He ought to be telephoning now,' said Anne in a troubled voice: for a while she remained deep in her own thoughts. Chantal could not find anything to say. At last Anne made an effort: 'Lucette is marrying that young man I told you about, André Naville, you know. A week ago Mama insisted on a firm answer and Lucette spent the morning running from one friend to another asking for advice. Everybody told her to say yes.' She jumped: the telephone was ringing. She lifted the receiver and Chantal watched her face. 'Yes . . . I see . . . very well,' she said in a choking voice: after quite a long pause she hung up. 'Pascal can't come,' she said. 'It was Marguerite who spoke. Things are difficult for them: Pascal has to stay.' She sat down, nervously twisting her handkerchief.

'It's ridiculous,' said Chantal. 'Something ought to be done quickly.'

'He'll let me know when he's free,' said Anne faintly.

'But still, two or three days one way or another doesn't make all that difference,' said Chantal in an encouraging tone.

'I had so relied on seeing him,' said Anne: her eyes were fixed on the ground and her face was grey. 'It's this uncertainty . . .' She looked up and an expression of extreme distress could be seen on her face. 'I can't go away: I'm not strong enough.'

Chantal winced: perhaps she ought to have taken more care of Anne; she had never seen her with this hunted look. 'A year soon passes, you know,' she said.

'And what then?' said Anne. 'Waiting, and then more waiting: but what is it that I am waiting for, Chantal? I don't even know that.'

Chantal put her hand on her friend's shoulder. 'You're waiting to be able to start building a life with Pascal; and it's only a question of time, Anne darling.'

Anne made no reply. 'When he's there, I can still believe it,' she said at last. 'But why should he be so fond of me, Chantal? I'm nothing. I've been trying to make him do my living for me.' She shivered. 'I flung myself on him with all my weight; and really it was so cowardly. He hasn't wanted me to get things wrong, and he is right – in spite of everything one has to remain alone. But I can't help thinking that at present it's only pity that he feels for me.'

Chantal remained silent. She had always been convinced that in Pascal Anne had found the most certain of all supports, but now she suddenly realized that, out of scrupulousness, delicacy of feeling and a meticulous desire to be sincere, Pascal had not been able to give Anne security. 'I can't know what conversations you are talking about, Anne,' she said. 'But what I do know is that Pascal loves you.' She had spoken with real warmth and she looked at Anne as though begging her to believe her.

'Perhaps,' said Anne. She shook her head: 'What is certain is that I shan't be able to stay convinced of it for a whole year: that's what is so appalling, Chantal. There's something in me

. . .' her voice broke.

Chantal looked at her with alarm. Never had she so urgently wished to come to Anne's aid, yet she could not find anything to say. Six months earlier she had hurriedly placed Anne's fate in Pascal's hands; and now everything depended on him. 'You'll be able to persuade Pascal,' was all she said.

III

'An express letter for you, Pascal,' said Marguerite, coming into the room where her brother was working.

'Thank you,' said Pascal with a smile. Unhurriedly he tore off the perforated edge.

'Pascal, I can no longer bear not seeing you,' wrote Anne. 'To me, these four days have seemed endless and I absolutely must talk to you. I shall be on the Luxembourg terrace in the usual place at four o'clock and I shall wait for you. Please forgive me.'

Pascal's face clouded: the urgent tone of the appeal astonished him, and with Pascal astonishment was always close to reprobation; and the ring of passion seemed to him indecent. Anne's passion took him aback all the more in that she was poised, temperate and restrained.

He sighed. 'Perhaps it is impossible for me to feel what people call love,' he murmured. He had confessed this to Anne, confessed it with humility. It had grieved her: how difficult it was to be sincere! She said she admired this anxious attention to truth, but she would have been much happier if Pascal had simply said to her 'I love you.' She was always tormented. How could he make her understand that he loved her much *better* than if he had loved her *more*?

He pushed his books away: although it upset all his plans he would go to this rendezvous. If Anne had written, it must mean that she was most uneasy. Pascal's duty was to bring her a little strength and peace. He got up and walked along the corridor that led to his elder sister's bedroom.

Marcelle was lying on a couch with a table beside her loaded with magazines and papers; she had a fluffy angora scarf round her neck. 'How do you feel, my dear?' asked Pascal: he kissed her wide forehead – her hair was coiled at the back of her neck and her forehead was bare.

'Fairly well, really,' she said feebly.

He took Marcelle's pale hand in his and sat down by her. 'I shall not be able to have tea with you,' he said regretfully. 'I have to go out this afternoon: you wouldn't mind being alone in the house with Mama?'

'No. He wouldn't dare come back,' she said. 'Besides, we shan't open the door.'

'Poor dear.'

'So long as I still have a little strength to work and so long as I have you, I'm not to be pitied,' she said in a musical voice. She pressed her brother's hand. 'I don't look too ghastly?' she asked with a coquettish air.

The contrast between her white-powdered cheeks and her dark eyes made her appear a little feverish; but she seemed rested. 'You've never looked better.' He touched the pink bed-jacket, edged with swansdown. 'What a pretty little thing.'

'You like it?' said Marcelle. 'I used to take so little notice of my clothes before; but a sick woman who lets herself go is an ugly sight, don't you think?' She made a little face. 'One needs to beg the indulgence of others.'

'Silly creature,' said Pascal tenderly. 'Did you sleep well last night?'

'Oh yes, a little,' she said with a brave smile. 'Marguerite came home frightfully late. Didn't you hear? I said nothing to Mama, for fear of worrying her.' She sighed.

'Perhaps you ought to speak to her,' said Pascal.

'Marguerite? She would pay no attention to me,' said Marcelle. 'Everyone has to make their own experiments, my poor Pascal; and perhaps the cruellest thing about it is the knowledge that none of our sufferings allows us to spare the people who come after us.'

'She is our sister and yet she is a stranger to us,' said Pascal sadly.

'When life has bruised and beaten her she will grow more human,' said Marcelle. 'So far she has only known happiness.' She looked at the ceiling. 'Sometimes I think of describing the tragedy of a soul brought face to face with pain: horror at first, and refusal; then the slow coming of familiarity, still full of resentment and shying away; and then acceptance at last and happiness.' She paused. 'I should like my account to be as alive, as touching and as simple as a love-story.'

'What finer gift could you offer to people,' said Pascal thoughtfully, 'than finding that their sufferings have a meaning.'

'But they do have a meaning, Pascal,' said Marcelle in a trembling voice. 'Illness and betrayal have not passed over me in vain.'

He looked at her with deep feeling. These were the trials that had fanned the inner flame whose mysterious reflections Pascal saw in his sister's eyes: her wasted face was now no more than a pure spiritual effulgence. 'I'm afraid you work too hard,' he said, nodding towards the manuscripts spread on the table. 'You must not tire yourself, my dear.'

'Since I am forbidden all living contact with people, I have to try to make them love me by means of these little pieces of paper,' she said with a charming smile.

She was passionately attracted by people's souls and it was with intense eagerness that she studied new books and magazines, in search of fresh, sensitive minds.

'If you take great care of yourself . . .' began Pascal.

'Maybe, Pascal dear,' she said in an indulgent voice. She let herself fall wearily back on her cushions: 'I always try to go too deep into people's minds and spirits, and it exhausts me,' she said. 'You're the only one that counts.' She ran her hand through Pascal's black, wavy hair.

This hidden disease that was eating her away and that the doctors would not take seriously, no doubt because they could not give it a name, looked to Pascal like a kind of slow disincarnation: not all illnesses come from the body; too ardent a soul could wear its fleshly wrapping to the point of destruction; but in this attempt at self-purification did not the soul destroy itself, alas? In that ultimate moment when the spirit broke free, did it not disappear forever? Perhaps it stayed for a brief flash, poised in absolute lucidity. Pascal felt his head turn, as it did every time he thought about death. His meditations often brought him towards the subject, but he could not contemplate it for more than a few seconds.

'Why are you looking so sad?' asked Marcelle tenderly.

'I was wondering how they manage,' said Pascal. 'Those philosophers who calmly link ideas together, one after another, as though they were assembling a piece of machinery.' Marcelle looked at him attentively: there was no one else who studied Pascal's mind with such fervent interest; there was no one else in whose company he was so happily at peace with himself. 'A thought is a real presence for me,' he said. 'But it's too massive, too near for me to be able to distinguish its outline.'

'That's because you and I don't think with our brains only,' said Marcelle. 'We think with our hearts too.'

Pascal began to laugh. 'Or perhaps it's because we're not very bright,' he said with a kind of boyishness.

Pascal's highest rational ground for existence, the supreme justification for his being, were those ecstasies of tenderness or despair which sometimes arose from the slow pulsing of his thought: it would have seemed to him a crime against the spirit to exchange them for clear, abstract phrases. Apart from these precious visitations, his days passed simply, without a great deal of reflection.

'I must go,' he said. 'I'm late already.' He sighed. Anne would never know what a proof of love he was giving her by leaving a sister sad and ill, for her sake. 'We'll read Swinburne this evening,' he said with a smile full of promise.

Anne was already there when Pascal arrived. From far off he saw her, sitting under a chestnut-tree that had lost half its leaves. In the midst of the bare wood there shone one green branch loaded with white candles, and the sight filled Pascal with a strange joy. Anne's smile, lighting her grave face, was not unlike these late flowers, so full of life.

'Pascal,' she said, 'how very, very kind of you to come.'

'I too have suffered, not seeing you,' said Pascal, 'but my mother and my elder sister are having to bear such grievous troubles that I should have considered it selfish to think of our happiness.'

'I should have liked to share your worries,' said Anne. 'You need not fear that I should put them out of your mind, you know. I am not over-cheerful myself.'

'It is a question of other people's secrets – of secrets that do not belong to me,' said Pascal. Anne said nothing; she seemed very low-spirited indeed. 'Your letter hurt and worried me,' Pascal went on. 'Has anything happened?'

'Mama is absolutely determined to send me to England for a year,' said Anne with an effort. 'It was no good my begging not to go.' She clenched her hands. 'I should never have listened to

Chantal,' she said in a despairing voice. 'I ought never to have seen you again. Now it's too late: I am no longer capable of resignation.'

Her tone moved Pascal. 'I do not know how to love,' he thought with a humility that was not without its sweetness.

'That makes me happy indeed, Anne,' he said warmly. 'You know very well that I could not do without you.'

'Does anyone really need me?' she said.

'Anne!' he said reproachfully. 'No doubt I am not very clever at finding words, but in spite of my clumsiness you can believe in me – for me you are irreplaceable, absolutely necessary.'

'Is that true?' she said. 'Is it really true?'

'Woman of little faith!' he said tenderly.

'I'm cowardly,' said Anne. 'I don't amount to anything, Pascal; I don't deserve your fondness. I can't prevent myself from doubting. I feel that you see me through a mirage and that it will suddenly fade and vanish.'

'You must believe in me,' said Pascal urgently.

'When I can see you, I believe in you,' she said with a smile.

'Can't you persuade your mother to relent?' asked Pascal. 'I've made so many plans for this winter.'

'Mama cannot understand that you don't introduce me to Mme Drouffe, or why we don't get engaged right away; she is terribly mistrustful of you.' She gave him a quick glance. 'Pascal, forgive me for talking about it again,' she said unsteadily, 'but is it really impossible for us to be engaged? Afterwards we could wait as long as necessary. I quite understand what you mean to your sister, but nothing would be changed between you.'

He shook his head. 'It would not be the same,' he said. 'She would no longer think she had any reason for living if she no longer believed she was necessary to me.'

'Why should she be less necessary than before?'

'She would feel that it was so, I am sure,' said Pascal. 'I shall need a great deal of time to get her used to the idea that she is no longer the only one in my heart: I don't want to give her a sudden shock, above all not at this moment.' Anne gave him a sad look: there was nothing questioning about it. Pascal hesitated: he owed Anne an explanation. 'Listen,' he said. 'I will tell you how things are. You know my brother-in-law left my sister nearly three years ago, having treated her abominably?' Anne nodded. 'Marcelle was just beginning to forget and to recover when five days ago he turned up at the house when I was out, and after an appalling scene he took all Mama's and Marcelle's money by force. You can imagine what a horrible shock it was.'

'I do understand, Pascal,' said Anne submissively. But she still had a crushed look that hurt Pascal: she loved him and therefore she trusted him, but without wholeheartedly approving of what he did; he felt very much alone.

'After all, Anne, for us it's not a question of life or death; we are only giving up a year; and then, as far as we are concerned, we have all the future to be happy in.'

'A year!' said Anne in a toneless voice. 'Yes. Perhaps it's nothing really, a year.' She smiled painfully. 'A year without news of you; a year of waiting, a year of doubt.'

'We'll write to one another,' said Pascal.

'No,' she said. 'Mama will not have it. When she's there I can argue with her: when I am far from her all I can do is submit. She will no doubt allow me to see you once or twice before I go, but on condition that afterwards our break will be complete. I must obey her.'

Pascal did not protest; he had too much respect for Anne's religious beliefs to attempt to turn her from her duty as a Christian.

'I am afraid of being alone,' said Anne; she seemed to be about to add something, but she changed her mind.

The wind swept the chestnut leaves along the path; Pascal gazed thoughtfully at the young green shoots and the flowers blooming out of season. A fleeting triumph of life; in a few days this joy too would be extinguished. 'Ours will be a beautiful love, Anne,' he said with much feeling. 'Lasting and pure, because we shall not have bought it with lies of any kind. What is so rare between us, do you see, is that we value one another so much that neither wants the blindness of happiness for the other: so many loves are no more than a conjoined selfishness, a kind of sleep.'

'That's true,' said Anne. 'Yet it's so generous to lose oneself entirely in a passion – not that I am capable of it,' she added rather sadly.

'It is because we cannot deaden our minds,' he said. 'Diversions, in Blaise Pascal's sense of the term, are not made for us; and of all the diversions men have discovered, happiness is no doubt the most delusive.' He looked at Anne with a grave tenderness: she was very close to him – fraternal. She too felt life's pathetic nature, felt it to the point of anguish. This silent, mystic communion was the highest peak a love could reach.

'Still, it does seem to me that I could quite easily be happy,' said Anne. Her face relaxed and for a moment her expression was smiling and child-like. 'I was so happy when I was little,' she said. 'One day I must tell you what Mama made of our childhood.' She stopped. 'Perhaps it will be possible again.' There was a kind of appeal in her voice. Pascal hesitated: he knew what words she was waiting for, but he did not wish to lie.

'Being happy when one is a child is easy, because one is still ignorant of everything,' he said. 'Once one knows, one can no longer forget without being a coward. But the wonderful thing that you have brought me, Anne, is the revelation that one can do without happiness and yet not despair.'

How pleasant it would be to meditate without illusion upon the destiny of mankind, sitting in a warm room lit by Anne's quiet, gentle face, one's heart filled with serene tenderness; it would even be pleasant to feel a little tide of distress rise in one's throat.

'Oh Pascal, I will be brave,' said Anne. 'Does it really not frighten you to think that I shall be all you are granted upon earth? Sometimes I feel you ought to hate me.'

Pascal looked at her with apprehension: the thoughts that passed through Anne's mind were totally unpredictable: she wore herself out, asking herself useless questions from morning till night. 'I'm not so complicated as all that,' he said with a schoolboy laugh; and speaking seriously he added, 'It is the other way round, Anne: I am often ashamed of having so little to offer you.'

'Don't talk like that.' She reddened. 'You have transformed my life.' She looked at him with deep feeling. 'I told you how the idea of death attracted me in earlier days: now I no longer wish to die.'

Her words touched Pascal deeply, but they also made him feel uncomfortable: Anne lived in a stifling atmosphere – he breathed more easily when he was away from her.

They stood up and took a turn in the garden, walking side by side without touching one another. Pascal had never kissed Anne: physical gestures seemed to him too coarse to translate their hearts' inexpressible harmony. When he was a very young man he had had some rather squalid adventures; they had left him with a sense of great disgust and for a long while now he had been chaste. When he thought of the night when he would take Anne in his arms for the first time, he felt like sobbing.

'I shall do all I can to see you again before I go, Pascal,' said Anne as she left him: she shook his hand and walked off very fast without looking round. For a moment Pascal stood there motionless, leaning on the stone balustrade. The sadness of this farewell made him feel uneasy; Anne bore him no ill-will for it, but she had not succeeded in understanding him. She was a woman, after all, and, for her, happiness possessed a reality that had to be reckoned with: for his part, he had never made a strong distinction between his worst torments and his greatest joys.

Two days later Pascal went to have tea with Chantal. 'Anne will come if she can and spend a few minutes with us,' said Chantal as she let him in. 'She telephoned. She is shockingly taken up with getting everything ready for her journey: for you are letting her go,' she added reproachfully.

'Anne knows my reasons and approves of them,' said Pascal.

'There are cases where leaving one another for a year does not matter much,' said Chantal. 'But, Pascal, Anne is not strong enough to bear it just now. The last time I saw her she frightened me.'

'The cares and anxiety I inflict upon Anne,' said Pascal rather curtly, 'hurt no one more than they hurt me.' He valued Chantal and he knew what she had been for Anne; it was Chantal who had helped Anne to distinguish between actions of social conformity and those belonging to the life of the spirit, and she had broadened her outlook enormously; but that was no reason for her to adopt a patronizing attitude towards Anne. It had often vexed Pascal that Anne herself should look upon the freedom of Chantal's life and her culture as evidence of superiority. 'If it were only a question of myself, there is nothing that I should not gladly sacrifice for her,' he said more gently.

'But there is no one more in need of help than Anne,' said Chantal. 'If you let her go, how do you expect her to believe in your love? And if she does not believe in it . . .'

Pascal gently shrugged his shoulders. He had often been irritated by his friends' want of comprehension; but now that he had gone farther along the paths of solitude he found a certain pleasure in being misunderstood.

Anne

'Anne feels responsible for her mother,' Chantal went on, 'and what is worse she herself is beginning to condemn Mme Vignon: Anne still believes in God, but she no longer knows what God expects of her. If she doubts you as well, who is there she can turn to?'

'She has not the least reason to doubt me,' said Pascal firmly.

'And yet she does,' said Chantal. 'It's years now that Anne has been torn apart: you are the only person who could allow her to remain a Christian and yet at the same time really live. I don't know what will become of her.'

'You are talking as though I had left her,' said Pascal. 'I love Anne and she knows it, Chantal: set your mind at rest.'

'Very well,' said Chantal. She changed the conversation; but she was still visibly concerned. It was a relief to Pascal when Anne rang the bell.

Anne's face was as white as a sheet, but she seemed very cheerful. 'I've come to my senses, you know, Pascal,' she said abruptly. 'I'm ashamed of having treated you to such a sad face the day before yesterday.' She smiled. 'Poor Pascal, he was quite overcome when we parted.' She sat down on the divan and Chantal offered her a cigarette. Anne rarely smoked, but she now accepted it. 'When I think that I have so much and that I dare complain,' she murmured. She turned to Pascal: 'I saw Lisa this morning, when she came to give the children a lesson: I was overwhelmed with remorse – she bears her lot with such dignity and courage, although it's so sad a life. I was ashamed of myself, I who have everything.'

It was so unusual for Anne to speak of herself spontaneously that Pascal was taken aback; Chantal seemed embarrassed, too. 'Is the date of your going settled?' she asked after a short silence, pouring out a glass of sherry for Anne.

'I leave on Monday; but that's no longer of any importance, Chantal. I have thought it over thoroughly: my happiness is not at the mercy of a separation. It is something which cannot be destroyed: the knowledge suddenly came to me like a revelation.'

Her voice had a kind of fervour in it, and Pascal looked at her with kindness and approval: in Anne he had found a worthy object for his love; she was neither weak nor selfish; after a short period of confusion and distress, she had come to understand.

'I'll try to come to England at Easter,' said Chantal. 'I'd like to see London again with you.'

Anne smiled. 'That would be lovely, Chantal,' she said. 'You know, I mean to make the most of this stay. You must tell me about the museums and the theatres. And perhaps I shall try to translate one of Meredith's novels; that would surely be an interesting thing to do.'

'What a good idea,' said Pascal. 'But Meredith . . . there's nothing really of great importance in him. Why not translate a poet instead – Swinburne, Browning? They are scarcely known in France.'

'I re-read *The Egoist* last night,' said Anne, 'and I do assure you, Pascal, I was so enthralled that I read it from the first page to the last. I found a whole mass of things in it that I had not seen before. A whole mass.' She drank off her glass of sherry in one gulp.

'Do you know *Evan Harrington*?' asked Chantal.

Pascal gave up following the conversation – he read scarely any novels. He liked hearing Anne speak with that liveliness and enthusiasm which had surprised and charmed him six months earlier; yet at the same time he felt a great sadness come over him. He suddenly realized that Anne was really leaving, and he found these literary discussions rather futile.

After about an hour Anne glanced at her watch. 'I must be off to a tea-party,' she said with a little sigh. 'I do have a busy life, don't I?'

'That will change, Anne dear,' said Pascal, gently pressing her hand.

She smiled. 'It's changed already,' she said. 'Pascal, I'll say good-bye to you on Sunday: Mama says I may.'

Pascal bowed his head without replying: he would not have believed that he could be so deeply moved.

'I'll telephone to tell you when and where we can meet.' She smiled again, with an effort, and followed Chantal into the hall. The door slammed.

'I have not seen Anne so full of life for a great while,' said Chantal coming back into the room. 'She has rallied most surprisingly.' She looked almost disappointed.

'One can always rely on Anne,' said Pascal. 'She is equal to any trial.'

'When all is said and done, perhaps this going abroad will be a good thing,' said Chantal in a conciliatory tone. She sat down opposite Pascal and they talked affectionately of Anne, of her qualities and of her future, until the evening.

IV

It was at about six o'clock on Saturday afternoon that Anne rang at Pascal Drouffe's door: the only person in the house was Marcelle, and she was writing a poem about loneliness.

'Who is it?' she called through the door: she was afraid it might be Denis.

'Anne Vignon,' answered an unknown voice.

Marcelle had heard Pascal mention the name: she opened the door and saw a young woman with dark hair and brilliant eyes, wearing a red dress and no hat. Marcelle stared at her with surprise.

'Please come in, mademoiselle,' she said. 'No doubt you wish to see my brother? He will not be long.' She gave a welcoming smile.

Anne stood there, examining her suspiciously. 'You are his sister?' she asked without moving.

'Yes, I am Pascal's sister,' said Marcelle, rather taken aback.

Anne gave a little laugh. 'Forgive me,' she said, 'but it's so . . . so unexpected.' She looked closely at her hand, hesitated, and then held it out to Marcelle. 'How do you do, madame,' she said. Marcelle urged her towards the drawing-room and asked her to sit down: she was deeply shocked. There was a long silence: Anne stared into vacancy: Marcelle coughed to clear her throat.

'You are a friend of Chantal Plattard's, aren't you? How is she? I have not seen her for a long while.' The look in Anne's eyes appalled her.

'Of course I am not worthy of Pascal,' said Anne slowly. 'I don't want to try to deceive you. But I am not ill-natured: has he told you I was ill-natured?'

'He has not talked to me about you,' said Marcelle coldly.

Anne's voice took on a passionate ring. 'You have a wrong idea of me, I'm sure of it. I've never wanted to take him away from you: I'll not prevent him from loving you.' She wrung her hands. 'Don't force me to go away: it's just not possible: you don't want me to be unhappy. You mustn't hate me!'

Marcelle did not understand this scene at all, but she was vaguely frightened: women who went to see their rivals with a bottle of vitriol in their handbag must have just those feverish eyes. 'I shall never set myself between my brother and you, if that is what you are afraid of,' she said cautiously.

Anne stood up and began an agitated pacing to and fro. 'I too shall love you, and perhaps in the end you will like me a little,' she said. She put her hand to her forehead: 'I am very miserable,' she said. 'I do not deserve his concern. I ought to tell you the whole story of my life – it would be so long – but after all they did tell me that I should be trusting. It's not wrong to want to be happy – it's not a sin?'

'Certainly not,' said Marcelle.

Anne's face softened, and she leant against Marcelle's armchair with a familiar look: 'I thought that between people who respected one another the best thing to do was to talk,' she said with a kind of archness.

Marcelle drew back slightly. 'You were perfectly right,' she said.

Anne sat down on a settee and smoothed her skirt with a fashionable air. 'Everything went wrong, you see,' she said in a confidential voice. 'Mama and Pascal don't understand one another: they are so young – they don't know what is important,' she added indulgently.

Some reply had to be made: there was an unbearable threat in the air and it was only waiting for silence to become explicit. 'They will surely understand in time,' said Marcelle at random.

'Of course,' said Anne, 'it's a trick.' For a moment the smile stayed there, fixed, intolerable: there was not a sound to be heard in the house.

'She is mad,' thought Marcelle, and she felt calmer.

Anne buried her face in her hands and sank a little in her seat. Marcelle watched her without saying anything: there was no longer any point in labouring to maintain a conversation.

Abruptly Anne sat up again. 'What did I come here for?' she said. She broke into a hysterical laugh. 'To see you – I came to see you.' She took Marcelle's hand. 'I was sure you were kind; I was sure you would pity me.' Then she lapsed into silence again: she seemed exhausted. This was how Pascal found her when he came in a few moments later. 'You here?' said Anne, surprised; she got up and dropped a little curtsey. 'I am delighted to see you.'

Marcelle made her brother a sign that he did not understand. 'Mlle Vignon and I have come to an understanding,' she said hastily.

'Yes, Pascal: let me introduce one of my best friends,' said Anne: she gave an apologetic smile. 'I'm afraid I have been rather a nuisance.'

'I'm going to lend Mlle Vignon a coat, and you will take her home,' said Marcelle. 'Will you excuse us for a moment?'

'Why, of course,' said Anne.

Marcelle drew Pascal into the next room and quickly explained the situation. 'I still don't know what it was all about,' she ended.

'I will tell you everything later,' said Pascal, taking her hand. He went back to the drawing-room. 'Here's a coat for you, my dearest Anne,' he said. 'I am going to see your Mama with you.'

Anne flung the coat over her shoulders. 'Good-bye, madame,' she said gravely to Marcelle. As they went down the stairs she looked apprehensively at Pascal: 'You aren't cross, Pascal?'

'Everything is perfectly all right, dear Anne,' said Pascal. 'Don't worry.'

'I have such a headache,' said Anne, taking her place in the taxi: she leant against Pascal's shoulder and said no more. Only towards the end of the journey she opened her eyes. 'Won't you kiss me, Pascal? You never have kissed me.'

He clasped her tight against him and put his lips to the childish face held up to him: he felt torn by a pain that had nothing in common with his ordinary sadnesses – something bitter, merciless, unbearable.

Mme Vignon put Anne to bed at once: she allowed Pascal to go and say good-bye. Anne raised herself on her pillows and seized Pascal's hand with a certain over-excitement. 'You really agree?' she asked. 'I shan't be going away?'

'No, darling,' said Mme Vignon. 'Don't upset yourself: you will do just as you please.'

Anne looked at her. 'I do cause you a lot of anxiety.' Her features collapsed. 'I must manage not to love anyone any more,' she said: for a moment she remained vacant-eyed, with her jaw drooping. Pascal touched her shoulder: this face was too appalling.

'We are engaged now,' he said. 'Your mother gives her consent, Anne.'

'It doesn't matter,' she said.

Anne's death was a surprise: before being taken to Uzerche, her body lay in a mortuary chapel. The face was yellow and emaciated: the long black hair, rooted in that dead flesh, was spread out on the pillow, brittle, dull, still living.

Pascal pressed his fingers against his eyelids: he did not want to look at this wasted corpse surrounded by candles and autumn flowers any longer. There was nothing left of Anne in these mortal remains, and if he wished to reach her in her essential truth it was in his own heart that he must look for her. 'Just as eternity changes him into himself at last': he murmured the quotation aloud. Anne had entered eternity. He shivered: Anne's image had just appeared before him. 'Won't you kiss me, Pascal?' She smiled; and through this smile, which had haunted him the whole week, something horrible threatened him. Above all do not try to struggle by means of words: if words are uttered they can never be forgotten again and perhaps they may make life impossible for ever: one must accept anguish without resistance; let it wring one's heart and dry one's throat, without forming a single thought. Pascal stiffened: this evening it was hard to confine these equivocal pains solely and entirely to his body: the heart's distress became a thought, and a cruel, exact meaning loomed through the burning of his throat – quick, try by some exorcism to change it before it became wholly explicit. 'Anne, dear face, I shall never see you again,' murmured Pascal. Anne was dead and he loved her; he sighed; he was there in the heart of a great pure suffering once more. The danger had vanished.

'Anne, it is not sterile regret that you expect from me: you would not have wanted us to see your death as a diminution but rather as a source of inexhaustible wealth. You had a message for us; imperatively you require us to hear it, and then your destiny will be splendidly fulfilled: it is for us to fulfil it; but how hard, how hard it is, beloved, to give up all that joy you gave me. I am alone, Anne: you have abandoned me to loneliness. Now that we are far apart, how can I be worthy of you?'

Pascal heard a sob just at hand: it was Chantal. For his part he had no tears left. The sleepless nights, the hours of hopeless waiting, and the violence of the last blow had broken him and now he felt that he was beyond pain. When one is wholly lost oneself, then one can gaze upon the world serenely. Was it this that Anne was teaching him? He could no longer resist, and opening his fingers he saw Anne's face. The doctors had talked about inflammation of the brain, but a sudden attack like this was hardly credible; it was much more likely that Anne had been suffering from a tumour for a long while; for a long while her days had been numbered, and her excessive reactions of these last days were to be put down to this hidden disease. Marcelle had been overwhelmed: how deeply they had all felt this death at home, even Marguerite. Perhaps it was only in death that Anne could make such an astonishing impression: her death was the wonderful stratagem of a love too great for this world. Pascal bowed his head; a great peace came down upon him. 'How could I presume to mourn for myself and how can one mourn for you, you who have succeeded with such smiling, such terrifying audacity in escaping for ever?' All at once he understood the ineffable message. It was in death that this death-oriented life found its meaning: life was fulfilled by death and death was the source of life: no curse whatsoever weighed upon the earth . . . Pascal began to sob: Anne's radiant soul dwelt within him for ever, and she poured certainty and peace upon him: wholly and utterly he accepted the world.

Not many people followed Anne's coffin along the icy roads that led to the Uzerche graveyard, but Mme Vignon had the consolation of receiving a great many letters that gave moving testimony to Anne's rare qualities: this beautiful example of a Christian should not remain unknown; for the edification of other souls, God did not wish one's light to be hidden under a bushel, and Mme Vignon decided to have a booklet published in memory of her daughter.

A very simple little memento: a portrait of Anne and a few extracts from her private diaries and favourite prayers. Mme Vignon sat at her desk: she had sorted Anne's papers but she had not yet had the strength to read them through – it was a painful task. She drew the black notebooks towards her and the letters that Pascal and Chantal had lent her; she prayed that God would help her to climb this Calvary.

There were photographs spread out on the table: Mme Vignon took one and, wounded by too sharp a pang, she closed her eyes. And it had to be from me that all her sufferings came, oh Lord! Her end had to be hastened by me! If only I had known she was ill . . . She raised her head. Lord, Thy ways are inscrutable. She looked closely at another photograph: how Anne hated these sittings. A fixed smile above the gauze-draped bust; eyes devoid of expression. The snapshots were better, and perhaps it might be worth trying an enlargement. Mme Vignon pushed the photographs to one side and took a pencil to underline the passages in Anne's notebooks that were to make up the memento.

From as early as the first pages, tears poured from her eyes. Anne had loved her mother passionately, but she had often found it extremely hard to obey her, and it was only at the cost of a very great deal of suffering that she submitted to the kind of life that she was required to lead. How could I tell that what was good for others was not good for her, oh Lord? I am only one of Thy humble servants and it was a saint that Thou didst entrust to me! Thou knowest, God, that I acted according to my conscience; and if Thou didst not see fit to enlighten me further it was because these trials were necessary for her glory and for Thy glory. I was no more than an instrument in Thy hands.

Mme Vignon dabbed her eyes and carried on with her reading. Anne was an exceptional being: God had not made her to reach Heaven by the ordinary paths: He had led her soul by strange ways. A few years back He had allowed her to be tormented by doubt: she had never succumbed, but for a long while her acts of faith retained a tone of desperation. Mme Vignon underlined nothing: it was not right that these moving struggles against temptation should be laid out in broad daylight. Later Anne's faith grew stronger, but she was still uneasy: sometimes her reflections were upsetting, but she was young and God would have enlightened her in time, for she was humbly seeking the truth. Mme Vignon underlined nothing. In a very short piece it was impossible to give a notion of the private difficulties that Anne had struggled with; what counted was the fact that, throughout her cries of distress and her rebellions, the love of God never ceased to consume her. Mme Vignon underlined a magnificent page in which Anne placed her life and her salvation in God's hands. In the later passages the words surrender, acceptance and submission occurred again and again. Anne had even looked death in the face and had accepted it: in August she wrote, 'If I were told that I was to die tonight, I should submit without complaint and even with joy.' Mme Vignon underlined these words: they should be put just under the photograph. Later, in mid-October, Anne had written, 'At present I no longer wish to die.' Anne was human; the greatest saints had been human; but sometimes grace had raised her up to inaccessible peaks, and those were the moments of her life that must be given to the world as an example.

'Anne, my litle saint,' murmured Mme Vignon, 'pray for me, a poor sinful woman. Help me to accept having been the instrument of your suffering, of your salvation, without complaint.' She slipped from her chair and knelt with her forehead pressed against the table; and for a long while she remained there, prostrated at the feet of her daughter, a daughter radiant in glory.

Neither Pascal nor Chantal had been able to leave Paris for Anne's funeral, but when the Christmas holidays came round they decided to make a pilgrimage to her grave together. In the train that was carrying them to Uzerche, Chantal took a hard, objective look at Pascal: he was wearing dark clothes like a widower and his handsome face had acquired a doomed expression that made him irresistible: it was vexing – he had not been capable of loving Anne when she was alive and now he seemed to be setting himself up as the one guardian of her memory. 'In the end he will marry someone else,' thought Chantal. Hearts torn with compassion watched him from a respectful distance. His mother and his sister spoke to him only in hushed voices, and they surrounded him with unobstrusive attentions: never had his shoes been so well polished nor his linen so perfectly laundered.

'How hard I have become,' sighed Chantal, not without pride. She could feel it: she was evolving in the direction of cynicism. Anne's death had revealed the world's ugliness to her; her enthusiasm had dried up; and all she wished to set against the absurdity of fate was a clear-minded bitterness. Cynically she watched Pascal and Mme Vignon dressing up Anne's memory in their own way and becoming reconciled to her death: for her own part she did not accept it; she wanted to remain faithful to the true Anne and she knew that death had come to her friend as an enemy. That was the cruellest part of it – that Anne should have been destroyed before she had fully existed. And nobody tried to save her now she was on the far side of death: they turned her into a mystic, a votary. Mme Vignon had placed a saint in her heaven and the beautiful figure of the woman modelled by Chantal with such love had fallen into dust.

Chantal peered through the window. She did not know exactly what she hoped to gain from this pilgrimage: no memory could ever fill the emptiness in her heart. The only course of action that she had ever begun had been stupidly brought to an end: nothing could console her for this failure, yet she was expectant, passionately expectant.

They were getting nearer. A remote green light shone in the darkness; the train slowed down. 'This is it,' said Chantal, opening the door. The platform was almost empty: the thin ringing of a bell pierced the freezing air. It would be a good beginning to a novel, she thought, these two unusual travellers arriving at a little deserted station on a December evening: nobody is waiting for them – they do not get into the bus that goes to the town – where are they going? Who are they? A young married couple, an engaged pair, no doubt. They walk along the road side by side, almost silent, and gradually one makes out that the bond linking them is subtler than friendship or love: between them there appears a tragic figure, at first in shadow but little by little growing clearer.

She touched Pascal's arm. 'On this road Anne talked to me about you, Pascal,' she said with feeling. She was really fond of him, after all, with one of those rare affections between man and woman where there is no question of love. Curious looks followed them and she felt drawn closer to him by a kind of collusion: all those people were too vulgar-minded to have any notion of the precious nature of their relationship, too vulgar to suspect the reason for their journey. And indeed it was very strange to be here, on this road, with Pascal, and to have come solely to call up a ghost.

'Here is the house,' she said. They stood motionless for an instant at the bottom of the steps, then walked up them and knocked on the door. Mme Vignon opened it; she shook hands with Pascal and kissed Chantal. She had aged a great deal: her eyelids were red and swollen and the eyes themselves were dull.

'Mother, this is M. Drouffe,' said Mme Vignon, opening the drawing-room door.

Mme Boyer stared at Pascal. 'It has been my dearest wish to know the young man my grand-daughter loved,' she said, and she began a conversation with him, speaking in an undertone. Mme Vignon turned to Chantal. 'You received a memento, Chantal?'

'Yes,' said Chantal. 'Thank you for having thought of me.' She looked at Mme Vignon with resentment: this aging woman suffered without a doubt, but there was something triumphant in her suffering. The misfortune that had struck her was not a curse from heaven, it was a sign of divine election; she had won the game. Faced with Mme Vignon, Chantal was forever disarmed –death had abruptly cancelled all her efforts and now there was nothing left to her at all.

'I will give you back the letters you lent me,' Mme Vignon said to them. 'I thank you for having helped me to make my poor child better known.'

'I think you will like reading these,' said Pascal, handing Chantal the packet that Mme Vignon had just given him.

'And you will see what she told me about you,' said Chantal. They exchanged their bundles.

'The only consolation left to us,' said Mme Vignon, 'is the reflection that her death will not have been useless to the glory of God.'

Pascal nodded sympathetically.

'A pair of accomplices,' thought Chantal angrily. 'They both of them killed her.' She did not believe in this story of a tumour: they had made it up to ease their consciences. Anne had died from want of love. They did not choose to believe it; it would wound them and then again it would seem to them too romantic – the blind creatures supposed that romance was only to be found in books. Life was made up of a tissue of unlikely events; and Anne's very existence was in itself a miracle.

She clenched her hands: how distinct was Anne's presence between these old walls! Her gold-flecked eyes, her heavy blue-black hair, her autumn-coloured face – how I wish I could make her come to life again. It would need a whole book to show her as she really was, a being of flesh and fire, the bright, mysterious, and beautiful heroine with her ingenuous laugh and her passionate heart. – Why go on and on regretting the woman she would have become? There was a mission to be fulfilled towards the pathetic girl whose wraith haunted this old drawing-room.

Chantal leant towards the fire. A great wave of emotion came over her; after all these weeks of sterile regret she suddenly felt that she had not been cheated at all: her course of action had failed and the future had not meekly obeyed her, but in return she had been given a past. In the calm shadows of this old house she had at last found what she had been seeking for so long, something that belonged to her alone, something that others might envy her for: from now on her life would always bear the burden of a beautiful and tragic tale. From now on mysterious shadows would pass across her face from time to time; her movements and her words would possess subtle resonances; and people's eyes would dwell upon her, intensely eager to penetrate her secret. Chantal's head bowed lower. This wonderful burden weighed heavy on her heart: she could not yet foresee all the wealth it would bring her, but already she felt transfigured by its presence. She would be able to love, understand, enlighten and comfort better than before; and perhaps one day she might even be capable of transforming her painful experience into a serenely beautiful book.

'Anne, dearest, I never shall forget you,' she promised earnestly.

❧MARGUERITE❧

I N MY family it was always held that the things of the spirit came first. Papa devoted his life to the study of literature and Mama to the practice of the Christian virtues, while Marcelle and Pascal were dedicated to the worship of beauty and the inner life. As soon as I was three years old Marcelle taught me to read, and when I was seven I made my first Communion with an extraordinary degree of piety. I was always very advanced for my age because they paid so much attention to me at home: Papa used to read Pascal the tragedies of Corneille and Racine after dinner and I was allowed to listen; that forms one's mind – I was always first in examinations, and at the end of term the old ladies of the Institut Ernestine Joliet embraced me more heartily than any of the other pupils. These worthy school-teachers were not overburdened with diplomas, but as far as devotion and morality were concerned they were second to none: they wore long black skirts and plum-coloured silk blouses that caressed my cheeks when they pressed me to their bosom. There was one, rather younger than the others and endowed with a moustache, who was spoken of with some awe because she was studying for a degree at the Sorbonne. I was fond of lessons: the pupils sat round an oval table with the teacher at the head of it on a kind of throne, and from out of her frame Ernestine Joliet, a hunchback whom influential people were trying to have beatified, looked down at us with gentle severity. Beneath this portrait, sitting on a black leather settee, there were mothers and elder sisters, anxiously keeping watch on us; they hated one another, and it was impossible to look something up surreptitiously in a book or to whisper the right answer to a friend without being pitilessly denounced when the class broke up. By way of taking the bite out of this rivalry we were not given prizes: but in May, and in the presence of a bishop, there was a solemn handing-out of medals and honourable mentions in which everyone had a share. During the war half the class-rooms were turned into a hospital, and it was deeply moving to see these ladies walking about the corridors in Red Cross uniforms: we used to bring oranges and cigarettes for the wounded, and we were often taken to the Montmartre basilica, where we waved flags as we sang.

One matures quickly in an atmosphere of this kind: I hated the wicked Germans and I offered God my life so that He should grant our soldiers the victory. More than once I lay on the red carpet in the hall, at the foot of the grandfather clock, and waited for death. And Pascal was as patriotic as I was: when we were given a cake or a piece of chocolate we hurried off to put it into a tin kept for the poor wounded soldiers; the tin took a long time to fill, since delicacies were rare at that time, but at last it was brimming with wizened old pears, sticky sweets and stale gingerbread. Mama took it to the Institut Joliet, and in large letters on the wrapping-paper the headmistress wrote 'Marguerite's and Pascal's sacrifices'.

I loved imposing mortifications on myself – it was a positive game for me. At the beginning of Advent the Abbé Mirande, the Institut Joliet's chaplain, gave us little pieces of cardboard on which were drawn an Infant Jesus in violet ink: every time one performed an act of self-sacrifice one pricked the image with a pin. At Christmas, when I laid my card in the crèche that glowed at the far end of the chapel, it was riddled with holes. I certainly had a natural aptitude for the mystic life; I would often lock the lavatory door and whip myself with a little gold chain; I also rubbed my thighs with pumice-stone, which made red places that Mama dressed with ointment. The Abbé Mirande allowed me to take Communion three times a week and I made my confession to him every fortnight; he told Mama that I had a beautiful soul. I was very fond of kneeling at a prie-dieu in a dark chapel at dawn, when I was still heavy with sleep, and then coming home to a creamy cup of chocolate still talking to the Christ who had come down into me; but I was even fonder of confessing. The Abbé Mirande had a great many followers and I had to wait a long while before it was my turn to go into the confessional where he sat concealed. Vague shapes made the heavy green curtains bulge; all that could be seen was the feet of the kneeling penitents. My heart beat fast when at length I made my way into this secret holy place and even faster when the wooden shutter clicked open and on the other side of the lattice I saw the priest's pale face: it was a sensuous delight to hear the Abbé Mirande speaking to me about my soul in his kind, sugary voice, and I listened to him as I might have listened to Christ Himself. As for my fits of anger, my disobedience and my insolence to the schoolmistresses, I never accused myself of them at any time; I never looked upon either my mother or my elderly teachers as God's representatives; I set Him far higher – I had my own personal relationship with Him – and as I saw it His law did not coincide with the niggling code I was taught at the Cours Joliet. The older I grew the greater my love of God became, but less and less did I have any sense of sin: I did not think that talking in class, not washing my hands before a meal, filching five francs here and there, or reading Alfred de Musset in secret were any sort of obstacle to my spiritual progress. I should never have suspected God of assuming responsibility for the mean-spirited regulations that I found so wearisome. In spite of my piety I should have indulged myself in the vices of childhood if I had known them, but one cannot discover everything. Yet when I was seven I did very nearly make the acquaintance of sensual pleasure: as I was climbing a rope I suddenly felt a strange, agreeable, but imprecise sensation; I climbed several times one after another and each time the delightful promise came, but without growing explicit. I spoke about it to Mama, who blushed and told me not to talk nonsense. The gymnastics lessons stopped soon after. I still tried climbing trees in the country; but the bark was too rough.

From that point of view, we were well protected at the Institut Joliet: yet at an early date, because of the Hail Mary, I knew that children were formed in their mother's womb; but I thought they came out by the navel; and I saw marriage as a kind of blood-transfusion between the spouses. My theoretical knowledge grew a little more exact when I secretly began reading Zola, Anatole France and Maupassant. But it is no good looking for direct, lucid information in unspecialized books. There were astonishing contradictions about the duration of the sexual act, for example: in Zola it took five minutes to make a woman pregnant, while in Pierre Louÿs on the other hand it was a question of whole voluptuous nights. This left me deeply puzzled. Yet, after all, these problems did not take up too much of my attention: I was intensely eager to learn about the world in general and I did not like any field of knowledge to be forbidden, but I was not really depraved – indeed, in practice I was innocent. I remember Mama taking me to a cinema to see a documentary about the north pole (I was about fourteen), and the man in the next seat fondled and kneaded me with both hands: all I did was to clutch my bag against me with all my strength, being convinced that he meant to rob me. Another time, when the assistant in a small draper's shop led me behind a counter and undid his trousers a little way, I did not understand either. That is the advantage of a Christian upbringing – I might have let myself be raped without thinking there was any harm in it.

Of course I never talked about these things to the Abbé Mirande: with him I spoke of nothing but spiritual advances or defeats on an exceedingly high level and, when the old ladies told him that I was growing unruly and bumptious and that I was often given black marks for my behaviour, he was quite astonished. At the end of one confession he set about remonstrating with me. 'Is there nothing you have forgotten?' he asked me kindly, and without knowing why I blushed scarlet. 'No, I don't think so,' I said. 'Yet I have been told that my little Marguerite is not what she used to be: it seems that we do not pay attention during lessons, and that we are not very obedient.' I kept my head down: I was sick with shame: until that moment I had supposed I was opening my heart to God Himself, whereas it was a poor childish man that I had put my trust in. He went on in his gentle voice, 'From now on you must turn your efforts in that direction, and I will help you: sometimes one does not see one's own errors and mistakes.' I did not answer: I came out of the confessional overwhelmed and the Abbé Mirande never saw me again. Whenever I caught a glimpse of his surplice in the Institut corridors I ran away: he must have wondered what had happened.

That was my first disappointment with religion and priests, and I never really got over it. I had confused God and the Abbé Mirande in my mind for so long that now I began to wonder whether God too were not on the side of Mama and of the old fusspots who ran the Institut Joliet and of the books marked Y in the Family Library; but this God was so ridiculous that soon I began to doubt His existence. The first time this doubt came over me I was very frightened: it was in the country and I was lying on moss with the top of a birch-tree waving to and fro overhead; I was not thinking at all, but in the midst of a great silence it appeared to me that the world had suddenly grown empty.

Nobody ordered the trees or the sky or the grass to exist, and I myself was drifting at random among these formless aspects of the void; I got up, unable to bear this distress, and ran back to the house, back to human voices. When you have been living in a world peopled with angels and saints, under the eye of an all-powerful being, it is strange suddenly to find yourself alone amidst mere blind things.

I did not resign myself to it right away. I went to Saint Sulpice and asked a priest for his advice: he listened to me patiently and when I had finished my confession he said, with calculated abruptness, 'Now tell me the truth. What is this sin that has kept you from the sacraments so long? What have you done?' I protested: he did not believe me. He absolved me nevertheless, but as far as I was concerned it was over – I was sick of these spiritual consultations. That same year I went through my terminal classes with a fat, apoplectic priest who thought me cold-hearted and sceptical; without suspecting it, he certainly helped liquidate the last vestiges of religion in me.

There is no doubt that it left me with a feeling of emptiness. I used to have long, serious talks with Pascal in those days and he told me that it was not in a deserted heaven that we ought to look for God but in our hearts. Yet, as far as I was concerned, when I looked into mine all I found was a vast boredom. I remember the moment when the prospect of the long sequence of useless days I still had to live made my head swim: it was in the dining-room; newspapers were spread out on the table and I was cutting them into neat squares that I threaded onto a string so as to hang them in the lavatory; Pascal was reading and taking notes and I could hear Mama singing quietly in the kitchen. I felt completely hollow and soft, as though I were going down through layers and layers of emptiness. For a great while it seemed to me dreadful to exist without an aim.

I never was a frivolous creature; but at that time in my life I felt the vanity of human activities even more strongly than before. I no longer felt like taking any pains with my appearance and it was with reluctance that I washed and did my hair in the morning. When Mama called me into the drawing-room, I scarcely greeted people, but sat in a corner, swinging to and fro in my chair, staring affectedly at the ceiling, my mouth tight shut. What I loathed more than anything else was going to his friends' homes with Pascal: the number of friends Pascal had gathered at school and at the Sorbonne was quite horrible, and even more horrible was the fact that a great many of them had sisters too. They were ugly and dismal, but all these future teachers were so afraid of the solitary life waiting for them in the provinces that love affairs began. They often met, they danced, they talked about literature, eating little home-made cakes as they did so: Mama hoped that I too would follow one of these pleasant young men when he took up his first post and she compelled me to accept every invitation. I hated what I saw when I looked in a drawing-room mirror and saw myself in spinach-green taffeta with my hair all frizzed, my face sweating; and then I hated what dancing did to me – my face would flush and in my body I would feel a burning languor that left me feeling quite sick when it died away. I took to having such fits of crying when I got home that in the end they left me in peace.

Intellectual joys were the only ones I would still indulge in: I had been introduced to them so young that I did not think of questioning their value. The ladies of the Institut Joliet had told Mama that I would lose my faith and my moral sense if I were allowed to study for a degree at the Sorbonne among all those misled, wandering girls, and Marcelle had worked out a compromise: I was sent to the Institution Saint-Ange as a day-girl to attend private classes under the spiritual direction of Mme Leroy and Mlle Lambert. The teachers were young and full of enthusiasm, and I flung myself into my work with furious zeal. Pascal and Marcelle thought the time had come for a cautious unveiling of contemporary literature and I eagerly read all the works on the list they had drawn up after anxious debate. I was always deep in books and people looked upon me as a thoroughly repellent kind of freak. Marcelle tried to make me take pleasure in flowers, in sky-blue pullovers, and in all those delicate refinements that make up a woman's charm; but quite in vain.

I was far more willing to listen to her when she suggested my joining 'Social Contact' and lecturing young working girls on ethics and literature in the rue de Ménilmontant; it would add a little novelty to my life, I thought. From the very first study-group I saw how absurd the whole undertaking was, but I said nothing because I thought it perfectly wonderful to come home at night by myself, passing through unknown districts. I did not know how to look and I saw nothing, but as I walked quickly along the dark streets I felt the vague presence of the world about me and that was intensely exciting: drunks came staggering out of bars and in the boulevard de la Chapelle women stood waiting under the electric signs of hotels; the world was covered with leprosy – it could not be looked at without horror – and yet one had to brush by it, close by it, trembling as one did so, and listen to its breathing: this vast, monstrous, chaotic mass fascinated me.

I felt the same distress and the same attraction where Denis was concerned. To begin with I was very wary: he had married Marcelle, which was not in his favour; but I soon found that he was not like Desroches, nor like anyone else, nor anything I knew. His extravagant elegance, his spendthrift ways and above all his casualness were a living scandal in the house; it was the first time that our apartment had ever beheld anyone who could stay sitting in an armchair without doing anything. It shocked me too, and Denis' flashes of wit put me out of countenance; but I could not take him lightly. He was very young, but he looked as though he had come from a great way off; and the less he deigned to explain himself the deeper a meaning I attributed to his mysterious smiles. When he contradicted Pascal or when he poked fun at Mama I systematically took his side and he would thank me with a look – how caressing they were, those looks! I should have liked to deserve them often and to establish a real friendship with Denis; but he did not take much notice of me. Indeed, I was not particularly attractive – the awkward age never seemed to come to an end with me. Sometimes the mirror would send me back an unexpected picture, with the line of the eyebrows and the curve of the nose and chin forming an agreeable face with blue eyes shining and a fresh young mouth; but this was only a fleeting vision: I had pimples on the back of my neck, coarse red cheeks and greasy hair. Denis looked upon me as an insignificant little schoolgirl; I agreed with him and it made me suffer. He talked about bars and cafés and night-clubs, places whose very appearance was beyond imagination, and he liked books and painters whose names I had never heard. When I listened to him I had the feeling that I knew only an expurgated edition of the world: it did no doubt contain some part of the authentic text, but the cuts distorted it.

I was not exactly prevented from going out: when there was some show of unquestionable artistic merit we did not hesitate to go to the theatre or the cinema; but these amusements fell so precisely into place between dinner and the cup of chocolate that was waiting for us in the kitchen when we came back that they only just came up to the level of one more family celebration among the rest: they no more took me out of the house than walking along in a line takes boarders out of their school. Even when I went out by myself I still felt excluded from the world: as I passed by the little cafés in the rue de Belleville their steamy windows did not call up a gentle warmth for me, nor the taste of black coffee nor the nasal voice of a gramophone; they were a mere backdrop, with neither depth nor reality, because it had never occurred to me to give the door a good shove and walk in.

I was vaguely conscious of the highly-coloured cinema advertisements, but I did not plan to buy a ticket at the box-office some evening: I had no notion of the clacking of the wooden seats, the galloping of the cowboys on the screen, the sharp taste of the sweets sucked during the intermissions; no looking back, no looking forward extended my perception in either direction; I remained as it were on the surface of things, a bare surface with neither poetry nor promise, because I never made the least approach to an action that would carry me more deeply into them and make me more intimately acquainted with their reality. Denis had led me to suspect that they possessed hidden wealth, but I was so little used to freedom that I never thought I could seize upon it: in life I was like a visitor, who does not presume to touch anything. Mama and Marcelle and, in spite of all the people he knew, even Pascal seemed like poor relations; only Denis looked as though he were at home, and it was to him that one should turn for the key that would open all doors. I watched him for a long while: I was too shy to question him and he avoided conversation. One had to catch his sentences in flight when he launched them across the table; I turned them over in my mind, and although I did not understand them very well at first, in the end I found they contained a philosophy and a code; then at the moment of my discovery he would let fall another remark that seemed to contradict the first in every point. Fitting them together was another undertaking entirely: I could never see an end to it.

One day, when Denis and I were alone in the house, I was working on a Greek translation in the dining-room: he suddenly opened the door and walked in – his hair was on end and he had a green scarf round his neck. He sat on the end of the table, one of his legs swinging free, and he lit a cigarette. 'Don't you ever feel like tossing all those books out of the window?' he asked me abruptly. I gazed at him: he looked half asleep. 'And what should I do then?' I said. He smiled, tossing a small coin in his hand. 'Anything.'

'If I could find other worth-while things to do . . .' I said with a sigh (this was chiefly to make myself interesting: in fact I was quite fond of doing Greek translations).

'But nothing is worth-while,' he murmured.

I pricked up my ears: as soon as anyone spoke to me of an absolute it went straight to my heart. With some embarrassment I said, 'I'd like to leave home as soon as I can, you see; so I must get through my exams as quickly as possible.'

He stood up and began walking to and fro; from time to time, with a jerk of his head, he threw back the lock of hair that hung over his eyes; and for a long while we remained without speaking. My ultimate reason for living had just vanished: in a flash I had grasped that work too was only another futile activity.

'You are going about things the wrong way,' he said at last: his face was grave, his look keen and alive; it was as though he had been studying my case carefully for weeks. 'It is not by methodically searching for freedom, as you are doing now, that you will ever find it. Listen, Marguerite: you have to be capable of throwing even freedom out of the window: the day you no longer value it, nor anything else, then, and only then, you will have it.'

I felt appallingly humiliated: he was right: I belonged to a mean and reasonable breed – I was a dreary little bourgeoise. I was preparing my future liberty with the same careful economy as Mama, when she put money aside for her old age. Denis' magnificent and desperate unconcern dazzled me: a mass of questions rose to my lips, but I dared not ask them.

'But why does one live then, when one no longer values anything?' I said in a low voice.

He shrugged. 'One lives,' he said, and his eyes grew clouded. 'Why shouldn't everything be absurd?' he went on with a kind of flippancy. 'Dying is as absurd as living, and one can just as well twiddle one's thumbs as fire a revolver in the street. You can do anything at all, once you do not hope for anything. And sometimes you come upon the miracle.'

'The miracle?'

'Yes: a genuinely gratuitous action, an unlikely conjunction of words or colours, an illusion, a two-headed woman, anything at all. Sometimes the absurd makes its appearance – always provided, of course, that you're neither a doctor nor a philosopher nor an artist nor a gentleman.'

I listened open-mouthed: I was quite flabbergasted by these prodigious novelties. 'I thought you wanted to write,' I said.

His fine white teeth showed as he smiled. 'One can always hope the miracle will use one as an instrument,' he said. He gave me an amused look – 'I must show you the *Surrealists' Manifesto*; I'm sure you will find it interesting.'

From then on he lent me an occasional book: that, indeed, was the cause of a certain number of scenes with Mama. Pascal did not say much, but he looked at me sadly. They were all thoroughly mistaken. To be sure, several of these books described the most extraordinary perversions in a coarse fashion, but these descriptions did not affect me at all. My mind had a most decided turn for the sublime: as far as I was concerned all these novels, even the most obscene, were symbolic accounts of the eternal drama of man in pursuit of the absolute, and if the hero carried out an appalling rape or a sadistic act it was because he was trying to fill the emptiness of his soul. Of course, I could not bear the works in which eroticism was shown in its pleasurable aspect.

By this time I was as well informed about the sexual act as possible. In a surrealist piece I had found a list of the thirty-two positions, with their names; and masochism, sodomy and dung-eating held no secrets for me. In practice I was still pretty simple: I did not imagine any intermediate stage between shaking hands and making love – clasping and kissing seemed to me mere expressions of affection. I thought that when I loved a man we should look at one another after a day spent in conversation, with an open, direct smile, and that we should go to bed to enjoy pleasure as localized and as simple as those of the table: in practice I lost the clarity of mind I was so proud of and all my self-assurance when I saw a prostitute on a street corner stop a passing man – I was seized with distress and repulsion. I had to have my eyes opened by Denis before admiration and a kind of envy mingled with my horror.

I shall never forget that evening when Denis took me to a Montparnasse bar for the first time. Leaning over the banisters, Mama uttered tragic cries as we hurried down the stairs: I was wearing a mauvish dress (Mama delighted in those false colours that look cheerful and do not show the dirt), a beige coat and a hat that came down over my eyes: I knew perfectly well that it was horrible but I didn't give a damn. My only thought as we got into the taxi was that I was going to live in Denis' world for a moment – that genuine world I had never seen: I was beside myself.

The cab stopped in the boulevard du Montparnasse: a mauve, pink, and convolvulus-blue sign glowed over a half-open door. Denis joked with the black boy in red livery who stood aside to let us in and with a light hand on my shoulder he pushed me forward: through an orange haze I saw tables, pillars, violently coloured posters, dancing couples; a savage, uninhibited music rose above the sound of voices and laughter. That evening Denis was wearing a long beige overcoat: between the lapels of its upturned collar his face seemed hard and closed: I kept my eyes fixed on him. He shook a great many hands, smiling with an affable, blasé look; then he took off his coat and helped me climb onto one of the bar stools. 'What will you drink? A gin fizz?' he asked. I said yes, and the barman set a glass full of a yellow liquid in front of me: I sucked it through a straw and my mouth was filled with the taste of lemon and metal. There was a mirror behind the bar and beneath it bottles with multi-coloured labels; there were little American flags too. 'How you knock it back!' said Denis with amused admiration. 'Michel, fix another gin fizz for mademoiselle: we'll roll dice for it.' The barman put a little green-covered tray in front of Denis and, each in turn, they threw the dice. My eyes opened wide: everything was new to me and I lacked words to sort out this dazzling chaos: women were sitting on high stools next to me, and there was no adequate expression for the delicate stuff of their clothes, the colour of their hair or their complexions; it was beyond my imagination that their filmy silk stockings, their striking shoes and their brilliant lipstick could possibly be bought in a shop: by some unrivalled stroke of grace they had been endowed with all these perfections in a single moment. The young men leaning casually on the bar all had a disillusioned line at the corner of their mouth, like Denis: I had never known the sad, fine-spun thoughts, the complex feelings that showed in their eyes: I looked at them and I thought of sleepless nights, departures, encounters, waitings; I could form no distinct picture, but even these vague ideas overwhelmed me.

The things around me seemed plain enough: my neighbour was stroking a woman's knee and she was fishing in a jar for cherries in brandy; but I was not deceived; I knew that they were there, both men and women, waiting for the miracle and all ready to support it: this was the place of miracles, and I could feel them looming. I drank the last drops in my glass. The white horse on the bar next to a glass ball full of nuts, the notices hanging from the beams – 'If you want to fight, join the army' – Greta Garbo's smile, Maurice Chevalier's hat and Charlie Chaplin's boots made strange mosaics against the background of the light brown walls: I had already grasped their miraculous signification. 'Are you all right?' asked Denis and I gazed at him ecstatically.

At the same moment I heard shouting: a waiter opened the street door, dragging out a limp body by the feet – a pallid face under sweat-plastered hair. The waiter heaved the body onto the pavement and closed the door in the midst of laughter. Horrified, I asked 'What's the matter, Denis?'

He shrugged. 'He always makes such a row when he's drunk that they have to throw him out.'

'Does it often happen to him?'

'Pretty nearly every night.'

I was deeply shocked: that wreck being dragged out by the feet had seemed to me repellent. 'How disgusting,' I murmured.

Denis looked at me, shaking his head. 'Why? He's a very likeable creature. Does it upset you?' His tone was rather scornful.

'To do it once in a while – fine: by all means. But you told me yourself that one ought not to accept debasement in any form.'

His expression became thoughtful. 'I was leafing through a book on Baudelaire the other day, and I chanced on a passage that seemed to me to have a great truth in it: the writer – a Catholic –said that sin was always the space yawning wide for God.' He drew on his cigarette; he looked extremely pensive.

I understood what he meant at once; indeed it was an idea that had been familiar to me ever since I had read Dostoievsky, but I was still hampered by such a mass of preconceived notions that I did not apply it to real life.

I drank another gin fizz: nothing more happened. The walls took to turning around me a little, and in the street Denis slipped his arm under mine; the leaves of the plane-trees made a rustling sound; there were broad patches of scabby bark on their trunks; and at the far end of the boulevard could be seen the bright lights of the carrefour Vavin. I was more deeply moved than on the day of my first Communion, and I felt that from now on I was bound to Denis by an unbreakable tie, as though we had committed a murder together or crossed the Sahara on foot. We reached the Dôme: the terrace was almost empty, but there were some young men talking by the blue letter-box on the corner of the rue Delambre. Denis gave them a friendly wave and led me to the counter: he made me drink a cup of coffee. Everything was spinning; next to me a red-eyed face gave a sneering laugh; I felt Denis' hand on my shoulder. At all the street corners miracles burst out like fireworks.

During the next few days I saw much less of Denis than I had hoped, and we had no talk together. Then one evening, as we were sitting down to dinner, Marcelle stood there behind her chair for a moment and she said, 'You can take Denis' knife and fork away, Mama: he has left.' Mama was struck dumb: Pascal reached for Marcelle's hand and pressed it for a long while without a word. It was the next day that she took to her bed.

I was not really surprised: it was so like him to vanish like that, without warning. He was a man without ties, a man belonging nowhere. I waited impatiently for his letter and the rendezvous he would fix; in the morning I watched for the postman before going out and as soon as I came back I darted into the concierge's lodge. If it was shut I stood on tiptoe to look over the curtain covering the glass door to see whether there was an envelope in our pigeon-hole. But Denis did not write. Our friendship was just another of those countless golden bowls that he tossed into the sea 'so as to weep for them afterwards', as he had once said to me. For my part I was certainly grasping and mean, since I could not get over having lost everything at one blow: at first I sobbed all night long, and when I was working at the Bibliothèque Sainte-Geneviève or the Sorbonne tears would well up in my eyes so that I hurried out, almost running, to cry in the streets: sometimes I hid in a church, but usually I walked straight on, without any shame. I did not even believe in the value of work any more, and now that I had had a glimpse of the world family life grew unbearable: I was bored to death.

We lived on the fifth floor, and every evening after dinner it was my duty to carry down the dustbin. It was too small – for years Mama had been promising to buy another soon – and greasy paper, cabbage-stumps and potato-peelings often spilled on the stairs; I pushed them back into the bin with my toe, though sometimes I had to deal with them by hand: yet even that was less revolting than the feel of the cold, greasy metal handle against one's fingers. The main dustbins were lined up in an evil-smelling little courtyard near the concierge's lodge: I would lift the lid; they were often cram-full already and it needed a great deal of skill to heap our filth neatly on that of the other tenants. It was a disagreeable task, particularly in winter when there were ashes – the yellow dust blew into my face, and got into my mouth and nose. When I had finished I stood motionless for a while at the front door: I saw people go by, and cars, and far away the sky of Paris glowing red; between the black houses the street-lights drew a festal path. In other places, at the same moment, miracles were coming into existence; and somewhere there was Denis. I began to climb the stairs; often I stopped half way, not having the spirit to go on; I looked at the carpet and the shining brass stair-rods; after them would come the red carpet of our hall with great bald grey patches where the pile was worn to the thread: it was coming nearer, inevitably nearer.

To escape and live according to Denis' doctrine, money was needed; and that was difficult. Pascal was open-handed, but I did not like to ask him: I begged Mama to give me contributions for the 'Social Contact', and I stole small sums from Marcelle. The first time I had ten francs to spend I went to have a drink at the bar of the Rotonde. The place was almost empty: a few young men were talking among themselves in an intimate kind of way and I had the unpleasant feeling that I was thrusting myself into their private lives. I sat on a stool and I ordered a gin fizz: the little wooden tables, the Norman chairs, the red and white curtains over the windows did not appear to be hiding any mystery; nothing happened; I was deeply disappointed. But when I wanted to pay, the red-headed barman refused my money; and this good omen quite certainly pointed out the road I was to follow. I began to haunt bars and places where people danced, and the social work provided me with an alibi. To begin with I always used to spend an hour at the rue de Ménilmontant: and one evening, when I was to give a lecture on resignation, I arrived with my legs trembling, my forehead covered with cold sweat, having just thrown up two gin fizzes in the métro. They made me lie on a couch, full of admiration for my courage in coming. Presently I grew more daring and secretly resigned. After that I was able to spend a whole evening once a week at the bar Denis had taken me to: I went there as once I had gone to Mass, with the same ardour, and I had scarcely changed my God – the jazz moved me as deeply as the great voice of the organ in earlier days. Ever since Denis had told me that piece about sin being the space yawning wide for God, vice had given me the same ecstatic feeling that I had felt as a child before the real presence of the Holy Sacrament. Fundamentally, Pascal was quite mistaken in supposing that I was so far from him and in having such grave, sad confabulations with Marcelle: in my own way I too was serving the things of the spirit.

I accepted rape, incest, lechery, drunkenness: any satyr might be a Stavroguine, any sadist a Lautréamont, any sodomite a Rimbaud: it was with veneration that I looked at the red- or mauve-haired prostitutes sitting near me on the bar stools: there was so little lubricity in my imagination that even when I heard them wonder aloud how much they would charge for sucking off a customer I formed no distinct picture. I was playing with words, dark and magical words that filled me with a confused amazement and admiration. I had no sort of success at all with the whores, who mistrusted me; I should have liked to know by what series of initiations they had won the splendid freedom they enjoyed in relation to their bodies. They were beyond fear, beyond disgust; nothing was forbidden to them, nothing impossible: for my part I was ashamed of my virginity. But just as I never expected to buy clothes like theirs, merely with money, so I saw no human means of becoming one of them. A kind of election was required; and I had not been chosen. I had only a very narrow field of action.

'Go into a bar, do no matter what, and things happen,' Denis had said to me. Within the limits imposed upon me, I followed his advice. I went in: I still wore my mauve dress, lisle stockings often with holes in them, and heavy walking-shoes; my face was not made up, my nails were dirty; I did not care at all. I did not suppose that these people saw me or formulated thoughts about me: allegories have neither eyes nor awareness. I had the many-faced vices there before me – anxiety; futility; dazed, heavy stupidity; despair; and perhaps a genius or two; but not beings of flesh and blood. I climbed on to a stool near the door; and I began my drink; at first I was bored, and then I grew a little more lively; if a customer came in with his hat on his head I shouted 'Hat' at the top of my voice, seized it with both hands and threw it as far as I could; I joked with the barman, filching his cherries in brandy and slices of banana; now and then, when I had emptied my glass, I flung it to the ground, where it broke with a great deal of noise: once I had smashed four in a row. I was an exceedingly loquacious drunk and I hailed all the regular customers: there were some young men of good family among them, several little pimps and queers – I could not tell one from another. I had a simple-minded belief that I could have fun by deluding them, since it was common knowledge that delusion was a form of miracle: sometimes I claimed that I was a model, sometimes a whore; but I fooled nobody. I was furious when a hook-nosed fellow who said he wrote serials shrugged his shoulders and observed, 'You are a little bourgeoise trying to act the bohemian.'

In an irritated voice I said, 'It's not true. I come here to pick up clients.'

'You haven't the right touch,' said another man, a big man who limped and who wore horn-rimmed spectacles.

'You ought to have a more showy dress,' went on the writer of serials, 'and make-up on your face, and high heels.'

'And a more sophisticated look,' added a third. They laughed: there were four of them and they pinned me between the bar and the wall. The lame man showed me a drawing: 'That's what you have to do and let people do to you if you are a tart.' I gave it an indifferent glance: 'It's terribly badly drawn.' 'But it's quite like – have a look.' He undid his trousers: they all burst out laughing. I looked away: 'It doesn't interest me.' They laughed again. 'There, you see,' the serial-writer said to me, 'a whore would have looked and she would have said "Bah, I've seen better than that".' I was furious.

Yet one evening a man did ask me to go home with him. He had red hair and freckles and they called him Casque d'Or: he was sitting at the bar of the Jockey with a whore he had just picked up and a friend, a very young man with a childish mouth and blue eyes by the name of Marcel. 'Come along with us: it's better for dancing at my place.' I went with them to an apartment whose walls were covered with weapons and wild animals' skins; they put on some dance-music records and drank port and Casque d'Or disappeared with the blonde whore. Marcel sat on the divan at my side and tried to kiss me: I pushed him away, but quite kindly, because I liked him. 'Listen,' I said. 'You will easily find other women: there's no lack of them, particularly for a man as handsome as you. But I have a friend, and I mean to be faithful to him.'

He grew rather pressing. 'Well, I don't mind giving you a kiss,' I said, and I set a little peck on each of his rosy cheeks. He had drunk quite a lot and this moved him deeply. 'You're not like the others,' he said, and then remained silent for a moment. 'You're not immoral; one can see that right away. It's really touching to find a good little girl like you.' He took a flat tin out of his pocket, and his voice grew thick. 'As for me, you see what kind of a fellow I am: I never go out without carrying these gadgets with me. Sickening, isn't it? That's what life's like.' He began telling me about himself; sometimes he broke off and asked me, quite embarrassed, 'Do I disgust you?' I often saw him afterwards in Montparnasse and he always treated me with the utmost respect.

This incident gave me an exaggerated confidence in myself: I supposed that I should always be able to keep men at arm's length with fair words and pretty smiles. Very ugly things might have happened to me: I was moving in a world governed by rigid and finely-shaded laws and I was doing so without the least notion of its rules of behaviour, its hierarchies, or its points of honour; I did not know when one could let oneself be bought a drink and when one could not, nor when a woman, as a fair competitor, should refrain from speaking to a friend's client or when it was allowable for her to steal him. In my ignorance I trampled on all the conventions: I accepted all invitations and I let myself be picked up in the street, for I should have been ashamed if any hanging back on my part had hindered the coming of the miracle. I thought I could carry on the great game of gratuitous acts and of adventure just as I thought fit, and I looked upon my partners as mere supernumeraries. What saved me, I believe, was the fact that I aroused little desire: I was not very attractive. For my own part I had no prudence whatsoever. Thus, I agreed to get into a car that had followed me along the boulevard Raspail: the young man at the wheel was neither handsome nor agreeable, but he had civil manners. He made me sit by his side, and drove down the boulevard Saint-Germain at a great pace. 'What do you say to going out to Robinson?' he asked. I hesitated for a moment; it was clear that I ran the risk of being left in the lurch miles from Paris; but I had my principles. 'Never refuse anything,' said Gide and Jacques Rivière and André Breton and Denis. 'Let's go,' I said.

We stopped in the Place de la Bastille and drank cocktails on the terrace of an empty café. The fellow was gloomy; I made no advances, nor did I laugh. As soon as were were back in the car he began to fondle my leg; I pulled it away. At this he got cross. 'What, you let me trundle you about in my car but I'm not even allowed to touch you?' His face had changed and there was no trace of politeness left in his voice: I did not really know what to say. He put his arm round my shoulder and pulled me roughly towards him: I pushed him away with both hands and broke free. He stopped dead. 'With an ugly mug like yours you might at least be pleasant. Who do you think you are? It makes me laugh – there's nothing like a plain Jane for giving herself airs.' I got out quickly and as I hurried away I could still hear him insulting me. I was almost at the gates of Paris and the last métro had gone some time before, but I regretted nothing: I was delighted with myself for having brought an entirely absurd happening into existence. Still, I was quite glad that I had not gone as far as Robinson.

On one occasion things took a much more unpleasant turn. At a little fair in the avenue des Gobelins I was picked up by a fairly young man with a tough look and a pink scar on his cheek: we fired rifles and played with the football machine, and each time he insisted on putting the coin in the slot. He introduced a friend and the two of them invited me to go to the Dôme: the friend stood three cups of café crème. We talked for a while and then, seeing my last bus, I said good-bye in haste and set off at a run: I was just about to leap aboard when the fellow with the scar caught me up and took me by the shoulders. 'Trying to brush me off, are you? That's the kind of treatment I don't put up with.' He looked furious. The conductor hesitated, his hand on the bell, while I struggled to get away: in the end the bus drove off. I was speechless with anger. The friend intervened, explaining that I ought not to have let myself be treated to a drink and that my behaviour was questionable. The other man calmed down and when we had made friends again they told me that they were going to see me home. This time I made it quite clear that they could expect nothing from me, but they still came along: I put up with it; and in any case I could not very well have stopped them. A few yards from the house the man with the scar took me by the waist and asked me for a rendezvous; at first I refused, but then, when his face grew threatening I ended up by saying 'We'll meet whenever you like.' At that moment four policemen on bicycles went by: I very nearly called them, but I did not dare. We walked on a few paces in silence, and when the policemen had vanished the man took me by the shoulders again. 'Now I know you're making a fool of me,' he said. 'You fix an appointment and you don't mean to come. You deserve a good lesson, my chick: I grow nasty when I'm crossed. You got it all wrong, trying to string me along.' I was in a tight corner, in that dark little street: I struggled with all my might – I did not want him to kiss me. Yet at the same time I was very much afraid that he might hit me really hard. The friend stepped in. 'Come, we can put this right,' he said. 'He's angry about the money he spent on you, that's all.' I opened my bag at once. 'There,' I said, holding out ten francs, 'pay yourself back.' 'I don't give a damn about the money,' said the other, taking the bag out of my hands. 'What I want to do is give you a lesson.' There were only five francs left. 'I shan't even have enough to get myself a woman,' he said to me with hatred. He emptied the bag, and uttered a few more threats; then he took his friend's arm and the two of them turned their backs on me. I crept into the house, my legs giving way beneath me.

When I told Denis these stories some time later I was deeply disappointed. 'There was nothing funny about it at all,' he said. 'It's ridiculously stupid to go along with just anyone.' I thought I deserved at least some praise: I had made a blind use of my freedom, I had let myself drift on the currents of chance and things had happened – slight, no doubt, and even squalid, but that made the fragment of miracle hidden in the depths of the vulgar happening seem to me all the more precious.

Denis was disconcerting: often he did not admire actions although they were carefully carried out according to his own maxims – did not admire them at all. I thought there must still be a kind of middle-class heaviness in taking him too literally.

I met Denis at the Jockey, by chance, nearly eighteen months after he had left. It was in April, the year I was preparing to take my degree: at the Sorbonne I had made friends with a Polish girl whom I introduced to Mama – her collusion made my going out at night the easier. I worked all day at the Bibliothèque Nationale and several times a week I spent the evening in Montparnasse: the next morning I often attended lectures with an aching head and an upset stomach.

That evening I was sitting at the bar of the Jockey, deep in a kind of daze, when a middle-aged woman came up to me. 'Do you dance?' she asked. She had dark hair, a ruddy complexion like an Englishwoman's, blue eyes, thick lips.

'No, not very well,' I said.

She smiled, showing big, shining teeth. 'Then let's talk, shall we?'

I gave her a friendly look. 'I should like that: have you been here long? I didn't see you come in.'

'I was here before you.' She coyly put her head on one side. 'Tell me why you are here.' With a sudden movement she took my hand. 'May I read it in your palm?'

I laughed. 'If you can see anything . . .'

She nodded. 'I can see, I can see a closed room and sad people: there are three of them, an elderly woman, a young man, and another woman. You come here to escape from them.' I looked at her with surprise, but her face was hidden by the heavy mass of her hair: she looked closely at my palm. 'Soon everything is going to change for you.' She let my hand go. 'You are about to meet someone.'

Rather anxiously I asked 'A man or a woman?'

'A man and a woman.' She stared at me triumphantly for a moment. I inspected my hand, turning it one way and another; I was thoroughly puzzled. 'I just have to believe you,' I said. 'I wish I could read your hand too.'

'It needs a very special gift.' She smiled. 'I noticed you as soon as you came in. You're so young, and I love young people; and it was so strange to see you sit at this bar.'

'Am I so out of place, then?' I asked sadly.

'Delightfully out of place.' She gazed at me for a long while and there was something like tenderness in her eyes. 'Why don't you look after your face and hair? You could be absolutely charming.' She had a warm, rather resonant voice, with a slight accent. I blushed. She went on looking at me without saying anything and then abruptly she put her hand on my shoulder. 'Come along: I want to show you someone who'll be glad to see you.' Pushing through the crowd of dancers, she walked to the far end of the room and I followed her – her brown dress, cut as high as a Carmelite's habit, outlined a well-shaped body, elegant though rather stout. At a table I caught sight of Denis and I recognized that way he had of passing his fingers through his hair when he was embarrassed.

'What on earth were you doing here, my dear?' he asked, shaking my hand very hard. 'Have you left home?'

'No. But I often come back here.' He had not changed; I was deeply moved.

'Will you have a drink?' I sat down. 'Let me make the proper introductions – Mlle Drouffe, Mme Lamblin.'

'For you, it must be Marie-Ange right away,' said Mme Lamblin, smiling.

'So that was how you came to know so much,' I said to her.

'Did you really think I was a witch? She is perfectly capable of it: Denis, this child is simply adorable.' Denis looked at us each in turn with a rather uncomfortable air. 'I know what a help you were to Denis,' she said to me; and smiling at him she went on, 'I admire his genius too. Sometimes he's terrible, isn't he? But that's what poets are like.' Her eyes were brilliant. 'I think we shall be great friends.'

'Certainly,' I mumbled. There was a silence: like Denis I felt rather ill at ease. Marie-Ange took a mink coat from the seat and got up. 'I don't want to be in the way: you must have so much to say to one another. But tomorrow you'll come and have tea with me, won't you?'

'You're going home?' said Denis.

'Yes. But you stay with your little sister-in-law. Please do – I don't need you,' she added quickly, blushing a little.

When she had gone Denis sat there for a moment looking down. I tried to steady my voice: 'I never thought I'd see you again. Why didn't you write?'

'I'm no good at writing,' he said. 'And I'm shy.' His voice was full of regret. 'I thought you had forgotten me.'

'You were wrong.'

He ran his hand through his hair again and gave a little cough: he was like a child caught in the act of doing something wrong. For a few moments the silence continued.

'Lots of things must have happened to you!'

He made a vague gesture, and his face darkened. 'Things, yes . . .' He seemed to make up his mind. 'To understand properly, you would have to know Marie-Ange: she's an unusual woman.' He smiled for the first time. 'She's not a woman: she's Destiny,' he said lightly. He flicked the ash off his cigarette and leant forward. 'You see, Marguerite, before I met her, my life was nothing more than a series of challenges to fate.'

'Indeed, I always wondered why you married Marcelle,' I said.

'I've always felt irresistibly attracted to Disaster,' he said, giving me a rather ironical look.

'I see. Do you still feel like that?'

He shrugged. 'Who knows?' His tone wrung my heart. 'Marie-Ange took me over with almost supernatural strength.' He looked thoughtfully at the ceiling. 'It was chance, an extraordinarily disturbing stroke of chance, that took me to her house; and without ever having seen me, she had dreamt of me three days before.'

I stared at him, fascinated: all around us things changed their nature – without losing anything of their truth, the jazz, the women's laughter, the orange light and the coloured posters assumed the form of a stage set, and instead of living my prosaic life I was acting in the scene of a play – a play in which Denis was the hero.

'She's enormously rich, and at first I took her for an ordinary patron of the arts – she has a place in the South where she's collected a whole colony of artists. But the interesting thing is the way she recruits them.'

He stopped: and I remembered how he always used to stop. He never finished a story and indeed it was rare that he ever came to the end of his sentences. 'Go on, Denis,' I said impatiently.

'She's blind, like Fortune: or rather she only sees signs that no one else can detect. She obeys her every impulse and all the hints that come to her in dreams. Can you guess why she wanted to get to know you? Because you picked up all the straws on the counter just now and broke them into little bits.'

'But what about you, Denis? What happened?' He had to be badgered.

He smiled. 'Her dream had warned her that without me she could not succeed in anything she undertook. I had to go to the South with her and work under her orders: we did some terrific things – I organized avant-garde shows in a barn with marion-ettes as actors and gramophones to play the text. Prodigious.'

'Oh, I am glad, Denis! I was sure that in the end you would do something.'

He shook his head. 'You're wrong, my dear. The anonymous production of pieces that go beyond you, pieces in which you don't see yourself at all, that's fine; but I would never bring out anything of my own, any personal work. It would give me the feeling of prostituting myself.'

Fine feelings have never been my strong point, but they touched me in Denis: they were another mark of his superiority. 'Are you going to stay in Paris now?' I asked.

'How should I know?' He smiled. 'I'm carried along by fate, I tell you.'

He took me back as far as my door: it was as though I were drunk, overwhelmed with joy and an excruciating, wonderful anguish. I woke the next morning in a new world, a world in which, for me, everything was a threat or a promise.

Marie-Ange's apartment was full of equivocal signs. I waited quite a while in the room that took up the ground floor of her house in the rue de Ranelagh: for me a home that seemed neither to have been bought from a catalogue nor to have been inherited was something extraordinary, and gingerly I touched the masks on the walls, the wire dogs, the Negro carvings. Fascinated, I deciphered the dedications in the books; and with some distress I felt that I should never have a life that would leave its mark on a dwelling: I was quite empty within.

'How kind of you to come,' said Marie-Ange, giving me both her hands. She was wearing a long, brilliantly embroidered gandura, heavy bracelets and Turkish slippers: even the shape of her nails filled me with astonishment. At tea she gave me bread and butter spread with caviar or with guava jelly.

'You must tell me about yourself,' she said with a rather affected smile. I felt shy, but I wanted her to find me interesting: I talked, but too fast, without reserve, in a voice that was too loud and that rang false. She was not put out: she listened, her eyes shining and her red mouth slightly open. 'How charming,' she said, from time to time.

After this she flung herself back in her immense armchair, and, looking at the ceiling, she began telling me about herself, smoking cigarettes as she did so. She had had an extraordinary life: twice married, twice divorced, she had lived in India, in Mexico, in a château in the Ardèche, in Florence, in Paris and the country near Aix. Hers was a soul perpetually unappeased; she had been a Theosophist and a spiritualist, she had turned tables and for a year she had lived on beans and boiled rice, and she had spent six months in a nudist colony. All these experiments had disappointed her, but since she had known Denis she had at last come to understand her tragedy: she was possessed by a creative demon that struggled within her and that stifled her 'because,' she said, looking me in the eye, 'he is given no way of expressing himself.' In a way she was a maimed being, and to be at peace she had to find her completion outside herself –she had to surround herself with artists and poets capable of detecting the confused vibrations that worked in her and of transforming them into plain, direct sound. When this happened she felt delivered.

'I have never met a sensitivity so exactly in tune with mine as Denis',' she told me. 'I must show you some of the documents that I have so to speak dictated to him by my mere presence: the transcription is so exact it's unbelievable.' She laughed. 'When I suggested that he should live in the little house at the bottom of the garden, he did not like to accept. He's such a scrupulous child, and he was afraid it might make our relationship seem ambiguous; but I broke with those old prejudices long ago. I just have to have him at hand; it's absolutely vital.' Her cigarettes had opium in them and the smoke was going to my head; I felt very strange; and there was something disturbing about this woman, about the singing quality of her voice and the way her eyes dwelt on me. 'And Denis too – he needed the drive of this creative force that is in me to be able to produce anything.' She smiled. 'What do they call that in natural history? Symbiosis, I think.'

I very much wanted to see Denis. I wondered whether he was happy; and I was afraid for him. When I knocked at the door of his room the next day, my knees trembled with emotion.

'How are you, old soul?' he said, giving me a most affectionate look. He was wearing a smoking-jacket: he sat deep in an armchair, looking chilly, and he remained silent. I had the impression that I made him nervous. I told him of my adventures: I did not feel very much like doing so, but something had to be said.

He shook his head disapprovingly. 'You mustn't go on, my dear: nasty things will happen to you,' he said. He drew on his cigarette. 'Marie-Ange will be a very useful friend to you,' he said. 'You need someone to show you the way through life.'

'She is very interesting,' I said, quite sincerely: then I hesitated, looking for the right words. 'Do you like the way you live, Denis?'

He smiled. 'What a funny question: you don't choose, Marguerite – things happen and you submit to them; then another day other things happen . . .'

'But still, you're interested in your work?'

'We're not doing a damn thing at the moment, and anyhow . . .' He shrugged his shoulders.

'It seems to you as pointless as everything else?'

He got up and began pacing to and fro. 'My poor Marguerite, how do you expect anyone to live when he has discovered that nothing in the world is worth the slightest effort?'

'Oh, come! You used to tell me that it was the very fact of an action's being gratuitous that gave it its value.'

'You can't perform even a gratuitous action without making chains for yourself.' He stretched, and I heard his joints crack. 'Oh, I'm so sick of it all.'

I should dearly have liked to give him back some of the self-confidence that he had once had in such abundance. 'You're no longer very proud, Denis.'

'No: I can't hope for anything from myself, Marguerite: nothing can be hoped for from anyone, and no one is hoped for by anything. Perhaps, do you see, the only right action I could perform would be to do away with myself.'

That gave me a shock: I used to cry at times and I was often bored, but I had never thought of suicide. Feeling that I was a horribly superficial creature, I confessed, 'For my part I do love being alive, in spite of everything.' In a flash I saw that soon these words would no longer be true: Denis was going to carry me along into his own despair, and I wanted to go with him: I was very much afraid that I was going to suffer.

He offered me a cigarette; his face grew a little brighter. 'Little things, there are still little things that you can cling to for a moment. Look at this paper-weight that I picked up in a junk-shop the other day: it's my latest passion. It might be an aquarium, a fun-fair, a candy, a rainbow . . . I can look at it for hours.' He balanced the prismatic ball in his hand, slowly nodding as he did so.

When we parted he held on to my hand for a moment. 'You must come back and see me again,' he said earnestly.

I went back very often; it was no easy matter, loving a man in a state of total despair. When I was away from him I made plans and I worked out fine things to say. It seemed to me that Marie-Ange was fighting for herself and that she did not mind about Denis: he stayed shut up in his room all day, doing nothing, and in the evening he went to Montparnasse to get drunk – it was no sort of life. I should have liked to persuade him to prefer himself to Marie-Ange, to go off no matter where, and to work out his own salvation. But as soon as I saw his sad eyes and the lines of his mouth, words failed me. He would welcome me, showing his latest find, a ball, a drawing, a ship in a bottle. 'Isn't it terrific?' he would say. 'If only we knew how to open our eyes, Marguerite, we should see angels.' The poverty of my feelings and my dreams left me feeling abashed – how could I presume to give him advice? I remained silent; he did the same; and I felt a piercing sadness come over me. At the threshold of his room, all reasons for living left me; I lit a cigarette; he half-lay on the divan to smoke his pipe or else he paced up and down. I don't know how many afternoons we spent like that. Sometimes the atmosphere was so oppressive that I got up to go. 'Stay a little while longer,' he said; but that was all. With our foreheads against the window-panes we watched the rain falling and the first street-lamps lighting up. It hurt me to the point of anguish that I had nothing to give him: I should certainly have given him my body and my life, but those were meagre gifts, and I reckoned myself of such little value that I did not even want him to ask me for them. I looked for nothing from him, except that he should let me stew in despair like this beside him.

Sometimes I seemed to read an indistinct appeal in his eyes that overwhelmed me; and there was one day among the rest when I knew that my being there could be precious to him. When I arrived his face was haggard, his eyes swollen, his features drawn; the room was full of thick smoke and ties were lying about on the backs of the chairs. He cleared a place so that I could sit down. 'I did a horrible thing last night,' he told me suddenly. 'I broke a life, broke it like that, as you break a glass. When you were little did you never smash anything, just for the pleasure of smashing? Because all at once you felt as free not to smash as to smash? Or out of perversity? At this moment I feel as sick as if my mouth were full of blood.' I was terrified: I asked no questions – I never did: Denis' adventures took place in an unknown world, among faceless beings. He tossed back the lock hanging over his forehead. 'We say we refuse all morality; we admire Rimbaud and Lautréamont; and yet we lack that essential piece of courage – the courage to make others suffer. What a filthy Christian inheritance – it doesn't even need blood to make us throw up: the sight of a tear is quite enough.' His voice broke. Hearing him talk was often painful: it was as though the truth could be torn from his heart only at the cost of unbearable suffering. He shrugged. 'In any case, where does the game begin or the play-acting stop? I'm like a murderer who doesn't know whether he fired at a man or a puppet. Was it even a genuine revolver-shot?' He looked really overcome.

'And which would you prefer? That it should be genuine or that it should not?' This was just to say something: I had no idea what he was talking about.

'How can I tell?' he said. 'Oh, Marguerite, I'm so tired. I should like to carry out at least one action that is not merely a gesture; and I do assure you it may be that killing oneself is what is called for.'

I thought, 'If he kills himself I shall kill myself', and that comforted me a little: the fact of no longer holding any part of my fate in my own hands was miraculous, but it was also terrible. I said, 'That too may be no more than a gesture.'

He smiled and flung himself into an armchair. 'That's the very thing that stops me,' he said. After this we talked about people and things with more liveliness than usual, as though ghosts had to be exorcised. As I was leaving he said 'Thank you' in an odd kind of a voice, without looking at me.

I walked about the streets for hours: my life was transformed –at last it had rediscovered the meaning it had lost the day I lost God, and since it was now of use to Denis it was necessary once more. Living close to him and sharing his fate meant becoming more than an ordinary mortal.

But Denis did not always need me. Often he would receive me with a bored, distant or ironic look: impatiently he repelled any allusion to our earlier conversations, he did not answer my questions and he pretended to be wholly taken up with a party for the opening of a bar he was to go to that evening, or a poker-game in which he had brought off a bluff the evening before, or the legs of a dancer he had discovered with Marie-Ange. He set himself in front of the mirror, peering at the back of his throat for a long while; he talked very fast, saying nothing. This seeming levity did not deceive me: when Denis affected to consider only the most futile trifles as having any importance, it was in order to make a stronger assertion of the total emptiness of everything. But when he did so I felt the uselessness of my compassion and my affection most bitterly: the least glass of gin, or a silk scarf, were worth as much as I was. And indeed since I could not prevent myself from seeing our friendship as something more than a simple amusement, I sometimes deserved being treated with a kind of enmity; asking Denis to take anything seriously was an insult to his despair, and I saw that his frivolity might easily take on an aggressive character. I ought to have gone along with him, laughing at the stupid puns, the dreary old jokes, or the nonsense that sent him into a macabre kind of hilarity: instead, I remained cold, unmoved.

I envied Marie-Ange. She moved about in the absurd with an ease that stunned me – Denis called her 'the angel of the preposterous'. In practice this did not make being with her very agreeable: she had really taken to me, but I did not like going shopping with her, nor indeed going out with her at all. In cinemas or restaurants she would often be seized with inspirations as imperative as they were unexpected and if she met with the least resistance she became terribly violent. And I really did not quite know how to behave with a woman who saw only the invisible. We were sitting in a tea-shop, talking, when suddenly she grew pale. 'A syphilitic has drunk out of my cup,' she said. 'Look.' I saw nothing. She pushed away her plate, full of cakes, all nibbled, and called the manager. Sometimes – as, for example, on the day she found the traces of a tapeworm in her steak – she refused to pay: for fear of a scene, they often let her have her way. In any event she always went through the bill with the keenest attention. She was not mean: she was unpredictable. She might buy a dozen hats so horrible that she never wore them, and do so without bargaining: yet I have seen her stamp on very pretty frocks because the dressmaker would not give her a reduction. With me she was extravagantly generous; indeed, I found it embarrassing. I did not like to refuse her presents; I did not know how to thank her for them; nor did I really know what to say when she put her arm round my waist, calling me 'my sweet charmer', or when she kissed me effusively.

She set about dressing me from head to foot according to her own taste. I scarcely knew her before she took me into her bedroom and said, with gentle authority, 'Take off that hideous frock: I'm going to try one of my dresses on you – this green will suit you marvellously.' I took my frock off: it embarrassed me because my underclothes were often rather dubious. When she saw my madapollam petticoat she cried, 'But look what you wear next your skin, my poor child! How rough it is! You, whose skin is so delicate and fine.' She stroked my shoulder, her eyes almost brimming over with pity: it seemed to me that she exaggerated a little.

'Its ugliness is what really matters,' I said.

'You must take it off, the horrible thing: put on this slip.'

I was more and more embarrassed; I was not very prudish, but I had never undressed in front of anyone. I turned my back as I took off my petticoat and I could not prevent myself from blushing when she came and stood there in front of me with a critical look. 'You have a lovely body,' she said. 'You are quite right not to wear a suspender belt.' She smiled archly. 'I don't wear one either,' she added. 'Feel.' She grasped my hand and pressed it to her belly. It was indeed all soft.

A maid came to take my measurements and mark the necessary alterations: a fortnight later Marie-Ange made me put on crêpe de Chine underclothes, silk stockings, high-heeled shoes and a delicately textured green wool frock. She never took her eyes off me while I was dressing, and she seemed to think it quite natural. 'I know who you are like with those high little breasts and that slightly rounded stomach,' she said. 'It's the women Cranach painted. Not a regular beauty, but much better. A faultless body is less characteristic, less touching.'

I was astonished; but one astonishment more among all the rest hardly counted. And then I reflected that modesty was just another old Catholic prejudice, and I tried to smile naturally. When I was ready, Marie-Ange put a dressing-gown over my shoulders and made me sit in an armchair: I put my right hand in a bowl of warm water and, while the maid worked on the moons of my nails with an orange-stick, Marie-Ange began plucking my eyebrows. She stood behind me and my head rested against her ample bosom; the silk of her frock caressed my cheek like the blouses of the Institut Joliet teachers in former times; it was just a little repellent. Then she put eye-liner round my eyes with a tiny brush, rouge and powder on my cheeks, and lipstick on my mouth, and the maid washed my hair with ether. It went on and on: I could bear it no longer. But when I looked at myself in the glass I was perfectly amazed.

I hurried to see Denis that very evening – I was afraid that by tomorrow I might have become ugly again. He stared at me, surprised. 'You look charming, Marguerite.' He mumbled on a cigarette-butt and then abruptly threw it right away. 'Seeing you, one might almost start wanting to be happy,' he said indistinctly. I gazed at him and he looked away; I did not know what taboo he had set on me – it was as though he were afraid of something. 'He's afraid of happiness,' I thought, 'and afraid of making me unhappy.' But that evening I was sure that he loved me.

There were great scenes at home: I said that Wanda, my Polish friend, had given me these presents out of gratitude for the French lessons I had given her, but Mama wept, Marcelle nearly had a heart-attack again, and Pascal gave me a long, dismal lecture.

Wanda was quite astonished by all that I told her about Marie-Ange and Denis. On leaving the library I often went to have tea with her in her little hotel room, and we talked: she did not understand much about the situation. 'You must make him fall in love with you,' she told me. 'You don't know how to set about it.'

'But I don't want him to love me,' I said. 'I just want to help him save his life: there must be some way of doing it.'

She looked at me with affection and pity. 'You are an idealist,' she said. 'If you want to influence a man, you must begin by making him fall in love.'

She was flirtatious and much sought after by men and she readily brought everything down to a matter of sex. It was in vain that I tried to explain to her the nature of the relationship between Marie-Ange and Denis. 'Imagine a prodigious natural force,' I said, 'something like a great waterfall or a sand-storm that one day decides that it would like to be aware of itself: an outside consciousness has to agree to become *its* consciousness. Out of a kind of generosity and out of that wish for self-destruction that he has always had, Denis has let himself be enslaved. She's not to blame; she's obeying an irresistible need; but she has emptied him of himself – there's nothing of him left.'

'They certainly go to bed together,' said Wanda, unmoved.

'Wanda! She's almost old enough to be his mother,' I cried.

Her green eyes sparkled. 'You are so very naïve, dear Marguerite,' she said.

That year I went away for the holidays as late as possible and I came back at the beginning of September; Marie-Ange had not yet returned from her Norwegian cruise, but Denis had not left Paris. I saw him quite often, sometimes at his place and sometimes in Montparnasse, for he was going out a great deal at that time. He seemed peaceful enough and almost happy when I came back but then suddenly he turned moody again; I had never seen him so deeply depressed. He only made vague allusions to things that worried him and I could not guess what they were. I was overcome when I found that he too was capable of having anxieties of an ordinary human kind.

I began the evening of this discovery by waiting for him a long while at the Jockey. He had given me an appointment for ten o'clock; at midnight I was still there and I knew that now he would not come: I was used to it. He accepted no ties; even his promises did not bind him: and for that too I admired him. As far as I was concerned, all my actions were calculated – middle-class economy again – and I was incapable of sacrificing a moment of happiness for a chance encounter, for a whim, or for freedom. I loathed sacrifices; I was as grasping as an old miser: at this very moment it was no good telling myself again and again that Denis was proving his regard by treating me according to an ethic more fundamental than any form of politeness – I could not help suffering. I was disgusted with myself. I ordered a second glass of whiskey; I did not much care for that aftertaste of iodine, but I needed to get out of myself a little.

Dancing couples brushed past me: I felt a heart-rending pity for them. I could not tell a foxtrot from a tango: all I saw was an empty busyness by which people did their best to escape from the appalling tedium of living. I was sorry for them, and yet I thought that they were right and I was not; I ought to have copied these women whose bodies expressed total surrender, these women wholly immersed in the present, delivered up to chance without the least defence. They did not know whom they would sleep with that night and they did not try to find out; they danced, they drank, and some made fortunes while others became wrecks, like the red-haired old woman sitting next to me who got drunk every evening: not one of them thought about happiness. In the whole bar there was only myself who was inflicted with this guilty and impossible appetite: I could not manage to stifle it. I tried, but in vain; every one of my actions was an attempt at building – building thoughts, a friendship, a life for Denis and me. I should never attain the gratuitous; I should never renounce myself, nor all desire, nor all hope. I was doomed.

A dwarf woman with an aged face, dressed in a schoolgirl's smock, had begun to sing: her voice was husky, she screwed up her eyes with a roguish look, and the flesh on either side of her mouth moved in soft waves. I had often heard her before, but this time I could not bear it and I left, walking along the boulevard under a gentle autumn rain. I wanted to see Denis at all costs. I decided to go and look for him at the Goéland, a little bar he had often told me about but which he had never agreed to take me to: it was a bold stroke, and I was afraid he might be cross, seeing me appear unexpectedly. I hesitated a long while: a piano could be heard through the metal shutters: no one went in, no one came out. At last, the whiskey giving me courage, I opened the door; and at the first glance I saw that Denis was not there. The room was small – it might have been the inside of a tomb – and a smell of corpses rose from the leather banquettes; cellophane curtains half covered the mirrors, which sent back a yellow light; there were full-blown chrysanthemums in a vase on the piano. I sat at the bar: the tables lined up along the walls and covered with white cloths were empty: three young men were joking with the pianist, who now and then touched the keys with an inattentive hand. Close to me there were two whores, carrying on an earnest conversation in slow, penetrating voices: it was almost embarrassing to disturb this intimate atmosphere, but fortunately nobody took any notice of me.

'No one can say I have any luck,' said one of the women. A broad silver lamé Medici collar framed her fragile neck, and her head, as slender as that of a bird or a snake, was crowned with heavy black bandeaux.

'Don't carry on so,' said the other, a blonde with frosted hair. 'I tell you she'll drop him.'

'Then he'll no longer have a red cent: just when I was going to be able to treat myself to that astrakhan. The kind of bargain I'll never find again, you know – whole skins and only three thousand.' She sighed.

'Astrakhan is pretty,' said the other, 'and it gives you a distinguished look. But I'd rather have a really good ocelot: it's more striking.'

They argued for a while and I stopped listening: I drank my martini; the flame of a gadget for freshening the air glowed gently on the bar; the pianist played a few chords; and all at once the blonde's voice jerked me out of my torpor. 'I do assure you I'm very fond of Denis,' she said, 'but I've always warned you he wasn't a fellow you could rely on.'

The dark woman shrugged her shoulders. 'He's not told me anything yet, but I know he'll drop me like a stone. She's going to sack him, the bitch. They really are disgusting, these old bags.'

'What makes me wonder is how she gets him to do it,' said the blonde, breaking into a shrill laugh.

'As often as five times a night he has to stuff her,' said the dark one: then her face grew serious. 'It's not funny, you know: I had such a thing for him, you wouldn't believe it.'

'Yes . . .' The blonde thought for a while. 'If you'd like me to introduce Jacques to you there's still time – Ginette was just like you. It never really worked with me, but I'm sure he'd take to you.'

I heard no more of what they said. I threw ten francs on the counter, went out and collapsed on a bench in the boulevard du Montparnasse; it was raining quite hard now and the trunks of the plane-trees were all glistening, but I felt nothing. I wept, and there was a throbbing in my temples; I could not even form an idea. It was not until the next morning that I more or less gathered my wits again. I cut my lectures and went to walk in the Luxembourg Gardens; all I could manage as I paced round and round the pond was an endless repetition of the words overhead at the Goéland. I suffered; I needed to see Denis. I had scarcely any hope – the words could never be wiped out – but at least I wanted to hear those hideous truths from his own mouth. He himself must give me the right not to believe in him any more, so that my suffering should stop being a kind of betrayal; and I had an obscure expectation of some undefined miracle.

I found Denis in his room. My voice rang false when I casually said, 'When I didn't see you last night, I looked in at the Goéland. It's an agreeable place: and it so happened they were talking about you.'

He smiled. 'What did they say? I'm very sorry, my dear, but Marie-Ange came back last night and I had to go and fetch her from the station.'

'Of course,' I said. 'It's of no importance.'

He was sitting on the edge of his bed, swinging his legs: he did not look cheerful. I summoned up all my courage. 'At the Goéland there was a charming dark-haired woman who seemed very fond of you.'

He did not look up. 'Valia? That's an old story. I'll tell you about it one day, because there's more than one lesson to be drawn from it. There've been so many stories in my life, my poor Marguerite!'

All at once I was flooded with joy. How simple everything was! I should have liked to run to Denis and kiss him for this frank confession. I had been mad, but now the nightmare had vanished; Denis had never made a virtue of chastity and indeed his code required that he should not refuse any adventure of any kind; he had not lied to me, nor had he been guilty of any contemptible weakness. And at the same time I understood his going to bed with Marie-Ange – understood it with a wonderful clarity. He might do so out of pity or out of a kind of gratitude, or on the other hand out of perversity, out of disgust: it did not affect the essential nature of the bond that linked them. Cautiously and one by one I repeated the remarks I had heard at the Goéland: they had lost all their poison. Only the words 'As many as five times a night he has to stuff her' were hard to swallow: yet I was well aware that Denis took a horrible pleasure in debasing himself; he liked hiding his fine, clean features behind an ugly mask, and it was cowardly of me to be so shocked. At the present moment his handsome face was smiling at me: I smiled too. I loved Denis in his wretchedness and in his splendour, exactly as he was, without asking him for anything and without refusing anything from him: never until then had I reached that total disinterestedness.

The long silence did not surprise Denis: he too was deep in thought. Suddenly he sprang to his feet. 'Do you know what I should like to do now? Leave everything – vanish! I'm sick of these "inward departures", as Guillaume Apollinaire calls them. Have you never longed for a real setting off, a great leap into the unknown with all its risks?'

'Oh yes, Denis!' I said eagerly. 'I've often thought you deserved a splendid life, with all sorts of adventures: you ought to go off and travel. In practice it shouldn't be so difficult.'

'It seems that fortunes are to be made in Saigon, smuggling opium: I've a friend who has just come back and he's told me how to set about it. It must be terrific.' He made a quick calculation. 'I shouldn't need such a great deal of money – just enough to pay for a deck-passage along with the emigrants.'

'I know how you could get it,' I said, laughing.

'How?'

'Why, go and get it from Marcelle. Her friend Germaine left her I don't know exactly how much but certainly quite a lot.'

'What, is she dead, that old trout?' said Denis. He smiled. 'That really would be elegant! But she'd refuse.'

'Go at five o'clock. She'll be alone, and you can easily frighten her.'

He hesitated a moment. 'I'll do it, never you fear,' he said. 'You're a splendid creature, Marguerite: we could bring off diabolical great jobs together. I dream of a really tough life, with prison at the end if need be: it would make something of a change.'

'Listen, Denis,' I said. 'What if I asked for a post in Saigon at the end of the year? I could help you a little at the beginning and then when you had arranged the right set-up just imagine how useful I could be. I could be a seller or a receiver: with my official status no one would ever suspect me.'

'Terrific, Marguerite; you've no idea what can be done in those parts.'

Denis was very good at making plans; he gave me quantities of detailed information on the smuggling of opium, and from then on every time we met he talked to me at length about our life in Saigon. I began taking the steps necessary for obtaining a post there in October; and really, with a little nerve, we might have tried our luck. By way of a beginning Denis succeeded in making Marcelle sign a cheque for five thousand francs.

'Don't say anything to Marie-Ange yet,' he said to me. 'And try to be very nice to her. She's not happy at present,' he added mysteriously.

I was as nice as possible, but Marie-Ange embarrassed me more and more; indeed, I thought she did it on purpose – she seemed to find putting me out of countenance amusing. When we went out in the evening I used to go and dress at her place and change again before going home. Once she suggested that I should have a bath; it was a luxury that I was scarcely acquainted with and I accepted with pleasure; but I had hardly begun washing before she walked in, smiling.

'I'm not in the way?' she said. I was deeply embarrassed: I did not like to admit it, but I tried to remain half-hidden under the soapy water. She began to laugh: 'You wash as Valadon paints, bit by bit – how amusing!' I had to get out of the bath with her watching and she rubbed me down with a friction-glove. 'I'm a nudist, you know,' she said. 'I can't understand why people are ashamed of showing themselves naked.' She had no modesty; she often walked about the apartment in a brassière and panties, and she often obliged me to feel her breasts and her belly to see how young they had remained. She had a red, granular flesh that disgusted me. I also hated going to Montmartre or Montparnasse with her to dance. She had decided to teach me the rumba, but she was incapable of explaining anything: she pressed herself against me so that I felt her breasts against mine and breathed her heavy scent. 'Follow,' she said. 'All you have to do is follow.' I tried; but the smell of opium and *chypre* that permeated her went to my head; I swam in a kind of insipid sweetness and I blundered at every step. When she let me go I was dizzy, on edge and so miserable that I could have cried. Often she grew cross: 'You'll never know how to do anything with your body,' she said. 'What an idiotic way of bringing anybody up!' Some evenings I had the feeling that she hated me. At other times she gazed at me in an ecstasy: she kissed my cheeks and neck and stroked my hair.

'It's four in the morning,' she said to me on one occasion. 'Don't go home: come and sleep at my place. You can say you stayed with your friend the Polish girl.' She squeezed my arm. 'Do come. You are young and you don't know what loneliness can be like sometimes: after all this noise and these lights and your being with me I can't bear an empty room.' There was real distress in her voice.

'But I should like to come,' I said. It amused me to sleep in an unknown bedroom: Marie-Ange lent me silk pyjamas and I stretched out luxuriously on her broad, low divan. She put out all the lights except a little lamp over our heads and we smoked a cigarette: the sheet made a bright patch in the dimness, a twilight in which carpets and tawny furs glowed gently.

'I shall like waking up here tomorrow,' I said, sliding under the bedclothes. She put out the last light, and suddenly I felt her arms round my body and her breath on my cheek. 'I hope that here you'll have the best of all kinds of sleep,' she whispered.

My heart began to thump; I did not like to push her away, but my whole body grew rigid. I did not know quite what she was going to do, nor how far friendship and gratitude required me to put up with it: I did not want to make an unnecessary fuss, yet I did not want to encourage her either. I decided to lie there as if I were a corpse. Her hand moved all over my body, sliding under my jacket and down my belly: I clamped my legs together, making no movement at all. I think it must have been half an hour that she silently caressed me; but it was only when I felt her thick lips on mine that these manipulations took on a clear meaning for me. 'She wants to make love to me,' I thought, turning my head away and trying to disentangle myself.

'Let me kiss you, sweetheart,' she murmured.

'I'm sleepy, Marie-Ange,' I said piteously.

She clasped me tighter. 'I have been wanting you for months. Ever since the first evening I have loved you: don't you love me just a little?'

'Of course I do, Marie-Ange.' I was on the rack. Again she put her mouth on mine: I clenched my teeth and we struggled for a while in the darkness. Suddenly she let me go, put on the light and gave me a sombre look. 'What must I do?' she said. 'Throw myself at your feet? Kiss your knees? What do you want?' I was so upset that I began to cry. She put her arm round my waist: 'You mustn't cry,' she said in a tragic voice. She kissed me; she fondled my bosom. 'Don't cry,' she repeated slowly.

I was furious with her and with myself: I thought the whole scene odious. 'Leave me alone, Marie-Ange. I want to go home,' I said, rather violently. Her face changed; she turned pale and her eyelids fluttered; for a moment she could not speak, but then she reddened and looked at me with hatred. 'You might be a little kinder,' she said. 'Why have you let me kiss and caress you all this time? I'm not a fool. It was for you that I've put up with Denis so long. Do you really imagine I didn't know you were both deceiving me under my own roof?' She got up, took my clothes lying on a chair and threw them out of the room. 'Go if you like and never come back here again,' she said in a broken voice.

If she had not flown into a rage, I scarcely know how the night would have ended; but seeing her with that red, angry face made me quite easy in my mind. I darted out of the bed and went to dress myself in the passage. I heard her pacing up and down in the bedroom talking to herself.

At noon the next day I telephoned Denis: he told me to come and see him at once at the Dôme. When I arrived he was sprawled on a leather banquette right at the back of the café. He looked at me gloomily: 'My poppet, you managed things so well that Marie-Ange has flung me out.'

I sat down: I could not utter a single word. 'It had nothing at all to do with you, Denis,' I said at last. 'You know what happened?'

He nodded. 'You and your prejudices . . .' He checked himself and took my hand. 'Don't be upset; it was sure to happen sooner or later.' He looked terribly worried.

'It was so unexpected,' I muttered. 'She said the vilest things to me, Denis.' Tears came into my eyes. 'What are you going to do?' He made a vague gesture. 'Take a room in an hotel and look for a job.'

On consideration I could not really see why Denis was so low-spirited; long before this he had made up his mind to leave. 'I'll help you look,' I said. 'In any case, we haven't long to wait before setting off for Saigon.' Absently he said 'yes'.

A new life began for us. I no longer went out in the evening: the examination was coming nearer and I spent the nights in my room revising my subjects – with all my heart I wanted to pass so that I could take Denis to Saigon. During the day I took step after step to find him a temporary job: I no longer saw him much. We met at the Dôme at about six o'clock; he was always in the same place, drinking a café crème. He seemed lost in thought; he was badly shaved; his forelock fell untidily over his eyes; he was always ill-tempered. When I asked him how he had spent his day he only answered with monosyllables; he did not listen to my accounts. So I drank my café crème too and held my tongue. I remembered the day I had seen the Dôme for the first time –Denis' hand on my shoulder, his conniving smile. We were strangers then; now the day was approaching when our lives were going to merge at last. I ought to have been happy; but this transitional period was horribly long, and I felt that Denis found it unbearable, which killed all my joy. He no longer spoke of Saigon; he never talked about the future. Only once did he say, 'I have a mind to write to Marcelle: if I could make her feel concerned about what happens to me, perhaps Pascal would help.'

'But, Denis, what are you thinking of?' I said, amazed. 'Don't you know that there's no forgiving what you did to her?'

'Oh, I know how to deal with Marcelle,' he said with a queer smile.

We both fell silent again; but it was no longer the silence of earlier times. In those days we had not spoken because words were powerless to express the splendid despair that linked us – we had too much to say. Then there had come periods of tender intimacy in which we had broken the spell and talked. Now, all at once it was as though we no longer had anything to say to one another. 'Patience,' I repeated to myself, 'in four months everything will be different.' But I was rather disappointed that poverty could have made such a deep change in Denis.

I was really proud of myself the day I brought him the offer of a job as secretary in a picture-gallery; but he shook his head. 'Don't take such a lot of trouble, Marguerite: I have other plans,' he said. And then he vanished entirely. He no longer came to the Dôme: I went to his hotel in the rue de la Gaieté for news of him, being afraid that he might be ill, but his key was hanging on the board and he was not there. I went the next day and several days after that: I left notes suggesting rendezvous but he never came to any of them; on the telephone he told me that he was terribly busy at the moment – that he begged to be excused – and he rang off very quickly. I was completely overwhelmed: I could not believe in plain indifference after so many shared plans and promise-laden smiles and deeply moving handshakes. Perhaps my affection was burdensome and once again he wanted to break free. At all costs I had to have an explanation. One evening I posted myself at the door of his hotel: I watched for a long while and then suddenly I saw his big white macintosh and his smile; it was so strange to see him there, exactly as I had pictured him, that I stood motionless, feeling all the blood drain from my face. 'What a pleasant surprise,' he said in a voice that rang utterly false.

'I've just been to your hotel. Why are you no longer to be seen, Denis?' Such joy flooded into me that I was passionately determined never to let him go again. I should throw myself into his arms, I should at last tell him I loved him – he was there; he still existed; nothing seemed to me impossible.

'One can't always do what one likes,' he muttered: he looked terribly embarrassed.

'Shall we go and have a drink?' I said.

He hesitated. 'I have to meet some friends at the Goéland: but do come with me. I'd like that.'

I went with him. As soon as we were no longer alone his face cleared; he smiled at me affectionately. 'A gin fizz, like the good old days? Do you remember the first time we went out together, Marguerite?'

'Of course,' I said. It was rare that he called up memories: he looked quite moved.

'How young we were!' he murmured.

'We still are, Denis.'

He shook his head. 'You: not me. I'm no longer any good at all, you know, Marguerite. Carry on without me: you have strength – I can no longer keep up.' He turned away: he went to sit at the piano and I did not see him alone again for a single minute.

The next day I was in my room going over my Latin authors when Pascal came in – an unusual thing for him, since he did not like to interrupt my work. He looked grave; but then since Anne's death he always looked grave, rather affectedly so. He sat on my divan; I was in an armchair at my table: I turned towards him and said, 'You want to speak to me?' I was on the defensive.

He gave me a sad, affectionate look: 'Yes. Although you don't take much interest in what happens at home, there are certain things I should like you to know.' He paused. 'Marcelle has seen her husband again and they have talked matters over. He seems to have changed a great deal; he has matured, and now he is determined to work – in short, she has made up her mind to forgive him and to resume married life.'

I understood it all in a flash; yet I still asked, 'Denis suggested it to her? He's going to come back and live with her?'

Pascal nodded. 'The position will be rather delicate to begin with: I must ask you to use all your intelligence and all your tact.'

There was only one idea in my mind – not to cry in front of Pascal. In any case crying was not exactly what I felt like doing: on the contrary, I uttered a slight hysterical laugh. Marcelle looked upon Denis as the very lowest kind of heel. 'But it's utterly grotesque.'

Pascal's face darkened. 'How quickly you judge, Marguerite. Have you ever even tried to imagine the sufferings of a young married woman who sees the future closed before her? I don't pretend that I heard Marcelle's decision without anxiety, but I understand it and I respect it. There is a real magnanimity in being able to forgive.'

'Much good may it do her,' I said contemptuously. I had to restrain myself terribly to keep some kind of a countenance. 'When did Denis come back?'

'Three weeks ago. Marcelle hesitated: she only made up her mind these last few days.' He seemed inclined to carry on with the conversation.

Abruptly I stood up. 'Listen, Pascal: it is very kind of you to give me this warning, but now you must excuse me – I have a shocking headache and I want to lie down.'

He looked at me earnestly, said 'Have a good rest,' and left me. I walked over to the window and pushed the curtain aside: once again I saw Denis' bitter smile and heard his voice. I repeated to myself 'He is going to come back and live with Marcelle.' I was not exactly surprised: I was dazed. I sat on the edge of my bed and stayed there a long time with one shoe in my hand; I could not carry any movement through; from time to time a picture came into my mind, the picture of that unreal, desperate being who had said 'thank you' one evening, looking slightly away from me. It vanished straight away, out of weakness, because I could no longer believe in it. The ghostly lamp hanging beyond the blue window was more easily grasped than these lightning-flash visions; my whole past was annihilated, and in my mind Denis' new face took shape without meeting any resistance, as though it had been roughed out long ago.

I dropped my shoe and began to undress: in spite of my obstinacy, my bad faith, and my love I had suspected the truth for a long while – ever since that evening at the Goéland – but I had gone on living in a world whose centre was Denis. Now the world was falling apart again; it was no longer a theatre and there was no longer any play going on; and once more it was only a chance collection of scattered objects. I really could not imagine what was going to become of me; and often in the course of that night I woke in extreme distress, wondering how I could set about living again when morning came.

During the days that followed I suffered less than I had expected, but nothing made sense any more. Fortunately this was the time for the written part of my examination, and that filled my mind to some extent: but as soon as I walked out of the Sorbonne I was overcome with the saddest feeling of having nothing whatsoever to do. I no longer feared anything, I no longer expected anything, and even my memories were dead; all that I could have grieved for was mere shadow – the man I had loved had never existed. At home they thought that the examination was tiring me, and they left me in peace. I shut myself in my room and read detective stories until I fell asleep. The night after the last papers I gathered my strength; I wanted to make an attempt at looking my empty future straight in the face. During the afternoon it had been insufferably hot and I had slept a little: as night fell I went out for a long walk, as I had so often done before. At first I felt unhappy, ill at ease; the pink and mauve lights of the carrefour Vavin still shone at the bottom of the boulevard Raspail, but they had lost their fascinating brilliance; and I no longer knew where to go. A vast, shapeless mass, swarming with people, stretched in all directions around me; I walked along the streets as chance led me, and my thoughts too wandered at random, forming a weak little eddy that led nowhere and that the slightest event drove from my mind.

I walked quite a long time, and suddenly I found that I was in the boulevard Barbès: I passed a woman walking the street with one hand on her hip; her opulent bosom filled a blue satin blouse; she wore high-heeled black boots, buttoned to the knee, and her massive face was flabby. When she stripped she must have kept her boots on. I pictured her with a whip in her hand, setting her foot with a masterful look on the pallid back of a kneeling man; it was a pitiable and seedy vision; the bed's cover would no doubt be yellow, with fringes, and its iron bars scaling. I waited a moment to see whether anyone would accost her; then I walked on, and all at once I caught myself smiling. This curiosity and this detachment were something new. A week earlier I should have seen this woman as the incarnation of all the temptations of despair and I should have hurried off, sad at heart, without noticing the colour of her hair; I should have pictured her calling Denis from the depths of the night to offer him a hideous and miraculous escape. Something had changed in me.

I went on walking, feeling strangely moved; the world too was changing – it was as though a spell were fading. Suddenly, instead of symbolic scenery, I saw around me a host of objects that seemed to exist in their own right. All along the pavement little cafés came into being, cafés where Denis had never set foot, and cinemas and popular little dancing places that he had never told me about: I could walk into all of them – I had no need of Denis to hear what they had to say to me. I went towards one: there were a good many people outside, and from the open door came the sound of an accordion. And the first thing I saw was the accordion itself, an accordion with shining sides and broad, silvery-white bellows: it was a band of children from twelve to fifteen, dressed in red, and they were playing a java in the back room of a little café that was also a tobacconist's shop – the platform was decorated with orange Japanese lanterns and paper festoons hung from the ceiling. I stared with all my might at the satin jackets, the brass cymbals, and the peroxided hair of a whore sitting on a banquette with its stuffing coming out, and unknown longings rose in me. I wanted to taste the plums that sat fatly there in their jar of brandy on the bar, I wanted to know the young band-leader with his thin, knowing face, I wanted to dance the java, to make friends with the fair-haired whore and indeed in some way to possess all those things that were offering themselves – offering themselves as if suddenly set free from the fixed meaning in which I had confined them; they had burst their allegorical wrappings and now they showed themselves naked, living, and inexhaustible. It almost made me dizzy: the more I looked the more new colours I found in the paper flowers, the lanterns and the lights; it was impossible to count them all. What treasures of time I had wasted! Slowly I walked off; the world was shining like a new penny, and although I did not yet know what I wanted to do with it everything was possible, since there in the centre of things, in the place Denis had left empty, I had found myself.

At the time I attributed too much importance to what I may call this kind of revelation: it was not a conversion of a spiritual nature that could rid me of spirituality. In fact my life had changed from the moment I was no longer engaged in merely inward revolution but in taking sides against Pascal's and Marcelle's code by outward actions; it had taken me close on two years to come to a full understanding of all the cowardliness and hypocrisy there was in their wonderful, pathetic dreams and to break with them. But that is a story I do not intend to tell; all I have wished to do was to show how I was brought to try to look things straight in the face, without accepting oracles or ready-made values. I had to rediscover everything myself, and sometimes it was disconcerting – furthermore, not everything is clear even now. But in any case what I do know is that Marcelle and Chantal and Pascal will die without ever having known or loved anything real and that I do not want to be like them. Chantal married a wealthy physician, Marcelle has just published a slim volume of verse, and the other day an archaeological journal mentioned Pascal's name with praise. They are not discontented with their lot.

Born in Paris in 1908, Simone de Beauvoir is France's most celebrated living writer. A lifelong companion of Jean-Paul Sartre and a pioneering feminist, she has written books famous throughout the world. Her works of fiction include *The Mandarins, All Men Are Mortal, The Blood of Others,* and *The Woman Destroyed.* Her nonfiction includes *The Second Sex, A Very Easy Death, Memoirs of a Dutiful Daughter, Force of Circumstance, The Prime of Life,* and *The Coming of Age.* She has just completed a book about the last years of Jean-Paul Sartre's life, *Adieux: A Farewell to Sartre.*

Simone de Beauvoir lives in Paris.

Pantheon Paperbacks by or about Jean-Paul Sartre

SAINT GENET
Actor and Martyr
by Jean-Paul Sartre, translated by Bernard Frechtman

The classic biography of the French playwright Jean Genet—thief, bastard, homosexual, convict, and genius.

"One of the most astonishing critical studies ever written about one writer by another." —*Time*

0-394-71583-7 $8.95

BETWEEN EXISTENTIALISM AND MARXISM
Sartre on Philosophy, Politics, Psychology, and the Arts
by Jean-Paul Sartre, translated by John Mathews

In this collection of his most important essays from the 1960s, Sartre takes stock of his work and his world, offering fresh insight into his most characteristic subjects.

"Strenuously...touchingly...powerfully part of the history of a mind."
—*The New York Times Book Review*

0-394-71584-5 $6.95

REASON AND VIOLENCE
A Decade of Sartre's Philosophy, 1950–1960
by R. D. Laing and D. G. Cooper

A concise guide to the three great works of Sartre's later years, *Saint Genet, Search for a Method*, and *Critique of Dialectical Reason*.

"A very clear, very faithful account of my thought."—Jean-Paul Sartre

0-394-71582-9 $5.95

SARTRE ON THEATER
by Jean-Paul Sartre, edited by Michel Contat and Michel Rybalka, translated by Frank Jellinek

A collection of Sartre's lectures, writings, and interviews on the theater and on his own plays, including *No Exit, Dirty Hands*, and *The Condemned of Altona*.

"Will no doubt become a classic."—*The New Republic*

0-394-73312-6 $5.95

LIFE/SITUATIONS
Essays Written and Spoken
by Jean-Paul Sartre, translated by Paul Auster and Lydia Davis

A collection of Sartre's last essays and interviews.

"We should salute such resilience....There is iron in [Sartre's] soul yet."
—*The New York Times Book Review*

0-394-72460-2 $2.95